The
Lucky Loser

The Lucky Loser

THE PERILS OF WINNING AT SEX, GAMBLING AND FRIENDSHIP

A NOVEL BY
DAN JAMES

Made in Charleston, SC
www.PalmettoPublishingGroup.com

The Lucky Loser

ISBN: 978-1-64990-155-2
ISBN: 978-1-64990-193-4 (eBook)

PROLOGUE

This is a work of fiction, that may offend some readers. Tough!

Any resemblance to actual persons, places or events is purely coincidental.

For those of you who lived through the high inflation, high unemployment, high interest rates of the 1970s, while getting high, read on.

If you endured the death of Jimi Hendrix, Janis Joplin, and Jim Morrison, and suffered through the endless torture of disco music you should be able to handle this book.

TABLE OF CONTENTS

I.

MONDAY 9:30 PM JAN 12TH 1977 SIX DAYS BEFORE SUPER BOWL X.

Our Bloomington Pleasure Palace

I had the night off so I was doing all the things that I normally do on a night like this: watching Tim clean the kitchen from the swell supper he had prepared; lounging in my easy chair, thinking about girls, smoking, sipping a cocktail or two, and admiring Tim's ability to know exactly when to throw the laundry around. I could read a book I suppose, naw, I never read books, or write a letter to a friend, but I only have one friend and he shares this townhouse with me. Monday night is the dead night in the bar business. Early part of the week, still five days from pay day, no hockey, basketball, football games tonight. Of course it was a typical Minnesota January night, dark, cold, really cold, windy, threatening snow. Ugh.

Now Tim came into the living room wiping his hands on a kitchen cloth, asking if we could go out for awhile.

When Tim and I decided to rent this Bloomington, a sprawling South Minneapolis suburb, townhouse together, he laid down some very easy to follow rules.

1. He did all the cleaning and housework.
2. He did all the cooking and shopping.
3. He handled all the bill paying and expenditures.
4. I stayed out of his way.

Easy. Works for me! I don't want anyone to think that we are a total "odd couple," on the contrary. I prefer to think of it as the two of us playing to each others strengths. In Tim's case it's cleaning, investing, sports betting, accounting, and planning for our future.

In my case it's, lounging, smoking, drinking, drugging, and bringing home as many wayward young, old, and anything in-between girls as possible for various sexual athletic events.

Tim did give me one living assignment, it was my job to take care of our car. Yes, our car. When we both got jobs at the same restaurant and boogie bar, Tim convinced me to sell our old cars and buy one really good vehicle for the both of us. Tim likes to take the bus around town anyway, and this way we would save on gas, license, maintenance and insurance was his plan. At first I was reluctant to part with my trusty, rusty, Pontiac GTO, but as always Tim was right.

So last year on a frigid winter morning the two of us went to this monstrous sized General Motors dealership on Highway 494 to look at cars. One point here, this was January 1976, just before the first of many gas/oil crises. Regular was going for about, (hold your breath here folks), 79 cents a gallon. Little did we know that those days would never come again. With my old Pontiac and Tim's ancient Plymouth crunching into the ice covered parking lot it wasn't like the salesman were wrestling with each other to see who could help us. Finally, some new hire was forced out into the wind and storm and asked, "What we wanted?" not, "Can I help you with something?" Not, "Hey guys, nice to have you on our lot, what can I do for you?" Just, "What do you guys want?" After snooping around and looking at stickers I saw something that made me call Tim and Mr. Personality over. There, in the middle of a long row of cars was a soft brown 1975 Oldsmobile. Even with a fresh dusting of snow and small icicles hanging from its wheel wells it looked great. Elegant, refined, classy interior, front wheel drive for winter driving, large soft cloth seats. The exterior was fabulous, perfect blend of sports car, muscle car, and luxury car. I was hooked and so was Tim. Plus it had a feature that sadly most car engineers failed to appreciate at the time. It had bench seating with a small soft retractable armrest cushion and the transmission was on the steering column. Now here I could let your mind wonder why two always horny young men would find this important. I could make some comment about what a smooth ride our new car had. Stop, what are you 13 years old? Listen up, in 1976 to say "Times Up" meant it was time to "Put Out, Girl", and, "Me Too", meant, I'll also have another beer. Of course we all know why this was important. If at a drive-in movie, parked over the Mississippi River Valley or slowly cruising through a Minnesota forest, and your girlfriend gets tired and needs to lay her head down on your lap while you softly, gently stroke her hair. So I ask you, "just exactly how is this poor girl supposed to navigate bucket seats and on floor transmission?" You have to think of her!

The windshield was painted with a price of $9,500.00. We hummed and hawed awhile and offered $8,000.00 and both of our old cars. The young salesman said it was getting colder and he was going back inside. I quickly offered him a cigarette and we all lit up.

"OK, $8,600.00 and our cars, and that's final," I said in my most authoritarian captain's voice.

The salesman thanked me for the smoke and turned to walk away.

4

Tim, always the wise business person decided to take charge. "Listen, it's not like there's a ton of buyers out here, why don't we work something out?"

The wind was really blowing now and all three of us were stomping around in the snow with our feet freezing.

The salesman tossed his cigarette in a small snow bank and said, "OK, here's what we can work out. You give us $9,500.00 and get those junky old cars of yours out of our customer parking lot."

Thus we acquired the, "Brown Bomber."

As I was saying, the only assignment Tim would trust me with was taking care of our prized Toronado. So once a week I would take it to a full service gas station, crack the power window and calmly slip a twenty to an earnest, oil splattered young man who would gas the car, check the oil, wash the windows, and warmly thank me for my patronage. I know, you really don't believe this.

Then once every three months I would drive the Toronado to a full service oil and lube shack where I would calmly watch earnest young men change the oil, check the tires, top off the fluids, while their unscrupulous supervisor would try and sell me supposedly desperately needed hoses and belts.

After that it was off to a full service car wash shop where I would calmly sit in the waiting room while dedicated young high school kids washed, vacuumed, and detailed our now great looking car.

Of course after all that hard work I needed to take a break.

"Go out? Tonight? Now? In this?" I replied looking toward our townhouse door. Without hesitating Tim cheerfully said, "Ya, let's go. We won't be long. Can you drive?" With that Tim flipped me my winter coat, which was never hung up, and headed to the closet door for his coat, gloves and stocking cap.

Slamming the brown bombers door shut and firing up it's eight cylinders I naturally asked, "Tim, where are we going? Or more to the point, what are we doing?"

Tim said, "Highland Park, my good man," in his sometimes used clipped English accent. "A little fresh air on a crisp Minnesota night is what we both need, yes indeed."

"Huh!" was my only thought. So off to Highland Park I drove. The great thing about the Toronado's massive engine is that the roaring mill could warm up the car fast. Ten minutes later we drove across the Minnesota River into Highland Park. Of course, I was thinking Tim wanted to hang out at one of our old St. Paul bars. Or maybe he knew a girl here and she had a roommate, or something when Tim said he wanted to hike the bluffs.

"You want to what?" The bluffs, big surprise, are the bluffs area over the Minnesota River, close to where it hooks up with the Mississippi River. High, open, windy, ugh!

I parked in the River Parking Lot, no other cars there of course. Tim bounced out of the car, jauntily skipping around encouraging me to join him. I creaked out of the car, the winter blast smashing me in the face.

"Tim, if you wanted to walk outside you could have told me so I would bring some gloves and hat," I growled.

"Oh John, you don't even own a hat, you never wear a hat. You and I both know that it would mess up all that dark hair you're so proud of." This was true. I hated wearing a hat, and I hated being out in the cold.

More of that annoying English accent of his, "Now Mr. Williams you have to keep up, high steps are best when marching in the snow. As they told us at military school, you are just one member of a large team, and we can't let the team down. Rah! Rah! By the way, how about a quick smoke?"

Trembling I reached into my coat pocket for my pack, sliding two out. Together we braced ourselves in the wind like football huddlers. My lighter balked at first, but I got one cigarette lit, got Tim's going off mine and handed it to him. There we were, standing like statues, smoking in the frigid night. Call me confused! Tim rarely smoked, and never outside.

"Remember when we were last here, John?"

"Of course I remember, it was the first time that we spent some time together," I said. "It was the night that I had gotten blown by that striking low-town-flat girl. Great night for me, years ago. I still look for that girl when I'm in St. Paul."

"Well I think we best be going Williams, the deed is done." Obviously Tim had read all the Sherlock Holmes books as a boy. Trudging back to the car, "I asked where to now?"

Tim replied, "It was getting late," (it wasn't) "and we best head home."

I stomped as much snow off me as possible entering our townhouse, blowing into my hands, shivering, and gasping for warm air.

"I'm proud of you Williams, you handled the elements like a truly tough Brit," said Tim in that now increasingly irritating British upper class tone. "Have a seat, I'll have the staff fetch you a hot toddy."

A few minutes later Tim came out of the kitchen with two perfectly prepared Perfect Manhattans. Straight-up stem class, top shelf Kentucky bourbon, dash of sweet vermouth, slight touch of dry vermouth and an olive, just the way I like it.

"John we need to talk," was his first remarks. "I doubt you will like what I have to say."

Hmmm! This did not start well.

"John, have you ever thought of living some-where other than Minnesota?" Have you ever considered that there are other towns, other bars, nightclubs, women, in far away places? Think about it John, Maxwell's is closing. Mickey Maxwell is retiring! You may or may not get picked up in the spring after the new owners' remodel is finished. Regardless, you'll have to re-apply, starting over at the bottom of the new pay scale. I'm positive the new owners will bring in their own business people, which means I'm out the door during a recession. That doesn't work for me."

I hadn't really ever thought about living anywhere else, but back then I didn't do a lot of thinking. Maxwell's Boogie Bar and Fine Dining Restaurant where Tim and I have worked for the last four years was closing after the Super Bowl. What the new owners had planned for the restaurant no one knew. However, now the boogie bar was getting a complete make over. No more bands, no more sports decor, just piped in disco music.

"But what about the money we get from the escort business we helped start? Then there's the bi-weekly poker game, you always win some nice walking around cash. If we leave that money doesn't follow us," I responded.

Tim and I played in a bi-weekly poker game and Tim almost always won. Some of the guys wanted Tim black-balled from the game. Some thought he must be cheating but I knew Tim would never cheat at anything. First off, Tim was an honest straight shooter. But more to the point if he cheated it would take the fun out of it for him. Tim was smart, real smart, and he liked to win, cheating would ruin it for him. Remember, down deep Tim was a businessman, money has always been his goal, the more the better. That's why I was surprised by his answer.

"John, you're a hundred per cent right, but I think it's time to go," he said. "The escort business has been good to us, but we are no longer really involved. It borders on illegal anyway and possibly crosses the line into criminal activity. No judge is going to take up prison space on us for helping squire prostitutes around, but the tax consequences could be an issue."

I looked at Tim, "Tax consequences? What tax consequences?" I asked.

Tim looked at me and began, "Well, you know the money that we get every month from the nefarious activities that you and I helped Boomer, his family and those other cohorts in crime start? Well, I haven't really been able find a way to declare them, so we haven't been paying taxes on any of this so-called ill-gotten gain. So, with the escort business, the illegal sports gambling we do, and tax evasion, we're starting to push things to the limit."

"What you're saying is, adding it all up might result in some 'Granite time' right?" I responded.

Tim looked at me and said, "You got it, but there's more.

You have developed an unfortunate appreciation for the nose blow."

This was true enough, last year at this time cocaine was new, novel, unique, and scarce. Parties didn't center around it, however, it was there to be had on rare occasions. What a difference a year makes. Now the blow was all over the Twin Cities, easy to get, inexpensive, and pure. Every party would have a glass surface with lines of the white stuff, and rolled dollars for all to participate, and I always did.

Tim went on, "If these illegal, and close-to-illegal activities blow up it's every-man-for-himself. Everybody will turn and blame everyone else. Guess what, all these bartenders, bouncers, cocktail servers, right down to the dishwashers are going to say? 'It was those two really smart college boys who led us astray.'"

I was starting to see Tim's point, add it all up and we could be reserving a room at that less-than-five-star Granite Hotel.

"Granite" is a clever nickname for the state prison in St. Cloud, Minnesota, north of the Twin Cities by about sixty miles. St. Cloud State Prison may be the ugliest prison in the world, and maybe the ugliest building in the world. I'm talking esthetics here. In the late 1800s the Minnesota pioneers, while clearing out the forests and Indian Tribes, decided they needed another prison to go along with the already established maximum security Stillwater prison. Hmmmm, where to build it and with what materials? "Let's quarry out all that granite near the center of the state and build the largest and ugliest granite structure in the world." Thus Granite, aka St. Cloud State Prison was born holding mainly 20-to 30 year old offenders of all ethnic stripes and criminal flavors. It is, and always has been a true reformatory, in that there are many programs in place to prepare the inmates for a bright and shinny future upon their release. These prison educational courses include woodworking, masonry, auto body, and so forth. All kinds of vocational training that most of the inmates went into crime to avoid in the first place. They even set up a college program with St. Cloud State College so many of the inmates would not be denied the joys of learning Art History, or Middle English Literature. Now I'm sure that there have been former inmates who fondly look back at their days at dear old St. Cloud State Prison, and think how lucky they were to have been part of such an enlightened institution, but I've never met one.

Little did the early pioneers of Minnesota know that by quarrying out all that granite and building that disgusting, foreboding looking prison, that many years later it would pay big dividends for the local college crowd. You see, once all the granite had been dug out of the fifteen or so granite depositories about ten miles out of St. Cloud, it left big holes in the ground. Over time these gigantic holes were filled in by rain water making great places for evening naked swims. This became a very trendy thing for some young college men, but, and more importantly young women to do. Let's have a picnic! Beer, pot, naked girls, better than the baseball game-of the-week. Better still were late night rendezvous' after the bars closed. How I enjoyed gallantly wrapping a warm towel around a shivering, giggling, lovely young naked girl on a moonlit night. 'Summer session should be more than classes and studying I always say.' What was interesting is that most of these liberated young coeds were only too willing to "bare-it-all" after endless winter months under layers of heavy winter clothes.

"So that was what this late night winter hike on the bluffs was all about. Get me really cold, then spring some idea about moving to a warmer environment on me," I said. "One little problem mister future MBA, what do we do for jobs, money, and by the way, where are you planning on leading us?"

"Fair question, sounds like you're interested," said Tim.

"I didn't say I was interested, please don't lead me on like that, but I am curious, so continue," I replied.

Tim reached out one hand to take my now empty cocktail glass, while reaching for a Financial Monthly magazine with the other.

"Page 48, start reading while I refill you," said Tim.

"Oh sure, ply me with alcohol and then spirit me away to some god forsaken hell hole of WWWOOOOOOOW, what is this?" I said, "are you serious?" was my first thought.

There on page 48 of Tim's Financial Monthly in soft green lettering with palm trees swaying in the background, with a near naked flower draped Polynesian girl shyly smiling was the heading, "Maui, Hawaii's Next Island Paradise."

The Financial Monthly was one of many magazines Tim and I would order. I'm sure our Postal Letter Carrier was a little confused about our various subscriptions. Tim would get his many business and sports issues and I always got Playboy, Penthouse and a few other "adult oriented" magazines.

Tim came back into the room with another cocktail for me while I perused our future island adventure.

2.

HIGH SCHOOL, PUBERTY AND ACNE

St. Paul Minnesota, Mid-1960s

Tim and I have been best buddies since our junior year at Cretin Military Academy in St. Paul Minnesota. As young people grow up they all go through various defining moments that chart their future. I was there for Tim's defining moments and he helped me through mine.

It was in my freshman year at Cretin that I started to stretch out over the other kids. I was 6'2" on my way to 6'4". Awkward, gangly, with big floppy feet, unruly black hair, huge clumsy hands, boney arms, legs and shoulders, and worst of all, a face full of zits. Ichabod Crane, with bad acne! Cretin High, like so many expensive Catholic Military Academies, was a power house athletic school; always winning championships in all the sports. Many of the football guys went on to play small college football and some even made it on the major college level. In the winter Cretin's hockey, wrestling and basketball teams were top notch. Same with baseball and track and field in the spring.

In my freshman year one of the young assistant coaches thought he could make a basketball center out of me. I was terrible, after ten minutes of running up and down the court he called me over and asked me to leave the gym. Muttering something about how, "John has feet like a drunken buffalo and hands like a blind surgeon, kid could trip over dust." You might think that these unkind digs and snaps might hurt me but it really didn't, because I didn't care anyway. What's more, I already knew that all the coaches were under heavy pressure to win. Cretin was a very expensive private school, and it was supposed to be good at everything. No excuses. It was all about the wins and losses academically, artistically, and athletically, and there better be a lot more wins than losses.

Because of my height it was hard to hide, which is all I really wanted to do. My parents were both very successful, Dad as a senior accountant at 3M, Mother was Assistant Chief Financial Officer at the St. Paul Public School District.

As an only child to prosperous parents I had everything I wanted. Great four bedroom, three car garage home in Highland Village, a very upscale burb of St. Paul. Swell downstairs rec room with a color TV, pool table, dart board, and my dad's liquor cabinet.

Because my hand-eye coordination was so bad my parents insisted that I take music lessons. It was my choice between piano and guitar. I chose guitar hoping that it would offer me better access to what was under the gray pleated skirts the girls wore at Cretin.

At Cretin the uniform for boys was dark shoes and socks, gray cuffed pants, white shirt, dark tie, gray blazer, gray overcoat. The girls wore dark shoes, white socks, gray pleated skirts, white blouse, green silk tie, gray jacket and gray overcoat. Catholics! If your religion is based on discipline, obedience, purity, chastity, virginity, and guilt, these are your colors.

It was a late fall evening of my sophomore year. I was down in the rec room practicing my guitar while watching TV when my parents came down for a chat. Mother began, "John, we've been talking with some of the counselors at your school, Cretin." As if I didn't know what school I went too.

My mother talked that way, always making sure everyone knew what she was referring too. It wasn't until I actually met some of the people that my mother worked with at the St. Paul School District that I understood why she had developed this speaking method. Mom had graduated as an elementary school teacher from St. Catherine's College in St. Paul and had immediately been hired to teach the tikes. Furthering her education over the summer breaks she earned another degree in finance and accounting. That led to her present job at the school district. It was her job to explain to Art, Science, History, and English teachers as well as coaches what educational curriculums the money could be spent on. Of course none of these people had the foggiest understanding of financial expenditures so mom had to be very precise, patient, and clear. "Your teachers and advisors have noticed that you're not participating in any of the social or athletic activities," Mom went on.

This was true, and by design. I was a loner! Not by choice, more by circumstances.

I tried not to reply, worrying where this was going.

"Well John, your father and I agree that you should try and join one of Cretins school sports teams."

I was afraid of this!

Mom continued, "My brothers, your uncles, *(there she goes again, as if I didn't know that my mother's brothers were my uncles)*, were on the sports teams in school and enjoyed it very much!"

"What team do you and the counselors think I should play on?" I asked, knowing full well I had no athletic talent.

Now Dad opened up, "Well the team sports are stocked with players already, but your counselor said there is one opening as a welterweight on the Cretin boxing team."

"Boxing! What makes you think I could to that?" I blurted.

Dad responded, "Now, John, I have a colleague, (*at the senior level of 3M you did not have coworkers, or associates, you had "colleagues" - wohooooa!*)

Gus Swenson, was on the boxing team in the Navy and he said he would coach you."

Of all the sports teams at Cretin, boxing was without a doubt the lowest level. It wasn't even a letter sport, more of a club sport. Back in the 40s and 50s St. Paul had been a hotbed of palookas, even developing some sluggers who made some noise on the national level. Now boxing was in its waning days, in fact the sport was discontinued at Cretin the next year due to lack of interest.

The way it worked was like this, all the school's boxing clubs would meet down at the St. Paul Armory on Saturday night and have matches. Six matches in seven weeks, after the seven weeks the top two of each weight class would meet again for the privilege of going over to Minneapolis to fight for the Twin Cities High School Championship. Cretins school boxing coach had retired the year before and nobody else wanted the job, that's how pathetic it all was.

So on a cold, windy early October day in 1967 I found myself in the dirty locker room of the dusty St. Paul Armory wearing a pair of gym shorts, tennis shoes and boxing gloves. I had the boxing shorts tied as tight as possible in fear of them falling down my skinny waist. Standing up, every bone in my body seemed to be visible. Good old Gus hadn't been able to train me once because he'd been called to Washington, D.C. to meet with some one and two stars about better ways to kill the Commies. Five minutes before my Dad and I were to go up for my first bout, Gus came charging into the locker apologizing for not being able to help.

"Sorry guys, I ran over here as soon as my flight landed in Minneapolis. How ya feeling champ?" he asked.

Even before I could say anything my Dad piped up that, "I was doing well, *(I wasn't)* and that I felt I was ready." *(I didn't).*

Gus began, "Alright now John look at me. I want you to keep your fists up." And he put both hands around his ears. "When you throw a hook remember to flatten the fist." Gus slowly threw a hook flattening the knuckles acting like it clanked against an imaginary opponents temple. "Now you try it," Gus coached.

I roped a roundhouse right hook and nearly lost my balance catching my knee on a bench. Ouch!

Little did I know that what Coach Gus was giving me was very possibly the worst boxing advice since the Marquess of Queensberry rules of boxing were drafted in 1865.

"That was pretty good," lied Gus.

Just then some old guy came in to the locker room and told us we were up next.

Gus again, "Go out there like you're ready for action and full of confidence." I was neither.

Dad opened up the second rope of the ring and I slid in facing away from my opponent. Finally, I had to turn around and I then realized what the term, "Scared Shitless" meant. I literally had to tighten my butt for all it was worth. There across from me was the biggest, blackest kid I ever saw. He was very short, and like so many black athletes had muscled out early. Thick legs, powerful arms, no neck, and without a doubt the largest nostrils I had ever seen outside of a National Geographic. The ref called us to the center of the ring, for the announcement.

"Representing East Central High, *(and he named the kid's name, I don't remember)*, and representing Cretin High, John Williams."

I returned to my corner and looked across the ring, at what I assumed was my opponent's Dad who had this very worried look on his face. I realized later that the kid's Dad might have been thinking that if, "My son kills that frail looking white boy, will I be lynched?"

"Ding!" Gus shoved me out in the ring yelling, "Keep your hands up."

I kept my hands up, luckily for me as strong and powerful as St. Paul Blackie was, he was slow and cumbersome. Unfortunately for me was that by following Crafty Gus' advice I totally exposed my midsection, ribcage and chest. I was so tall and the black kid so short he couldn't reach my head anyway. The black kid moved in and slammed a punch to my left kidney. Boom, it felt like a two-by-four blasting against my side. Then a straight to my solar plexus, that doubled me over, sending me to the mat. I gathered myself and tried to go on the offensive, what a joke, I sailed a hook eight inches over his head while he bombed me again in the rib cage. I stumbled to the neutral corner covering up only to be plummeted on the shoulder and arms. At that point the ref had seen enough and jumped between us. I wobbled back to my corner, sat on the stool and tried not to cry.

"OK, let's go home," I said.

"No," said Good-Old-Gus, "you have to go back out there."

"Why?" I said.

"Go on, the ref has to announce the winner," Gus ordered.

These were three round, three minute fights, with a scoring judge at ringside and a ref. The ref and the ringside judge each had an equal vote.

"What's there to announce?" I'm thinking.

So I got off the stool and out in the center of the ring holding each of our hands the ref in a very serious voice, like this was the world title or something.

"Winner by a knockdown from East Central High at the 48 second mark in the first round," and he named the kids name, and held his hand up.

The kid then came over to me and put his paw on my right shoulder and said, "Nice fight."

"Golly it was great I thought, I love getting the stuffing pounded out of me. Really we need to do this more often."

After showering I slid into the back seat of my Dad's massive Lincoln Town Car. St. Paul was conservative city and 3M was a conservative manufacturing company. The senior executives got the most conservative car on the road and that was this huge dark blue Lincoln with its 470 cubic inch engine. Some cars are big enough to have sex in the back seats, in this car you could have had an orgy.

We dropped Gus off at his house and drove back to Highland Village without talking.

The next Saturday was much the same. I slid into the ring and slowly turned to look at my new opponent. The first thing I could think of was, "What is the deal with me and minorities?" This little kid looked like something out of a nacho chip commercial. I didn't even think he was in my welterweight class. Brown skin, pointy nose, ratty teeth, jet black hair, and violent looking eyes.

He came out of his corner like a swirling sage-brush, arms and fists flying in all directions. Luckily for me this buzzing little bandsaw of a kid didn't really have the power to hurt me. In the first round the ref stopped the fight and looked at me while putting his hand behind his head and performing a tapping motion. Whatever!

Then in the second round he did again. What I found out was that I was grabbing the little Mexican tornado by the back of his head, which was against the rules. My feeling was, *"Ref, if you want to fight Frito Bandido, you go right ahead!"* In the third round the two of us were in the center of the ring and I corralled him by the shoulders and slung him down sliding him out of the ring. That was my third infraction and the fight was stopped. At the announcement he raised the little Hispanic Hitters hand and said his name, school, and that he'd won by disqualification. I just felt sooooo terrible!

I could hardly stand the idea of doing this for another five weeks. At school the principal would go out on PA system Monday mornings and give everyone an update on what happened over the weekend as well as what events were in the coming week.

"Good morning students of Cretin High, this is principal O'Brien. Congratulations to the wrestling team for their impressive victory over St. Johns, also the basketball team had a stand-out performance with their upset win over previously undefeated De La Salle. The girls choral group will meet on Tuesday in the school theater. Don't forget to bring your signed polio cards and two dollars for your shots on Wednesday. Thursday our highly acclaimed debate team will go head-to-head against Benilde-St. Margaret in the school lunch room at 3:00 PM, this could be a good one. The Chess club suffered a tough loss to Sacred Heart on Saturday *(bet they got rooked)*. Tryouts for the one act play competition will begin at 2:45 PM sharp in the communication room. Actors will be expected to do an impromptu performance of a farm animal, remember to bring a hall pass. Finally the boxing club came away with four victories and one loss, Stevens, Johnson, Nordlum and Jensen won, Williams lost due to disqualification. This has been principal O'Brien have a good week."

Occasionally I would be at my locker and someone would slide by and tell me how I was letting the school down. It hurt a little, but really I didn't much care.

The week passed and on Friday night I knew I would be alone with the house to myself. At the end of every financial quarter the senior executives of 3M would get together with their wives for a fancy dinner out at The Lexington Restaurant. The Lexington was strictly where the elite of St. Paul met, did business, entertained out of town big shots, had wedding receptions and so on. Dark wood paneling, plush red leather seating, classic dinner menu, sophisticated bar, 35 years of serving the best of St. Paul. 3M would rent out the private dining room and everyone would dress to the max. Back then men wore suits and their wives wore evening gowns with real jewelry. That week the ladies had visited their chosen beauty parlors and the mens shoes would be shined to a glean.

Cocktail hour would last for about forty minutes, followed by a few quick speeches and reports. A few hardy jokes, some back slapping and hand shaking, dinner, dessert, brandy, cognac and cigars. In the early 60s this was the way it was done in corporate America.

3.

FIGHTS, "THE BARBER," AND A REALLY CLOSE SHAVE

Before leaving in the massive Lincoln, Dad turned to me and said, "Gus came by my office today for a quick word about you. He said there is a fight tonight on the television he wants you to watch. Some guy named Doug Jones is going against Tony Alongi. Gus says both these fighters are really good. In fact Jones recently fought Muhammad Ali and almost beat him. Gus wants to talk to you after the fight."

The Gillette Cavalcade of sports came on live from Madison Square Garden in New Your City every Friday night. This was boxing night across the U.S.A.

So at 7:00 PM sharp I went downstairs and turned on the TV. The camera zoomed into the ring where two guys in tuxedos were talking as fast as they could about what a great night this was. What a great fight we were going to see. What a great crowd we had on hand. What a great sponsor we had in Gillette, and what great blades they made. It was all just great, except for one little thing, one of the fighters couldn't make it. Evidently the highly thought of Tony Alongi came down with an injury so he couldn't come out and play tonight. They went on, "But don't worry folks we're in great luck, because Billy 'The Barber' Daniels is Tony Alongi' replacement and we all know what a great fighter he is." (*We do?*)

At the last minute it had been discovered that Alongi' arm was shot due to bone spurs, and the poor guy won't be able to fight for months on end. Or until somebody shoots Doug Jones. After taking one look at Doug Jones I would come up with an injury too, in fact I would probably hide under my bed. Jones was a physical specimen, no wonder Ali almost lost to him. Muscles rippled all over Jones' coal black body. Power on power, sturdy, bulky, massive shoulders, gigantic back and legs, thick neck. Warming up in his corner the camera couldn't catch up with his flying fists.

Then Daniels entered the ring, I just thought, this is not going to end well for Daniels. Tall, lean, to the point of being skinny. Long thin arms and legs, light brown skinned. Jones looked like the fighter he was, a real knock-out artist. Billy "The Barber" Daniels looked like, well, the guy who would cut your hair. This was a bulldozer versus a palm tree.

The Ref called the two fighters to the center of the ring for the last minute instructions, "Alright men, I want a nice clean, blah, blah, blah . ." (*why are you bothering ref this isn't a fight it's an execution.*) The camera zoomed into the fighters, Doug Jones was giving Billy Daniels the big stare down. Jones looked so bad, so mean, so full of hate he was scaring me all the way to my parents rec room in St. Paul, Minnesota. I wanted to pull a cover over my face. All I could think of was, *"I sure hope they have a good fight doctor on hand because Billy Daniels is going to need one in about ninety seconds."*

"Ding" round one, both fighters charged out of their corners looking to set the tempo and make an early statement. Doug Jones moved in, hands up high, just like Gus-The-Great told me. Throwing big killer hooks left and right at Daniels head, missing but trying to let Daniels know who was in charge. I could almost feel the whoosh of his fists zoom by me. Daniels never retreated, hands low about shoulder height, kept Jones in front of him. The "Barber" slid to his left and slammed a sharp, penetrating left jab into Jones face, then another and another, smash, smash, smash. Jones kept coming, going low he tried to get to Daniels midsection. Again Daniels refused to retreat, blasting more left jabs into Jones' kisser. Jones made a full charge at

Daniels only to be greeted by a vicious right upper-cut that snapped Jones' head back. Jones shook off the blow and kept attacking. Daniels wrapped up the much shorter Jones in his left arm pounding away on the back of Jones' head with his right. "Ding".

"Do you want a close shave? Of course you do. And the best way to get that close shave is with a Gillette razor. Easy to use, and easy on your skin. Gillette razor now for the low price of $1.29.

"Ding" round two. Again Jones roared out of his corner determined to take Daniels down and out in short order. Daniels gave Jones more of the same as he had in the first round. Ripping that piston like left jab in to Jones' mutt whenever Jones tried to unleash a punch. It wasn't a defensive left jab - one that would give a fighter a chance to escape and regroup. It was an attacking, offensive, charging, crashing jab, rat-a-dat-dat-dat. Never stopping, relentless, keeping the much stronger Jones at bay, wearing him down, frustrating him. When Jones was able to get inside, "The Barber" would either slam a right uppercut into Jones' jaw, or wrap Jones up with his long arms keeping Jones' bombs from hurting him. "Ding"

"Do you think you're the only one who wants you to have a close, comfortable shave. Think of her, your wife, your girlfriend, your homosexual lover. No one wants to kiss a prickle face, especially not her. So

remember, the next time you buy razor blades think of her, and get the best, get Gillette. Now $1.29, sold in most drug stores."

"Ding" round three. And so it went for the entire ten rounds. Jones trying to get inside and knock the much taller Daniels out with a left or right hook, or going low attacking Daniels slender midsection. Daniels continued to slash that snapping, ripping left jab into Jones' face when Jones was at a distance, or firing the right uppercut when Jones moved in close. The rest of time Daniels would clutch and grab, often running his forearms into Jones throat. Banging him on the back of the head, and using his long arms like tree limbs to block the roaring hooks before they could land on his head while draining Jones fury. "Ding"

"That's the end of this great ten round fight here in Madison Square Gardens. What did you think of this match Bob?"

"Well Tom, I thought it was a great fight, just great, and what a great crowd we had tonight, just great, and isn't this a great arena. Now we're going to take a commercial break so our viewers can hear a word from our great sponsor, Gillette."

"This is Jack, Hi Jack! Jack has a swell car, Jack has a good job, Jack even has a nice dog. Woof!!! Until recently Jack never got laid. Why? Because Jack used bad razor blades. Since switching to Gillette, Jack can't keep up with the harem of starlets who keep dragging him

into dark alleys and ripping his pants off. Now a $1.29, sold at most drug stores and a few upscale gas stations."

One of the talking heads came back on the screen, "Welcome back boxing fans across the nation, we're here at ringside in the magnificent Madison Square Gardens and now for the call of this great fight."

The camera zoomed into some guy in a tux who reached up and grabbed a microphone. "Referee Joe Crooked scored the fight 6 rounds Jones, 4 rounds Daniels." I couldn't believe what I just heard, from my comfortable rec room two time zones away I had scored it 7 rounds Daniels, 3 rounds Jones. The announcer went on, "The two ringside judges both scored this fight 6 rounds Daniels, 4 rounds Jones. The winner by split decision is Billy 'The Barber' Daniels." Well that's better, I thought.

Doug Jones looked like he was ready to fight the entire New York Giant football team, all at once. Man was he pissed! I flipped off the TV, leaned back and stretched.

BRIIINNNG, "Hello" I said.

"Hi John, this is Gus."

"Hi Gus, er Mr. Swenson."

Gus went on, "Did you watch the fight John?"

"Yes, my Dad told me to," I said.

"Sorry it wasn't the fight we thought it would be, too bad for that Alongi fellow, hope he's alright," Gus replied.

Ya, a real shame, I thought.

More from Gus, "OK, well I'll see you at the armory next week, if you have any questions let me know."

"Sure," I said.

"OK, bye John," said Gus.

"Goodnight Mr. Swenson," I said and hung up the phone.

Wow what a great coach, I thought sarcastically.

By luck of scheduling I didn't have a match this week. It was my one bye week of the seven bout schedule.

That was good, it would give me plenty of time to think over what I'd witnessed tonight. What was bad was in eight days I was scheduled to get into the ring with a fine young scholar from the Low Town district of St. Paul by the name of Ricky Robinette. Low Town was an area in St. Paul that was low, (big surprise) in both elevation and economic and social status. Almost every spring the Minnesota River would overflow its banks and the residents of Low Town, also referred to as The Flats would have to evacuate. The St. Paul Pioneer Press newspaper would send a photo team down during the evacuation and take the same picture ever year. There would be mom wrapped in her old coat and scarf carrying a baby. Trudging behind would be dad clutching all their prized possessions. To round out the picture would be the huddled grandparents wading their way up to 7th Street where the Catholic Charities would pitch tents and serve them hot meals until the water receded. Most of the families were of Italian or Greek descent, (at the time I wondered that if you were from southern Europe you must have wanted to be near water). If the men worked at all, it was usually at the stock yards. The Chicago Stock Yards was the only operation of its kind bigger than St. Paul. It was here that Bessie, Bossy, and Porky would be hauled in, zapped, and turned into Sunday Dinner. A massive operation, and on a hot summer day you could smell the revolting odor all over town. Fortunately Highland Village was far enough away so it rarely was a problem for us. The Stock Yards served another purpose in the fall. It was here that the Midwest Deer hunters would haul in Bambi and Thresher to be turned into steaks, roasts and those oh so delicious venison burgers. Disgusting! With the deers eyes glazed over and it's tongue hanging out the mighty hunter would lash the Buck or Doe to the hood of his car and drive around the Twin Cities of Minneapolis and St. Paul proudly showing off his kill. Then you had to have your photoshoot. It was always the same, deer hunters only had one pose. With their rifle hoisted over their left shoulder, right foot on the front bumper, and right hand on the dead deer antlers, sporting a bright red hat and coat, big smile now, click. That's one for the Christmas cards.

Of course what I could never fully understand is why the people of Low Town/The Flats, were so proud of their area. What was so great about living in a shanty shack with a rusty old car out front? But they seemed to wear their poverty as a badge of honor. Like all poor areas of the Twin Cities, Low Town had a street gang. The Low Town Flat Rats were probably the most notorious street gang in St. Paul and maybe the entire Twin Cities. Bats, chains, wrenches, hammers, fists, knives, whatever was handy was their weapon of choice. Here again, was another thing I never understood. The Low Town Flat Rats seemed to think they were guardians of their community, protectors of their people, daring defenders of their hamlet, barriers to an evil that would befell the poor folks of Low Town if they weren't there. Huh! I didn't get it, who would go into that filthy place anyway? And to do what?

But if you were in Low Town you better have a good reason for being there or there was a very high probability that your car would be trashed, and the shit would be kicked out of you.

I'd already done a little research on my next match and I was not optimistic. If I was scared before, now I was full blown petrified.

My next opponent was famous for two reasons, A. Naturally he was a charter member of that dedicated community minded support group called the Low Town Flat Rats. And B. he was a fantastic boxer who had won the St. Paul light-weight division last year by going undefeated and then knocked out the Minneapolis champ in less than two rounds. The Minneapolis champ was a silky smooth black kid who fashioned himself as the next Sugar Ray Robinson, a brilliant boxer of the late 50s. The article I read said that Robinette tore into the kid like a wild dog. In the end Robinette slammed three quick short right hooks to the face of the supposedly next Sugar Ray Robinson followed by a clearing-house left that fired the black kids mouthpiece out and sent him to the mat.

With the TV off, and my inspiring phone conversation with Gus over, I sat back and reviewed my options. I had about a hundred bucks saved in my room, I could run away. Problem was I had no where to go, besides, I knew I was a spoiled suburban kid. At my age I'd never make in the real hardscrabble world. Truth is, I was starting to accept the idea that I would never make it at any age. My second thought was maybe I could pay some kid in shop class to take a hammer and break my elbow. It worked for Tony Alongi. I really didn't know what bone spurs of the elbow were, but I was willing to have them if it kept me away from that vicious Low Town Wop.

Finally I started to review the fight I had watched that night. Billy "The Barber" Daniels won, and I thought he had won decisively. What did he do to defeat such a talented, experienced and determined fighter, an opponent that was much stronger, and more powerful?

First, and this was going to be hard for me, he never showed any fear. On the contrary from the beginning Daniels met Jones in the center of the ring and traded punches, telling his foe that he wasn't going to be intimidated. In fact, whenever Doug Jones seemed to be mounting a serious attack, Daniels met the charge with even more thunder. Secondly, Daniels set everything up with his smashing left jab. Thirdly, Daniels always kept Jones in front of him. With his long arms he could keep Jones from flanking him and delivering a knockout blow, blocking those hooking bombs with his long forearms.

Daniels kept his stance wide, tall and slender he stayed in balance with a spread posture. When Jones moved in, Daniels would clutch and grab, if Jones was on the perimeter Daniels would thrust that blasting jab. I started to get goosebumps. That was a big part of it, spacing! Then there was Daniels uppercut, it was short, fire the uppercut then hold on and bang the back of the head. I stood up and started moving some coffee tables and chairs away. I held my hands out, lower this time, chest high, spread my stance and got on my toes. I looked at myself, Daniels was just like me or more to the point I was just like him. Long skinny legs, no defined ass, wide, thin undeveloped chest, ridiculously long wiry arms, boney shoulders, big clumsy hands. Aside from the fact that I was ten years younger, with bad acne, we were the same. Oh, and he was a black guy and I'm white. Same frame, same structure, same everything.

Without thinking I jolted out a left jab, hard and fast. Then another, and again, again, sliding to my left, head up, head back. I paused to think. I had the same advantages and detriments as Billy Daniels. I certainly didn't have knockout power, I wasn't muscled up, or blocky, but I had height, it was hard to get to my head. I had reach, long arms to block punches and keep my opponent at a distance. Like Daniels I was bony, if I could tie up an opponent inside I could rip and gouge with my arms and elbows.

There was no escape, in seven days I would be getting into the ring with the best young fighter in St. Paul, maybe the entire upper midwest. I was still scared, but at least I had a plan.

4.

A FAN, A FRIEND, A CONFIDANT

It was Wednesday four days from my fight with Ricardo Robinette, I was opening my locker when a note fell out.

"Good luck John, I'll be rooting for you, Tim." I had no idea who Tim was and didn't much care. But it was nice to know someone was on my side, even though I had no idea who this Tim guy was. I could have gone through the school directory and looked up all the Tim's but I didn't feel like it, besides for all I knew Tim could be one of the janitors.

Thursday afternoon I was washing up in the boys lavatory when Stu Oliver came in. Stu and I had never spoken to each other. The Oliver family was big into banking and his father owned banks all over the five state area. Stu was from a big family and all the kids went to Cretin and then on to college to take their place among the St. Paul business community. But that wasn't why Stu and I had never spoken to each other, we moved in different social circles. I suppose almost every school has a Stu Oliver or at least should. Stu was the kind of guy who everyone liked and could depend on. The kind of guy who was always in the middle of everything. In fact he played center on the football team, wrestled middleweight and was the catcher on the baseball team. Stu was everything I wasn't, powerful, athletic, friendly, optimistic. Ruddy faced kid with short blond hair, thick neck, and continuous smile. Like I said, we moved in different social circles, his was the entire school, mine was myself. Stu stopped me before I could leave the lav and looked around to see if anyone else was there. I didn't know if he had some secret to tell me or if he didn't want to be seen with a loser like me.

"Listen John," he began, "you got a tough draw Saturday night, there's nothing to be gained by you letting that dirtbag kid hurt you."

I stood there not really thinking, finally I muttered, "I should be OK."

Stu finished by saying, "I got to run, John, in six years you'll be in grad school and that rat will be in prison. In twenty years you'll be a big success and that bum will be dead, so who cares? Just don't get hurt." Then he was gone. *First I thought how nice of Stu to be concerned, then I thought, gee thanks for the vote of confidence.*

The rest of the week passed and Saturday evening Dad, Gus and I were cruising to the armory.

I could tell that neither of them thought much of this boxing idea of theirs. But midwestern men don't quit, if our ancestors had been quitters they never would have gotten to this garden spot of Minnesota in the first place. I slumped down to the locker room and got ready. All week long I had been practicing in the school gym. Keep my opponent at a distance, or keep him close, it's the middle space that could hurt me. Use what you have, height, reach, speed. Keep moving, but keep him in front of you, but most of all be relentless. MUST BE RELENTLESS, MUST NEVER LET MY COMBATANT THINK HE'S IN CHARGE. MEET FURY WITH MORE FURY, THUNDER WITH BIGGER THUNDER, it had worked for Billy 'The Barber' Daniels.

As I said the people of the The Flats were a proud lot, and very proud of anyone who was succeeding from there. Thus, Ricky Robinette had a big cheering section including parents who couldn't afford baby sitters, they just brought the kids along. I looked over at his corner, no point in hiding, and there he was. The newspaper articles I read about him described him as having feet of a tap dancer, hands like mercury. The way he was warming up sure looked like it. Robinette's Dad was his trainer, a big man, with a loud voice, always trying to make it seem to everyone that he was the reason for his kid's boxing prowess. Then I took another quick look, in Ricardos corner was a girl. She was there with the stool, bucket, sponge, towel, water, she was dressed in old jeans and shirt, hair looked bad, but she sure was slender and pretty. She had all those Italian beauty qualities, dark skinned, high cheek bones, perfect nose, mysterious dark eyes. That was Robinette's sister.

The ref called us to the center of the ring, made his announcements and had us tap gloves. It was here that I noticed that Ricky R. wasn't trying to give me the old stare down, but was smiling at me, really giggling at me.

I went back to my corner and waited for the bell, for some stupid reason I wasn't scared. I knew I had nothing to lose, no one gave me a chance, if I lost everyone would just shrug and think, 'Eh, it's Williams, figures'.

"Ding," I took three giant steps out into the center of the ring, got on my toes, legs spread wide, hands low, I could hear Gus screaming at me to, "Get your hands up."

I waited, and waited, that mean little smart ass paused coming out his corner, looked around at his crowd of worshippers and grinned.

*A man with nothing to lose is a dangerous man, a **mad** man with nothing to lose is a **very** dangerous man.*

Finally Ricky dickhead decided he would honor me with his presence in the ring. Jumping out of his corner he started dancing around like the next Gene fucking Kelly, a famous dancer of the 50s. Here he comes, bobbing, weaving, rolling, flashing that sinister grin, he was in range, bam. I fired a left jab with everything I had in my skinny, boney body. I was aiming for his face but I just missed and banged him square in the forehead. Robinette rolled back with a fast backpedal to the ropes which saved him from going down. The crowd went silent. It was here I made my first mistake, I momentarily stopped to look at my work. Billy Daniels would have been all over him smashing away with more powerful jabs. But I stood there for a second, eyeing the sagging Robinette. From over my corner I heard some kid scream out, "John, go get him." Robinette quickly tried to recover and shook his head smiling, but I'd sent a message. The rest of the round amounted to me stalking Ricky slamming the left jab, with Robinette on his bicycle trying to avoid me. "Ding."

I went to my corner positive I had won the round. Gus put the stool out and immediately leaned into my ear and said, "Nice round, here's what we're going to do now." I put the back of my glove in his face and said, "I was fine." Gus looked over at my Dad and shrugged. Over at Robinette's corner his father was standing over him screaming at him. "What the hell was that, I told you to get inside! You better shape up Ricky, that was a total disgrace."

"Ding" round two, Ricky wasn't fooling around now. I thought back to my mentor Billy Daniels, "Be relentless, meet fury with more fury." I kept snapping my penetrating jab. I was at least three inches taller than Ricky and a lot longer. Robinette threw a big left hook and I blocked it with my right arm. It was here that I made my second mistake. After blocking the hook, I lowered my arm and that mean 'Rat Flatter' doubled up his hook and caught me hard above the right ear, sending my left knee to the mat. I put my left hand on the second rung, the ref came over and I waved him away. Any other time John Williams would have just quit. This time John Williams got back on his feet and kept fighting. The rest of the round dissolved into Ricky trying to finish me off and me holding him tight and banging him on the back of the head.

"Ding" round three. Last round. I made a point of being out in the middle of the ring first. On my toes, legs wide, fists low, blasting away with everything I had, bang, bang, bang. Robinette slipped under and caught me with a shot to the ribs. I cracked my left elbow over his cheekbone. I could sense that Robinette was desperate, this fight, this match, this time, was in doubt. With a minute left Robinette made a furious charge at me. I kept thinking, "Must be relentless, absolutely relentless, must not submit." I shoved Robinette aside and powdered him with another jab, then another. Robinette went even lower and double hooked my left kidney, then tried to go upstairs but I blocked him with a forearm. Finally the bell sounded and that little bastard whirled around raising his hands in victory imploring his faithful while trying to sway the judges.

Hands burning, legs wobbly, gasping for air, but still full of fight, I turned to my corner. It was here that some kid jumped into the ring and threw his arm around me, "John, John, you did great, just great! You won the fight! You did great, wait till I tell everyone at school!"

I said, "Thanks," feeling too tired to figure who this kid was.

As I got to my corner I glanced at my Father and Gus. They both had this wide eyed, "I don't believe what I just saw," look in their eyes. This was a John Williams no one had ever seen before.

Out in the center of the ring the ref made the announcement. "Ring judge, *whatever his name was*, has the fight Williams one round, Robinette one round, one round a tie. Ref scores the fight the same way, this fight is a tie."

It was what it was! I made some mistakes, but I stayed aggressive through out the fight and really thought I'd won it. Robinette's Dad was now in full rage, and there were more than a few boos from the crowd.

I was still trying to gather myself when I noticed my Dad had gone over to meet Robinette's Dad. I glided over to Rickys corner to see what was going on.

Dad stuck out his hand to shake Old Man Robinette's, who looked mad and confused. Dad dressed in his expensive yellow overcoat said, "Nice to meet you, both of our son's did real well, don't you think?"

Ricky's Dad replied, "Huh? Oh ya."

"Since both of our sons tried so hard I thought we could all go out for a little bite to eat, maybe some burgers and shakes for the kids, my treat," Dad remarked.

Robinette's Dad now looked even more confused, "Huh, ah no, we eat at home," he dismissed to Dad.

Dad and Gus turned to walk away and my view rolled to Ricky's dowdy dressed but startling good looking sister. With her hands now on her hips flames were roaring out of her eyes, glaring holes in her Dad's face. There was no question who was really in charge here.

Looking at his daughter Old Man Robinette's eyes went wide, and his mouth went open. He turned to Dad and said, "Hey, look, OK, sure, I guess that would be fine, where did you want to go?"

"How about Porky's, they have the best shakes in town," said Dad.

Ricky's Dad wiped his chin and said, "Sure, Porky's, see you there."

5.

BURGERS, STEAK FRIES, SHAKES, AND CONVERSATION

I'm sure every major city in the country has a Porky's. Burgers, fries, and shakes, formica counter, hefty, waddling server ladies that have been there since statehood was granted in 1858.

Thirty minutes later Dad's massive, shiny, Lincoln pulled in to Porky's lot next to Robinette's aging, rusty 12 year old Pontiac. Gus, Dad, and Mister R put their rumps into one booth. Ricky, his slender sexy sister, and little brother about 8 years old lined up across from me in another.

I was too excited and too exhausted to eat anything, but in short order four huge burgers, with steak fries, and shakes arrived on our table.

Back then shakes were served in a large glass jar, and then the server would put a large canister of even more shake next to it.

Trying to be friendly, I asked Rick and his sister, "What courses are you taking in school?"

"None of your business," was Ricky's pleasant reply.

I tried another tact, "What did you guys do over the summer?"

"What do you care?" snarled Ricky.

"What are you reading in English class?" trying to change direction.

More glaring, more snarling, finally his intriguing sister opened up.

"Rick has a little problem with grammar, terms like predicate nominative, dangling participle…"

I interrupted, "Well that's easy, I can teach you that stuff in no time, here…."

"Shut up asshole," was his pleasant response.

The little brother on the end of the booth was starting to giggle. Evidently watching his older brother verbally and physically pound people around was high entertainment for him.

His slender sister now placed a controlling hand on Ricky's shoulder. Evidently other than going to school this girl's real job was was keeping her angry father and temperamental brother in check. Looked stressful.

It was here that my new best bud Ricky looked over at my untouched plate of burgers and fries and said.

"You going to eat that or not?"

I slid my plate toward them, the girl performed an equal one-third surgery on my sandwich and than poured a few fries on her plate. Watching her distribute the remaining food to her brothers I started to get it. They were hungry, and they shared things, equally. I realize now how stupid this sounds but as an only child to successful parents I'd never seen anything like this.

The convivial meal broke up and we headed out of Porky's. I opened the back door to my Dad's expensive Lincoln and sat down on the fine leather interior. I then turned to watch the Robinette's get in their Dad's shitty old Pontiac. They were walking together, Ricky in the middle with his left hand on his little brother's shoulder, she had her left arm around his waist. They got in their Dad's car and just for a moment I could see her looking at me with this blank stare. I looked back. Man was she pretty. After much goosing and coughing old-man Robinette's monster roared to life and drove away. What a strange night!

School and the weekly Saturday night fights went on. Naturally, after fighting the infamous Ricky Robinette to a draw my life changed. First, my classmates stopped sneering at me. Secondly I had gotten a major jolt of confidence. The next three fights were all very one-sided events. Using my long reach and height it was almost impossible for any of these punk pugilists to hurt me. Also my cheering section had stayed the same. This one kid who was about 5-8, maybe 150 pounds would come down to the armory and clap, whistle, and roar his approval. Finally, I spotted the kid sitting by himself in the school lunch room and with great trepidation went over and asked how he was doing? He looked up and asked if I would sit with him. As it turned out we had a lot in common. Both were very shy, introverted, and insecure. Both had successful parents, his father had just been promoted again to be some high, senior, senior, mucky muck with a major clothing company. Most surprising was that like me, Tim, that was his name, Tim Langford was an only child. This was very unusual for the times. Back then you could say there was three "no's". No pill, no abortion, and honey, snookums, darling, sweetie pie, was not suppose to say, "No."

"So Tim, before we go back to class can I ask you a question?" I asked.

Before I could continue Tim interrupted, "I just didn't think it was fair," he said.

My only thought was, 'Huh!'

"It wasn't fair," he said again. "All the other athletes and sports guys in this school have people supporting them, so I thought I would support you."

We've been good, ok only, friends ever since.

Practicing everyday in the school's gym the left jab got faster, harder, and meaner. Snap, snap, snap, bang, bang, bang. Foot work was still a problem. I was still growing, my big floppy feet were still catching on things. I had risen in the ranks to second place and now would fight for the St. Paul welterweight division title. My opponent would be, you guessed it, that charming young fellow from the Flats named Ricky Robinette. I knew this was going to happen, and I also knew that old Ricky Robinette would not be unprepared this time. I may have blindsided him once, but now he would be looking for revenge. As was to be expected Robinette had finished the rest of his schedule without a loss. Thus, I was the only thing keeping him from fighting some kid in Minneapolis for another Twin City title. As if old Ricky needed any extra motivation, some writer for the St. Paul Pioneer Press did some digging and found out that what Robinette was trying to do had never been done before.

"Ricky Robinette the 'Pride Of Low Town' will be trying to reach a level that has never been achieved in the boxing annuls of the Twin Cities. Last year's Twin Cities Lightweight Division Champ is now only one small step away from fighting for the Twin Cities Welterweight Championship. Robinette, aka 'The flattener from the flats' has but one blemish on this years record, a draw in the third week of his schedule. *They didn't ever bother to mention my name, assholes!*"

The article went on, "Aside from this minor hiccup, Robinette has dispatched his opponents in quick order.

Ruthless Ricky Robinette could then be the first St. Paul fighter to win successive Twin Cities championships in different weight classes."

That week in school was not easy. Some smart-ass clipped the story out and taped to the wall in the school cafeteria. Nice! Real nice! Not only that but the wise-ass highlighted the words "blemish" and "minor hiccup." For the rest of the week I was referred to as "Blemish." Trust me, no kid with acne likes to be called "Blemish." What was worse was what happened in English class that week. Our English teacher, Mr. Larson, dressed as always in a plaid tie, plaid shirt, and brown dress coat with patches on the sleeves, (*Who came up with that fashion statement? Very popular with male English teachers in the 60s who were sure they were the next undiscovered F. Scott Fitzgerald*) was lecturing about the undercurrents of animosity associated with Arthur Miller's Death Of A Salesman. Then turning to me Mr. Larson asked, "Maybe Cretin Highs 'minor hiccup' could tell us about this?"

The whole class laughed and some even pointed to me. I smiled my golly-gosh-midwest-grin like I was in on the joke. But I didn't think it was funny. I never met anyone who liked being called a 'minor hiccup'.

6.

TO DIVE OR NOT TO DIVE, THAT IS THE QUESTION

St. Paul High School Welterweight Championship Bout:

Sat. Night 7:20 PM Mid November 1967

As we drove to the Armory Gus turned to me to give me some more of his savvy, sage boxing advice. He kept it short, "John" he said.

"Yes, Mr. Swenson," I replied.

He continued, "Just one thing, I've been watching this kid Robinette you're fighting tonight. He's not above fighting dirty, keep your hands up."

He looked back at me, "What I mean is, on the referee break, or at the bell, he's still looking for an opening. Don't let your guard down until he turns from you."

Hmmmm, good to know.

"Representing Blah, Blah, Blah Ricky Robinette, the roar was loud and enthusiastic, they'd come to watch their local hero take care of that one 'minor hiccup' and move on. And from Cretin High John Williams," Gus and Dad clapped and my new and only friend Tim jumped up and cheered.

This time Ricky Robinette was not smirking or smiling. We met in the middle of the ring and he was giving me his, "Suburban boy you are about to deal with an inner city killer," stare. It was not comforting, such a fine sportsman.

"Ding" Round 1.

Robinette stormed out of his corner like the second coming of Hurricane Carter. I swear somebody put firecrackers on his ass. He didn't dance, or glide over to me, he flew at me, fists roaring from all angles. I immediately found myself pinned to my corner, Gus screaming at me to "Move left." Tim screaming at me to "Move right." Dad screaming at me to "Get out of the corner." It was very obvious what Robinette's fight plan was. Pin me down, trap me against the ropes and whale away. Eliminate my height and reach advantage, tear into my midsection. I faked left and tried move right but Robinette was right on top of me almost inside me. Ricky let loose a right, left, right combination to my ribs that sucked the gas out of me. Finally, I locked my two forearms around his head, spun him around and retreated to the middle of the ring.

Robinette came at me like a vicious badger, going low he forced me into the ropes near his corner. Windmilling shots from all directions, I could hear his cultured Father roaring at him to, "Stay low, work the midsection." From the peanut gallery his super-brat little brother was laughing, and jumping, with great glee.

"Ding." Robinette kept swirling, just like Gus had said. Finally the ref jumped in between us. Robinette went to his corner mumbling something about, "Not hearing the bell." A-Hole!

I limped to my corner, my arms, shoulders, and ribs felt like they'd been pulverized, maybe even tenderized. Gus, Dad and Tim looked glum, they wiped me up and asked how I was doing?

I didn't bother to respond. The only advantage I had was I knew exactly what Robinette was going to do. I also knew that clutching and grabbing hadn't worked, and retreating had totally failed.

"Ding." Round 2.

Here comes guess who! I forced myself into the middle of the ring, I had to stay off the ropes. In came Robinette low, and ready, time slowed, I suddenly thought of what Billy "The Barber" Daniels did at a time like this. If you've never boxed or even been in a fist fight you probably won't understand what happened next. A fighter knows when he's scored a decisive blow, a striking shot, a fight turning smash. I stepped forward and let fly a short, intense, crunching right uppercut to Robinette' nose, my four knuckles plastering Ricky's upper bridge. It felt like his head exploded against my right glove. Time slowed more. I saw Robinette's head turn, and his right leg quiver, he sagged to the mat, blood flowing from his nose and mouth. I saw the ref bouncing in front of me screaming, "Williams neutral corner, Williams neutral corner." I saw my Dad, Gus, and Timmy frantically trying to get my attention, all with their arms and fingers pointing to my neutral corner. I saw the ref looking over Robbinette. I saw Ricky's beautiful sexy sister grab a towel and try to throw it in the ring to stop the fight. I saw her angry Father rip the towel out of her hands and throw in the crowd. I felt a whoosh of silence from the Ricky Robinette's faithful, all in slow motion. Time restarted, the ref had asked Ricky if he was alright, he said he was, he wasn't, the fight continued. But there was no fight in Ricky Robinette. From my corner I heard, "Stay aggressive, stay aggressive." I moved in slashing left jabs to the wobbling Robinette. The first one landed, then the second, one for each eye socket. Somehow I missed with a third nearly tearing Robinette's right ear off.

"Ding."

I went to my corner, Gus set the stool out for me, with my left foot I slid it back. I then casually turned and stood there arms out stretched on the third rung, lazily crossing my leg. Time to play some mind games with Robinette and his corner gang. I tried giving the whole scene a detached, uncaring look. The mood and emotion I received from the crowd was now distain, bordering on sheer hatred. For some reason I started to like it. This was the first time in my life I felt powerful. What a rush! Ricky looked awful, blood was coming out of eyes, nose and mouth, his right ear was turning purple. Robinette's sexy sister was running low on towels, and his bratty brother was hiding in his seat. The ref checked on him, asking his Dad if he really wanted to continue? Old man Robinette ordered poor Ricky back in the ring. Ricky didn't want to go, didn't want to get off his stool. Finally he rose, took a deep breath, mustering up some bravado from somewhere deep in his DNA. It was then that I saw it, it was fast, it was private, it was pleading. Ricky's sister had scurried her long legs and perfect butt back behind their ring corner. Shielding herself from her roaring Father she shaded her face with her left hand, eyes wide, making contact with only me. She then took her right four fingers and made a small, flat wave. It was easy to read, "I surrender, please don't hurt my brother." Time slowed again.

"Ding" Round 3.

I put my gloves out, John L. Sullivan style, thinking, "What was I getting out of all this?" Sure I could rip Ricky up. But then what? Next week I have to go fight some guy in Minneapolis who just might knock my head off. The boxing program at Cretin High was going to be discontinued anyway. I never wanted to do this in the first place. I had a winning record, nobody could say I hadn't tried. What's more that beautiful girl in the corner had asked me to help. I had everything, successful parents, plenty of money, private school, Ricky Robinette didn't have much. Problem was, it was going to be a tough sell.

I moved in to Ricky. He started to retreat. I made a valiant lunge for him, missing by two feet and landed on my left shoulder, legs crossed. I could hear and sudden burst of enthusiasm from Ricky's crowd. Hoisting myself up, the Ref asked if I was OK, I gritted back, "That I was fine." Again, I moved on Robinette finally shouldering him into the far ropes. I let him pin me to a neutral corner, hands over my ears I made it look like I was out of steam. He started going to work on me, but didn't have much left in his tank. His lefts and rights to my body were almost pitiful. My corner was screaming at me to move. I continued to cover up, putting a worried, beaten expression on my face. Robinette was coming to life now. I let him bang away, picking almost everything off. He stepped back and delivered a big left hook, always his best punch. I blocked most of it, but felt part to it connect with my head. That was what I was hoping for. I fell on my right side, face away from my corner. I stayed down, finally rolling to a sitting position with the Ref looking down at me. "Are you done?" he hollered over the now near bedlam. I shook my head up and down. The Ref waved his hands over me, indicating he'd stopped the fight.

I slouched to my corner and had Gus put a towel over my head.

At the call the Ref announced that at the two minute and twenty second mark of the third round the fight had been stopped. Winner by technical knockout Ricky Robinette.

I was so glad to get out of there.

On the ride home Gus and Dad were really quiet. Finally Gus turned to me and asked, "If I was alright?" I said, "I was OK, and thank you for asking Mr. Swenson, and thank you for all you've done for me." Faking disappointment was not easy for me.

"What happened in the third round?" Gus questioned.

"Just didn't have anything left, couldn't raise my arms. You saw what he did to me in the first round. I guess it caught up to me," was my response.

There was a long silence and I thought I had convinced them when Dad asked, "If you were so tired why didn't take the stool when Gus offered it to you?"

That was a tough one, I had to think of something and it better be good. Finally I said, "Dad, I was so tired I didn't dare sit down because I didn't think I could get up."

They both just nodded.

I didn't know if they believed me or not, and I didn't much care.

At last my endeavor into the wide world of sports was over and I hoped that would be the end of my parents trying to make an athlete of me. I just wanted to get back to doing what I liked to do. Hang around by myself in my rec room, listen to my records, watch TV, shoot pool, play my guitar and of course, think about girls.

7.

BLOW JOBS AND BREATH MINTS: NOT THE SILVER BULLET, BUT AT LEAST THE BRONZE:

A week after the "Dive."

Football season was also wrapping up, and school was almost ready to break for Thanksgiving when Tim asked if he could speak to me privately. Why did Tim talk to me like this? Of course he could speak to me privately. I'm a total loner. I'm not part of a crowd, speaking to me privately is the only way anyone ever talked to me back then.

Cretin was a very large school, but there were very few hideaways that were out of the eyesight of watchful teachers, hall monitors or nosey students. However, there was a small room between the music center and the school theater. It was here where a guy could duck in for a quick smoke, a short snort of bourbon, and if you were one of the popular jock types you might even cop-a-feel from an admiring Cretin girl. This was about a week after my last fight down at the Armory. Tim led me to the room holding a copy of Moliere' The Miser which was the fall play that year just in case anyone got suspicious. Closing the door, Tim said, "This is the deal John, that friend of yours got a hold of me last night and says she wants to see you."

My first thought was, 'I don't have any other friends than you', my second thought was, 'Did Tim say she?'

Tim talking fast in a hush tone, "Ya, she says to meet her behind St. Marks Church off of Selby tomorrow night. I don't know how she got my number but I think she must have some family member work at the same company Dad runs."

I first said, "Tim back up, what girl? Why St. Marks? And do I have to come alone?"

Tim whispered, "The girl at the fight, Robinette's corner girl, you know, the one who tried to put him back together after you decked him."

"Her!" I exploded.

Tim with an alarmed look on his face, "John keep it down."

"Why does she want to see me?" I asked.

"I don't know, but actually she didn't say she wanted to see you, she said she needed to see you," Tim answered.

"I don't think I like this Tim, that church is over by the Flats, I don't think either of us would be welcome in that part of town."

Tim said, "John that's what I first thought too. It must be a trap to lure us there so that a bunch of Low Town Flat Rats can beat the crap out of us. But why? Robinette won the fight."

"Will you go with me?" I asked.

Tim was thoughtful for a moment, he had screamed his head off cheering for me to beat the Pride Of Low Town. I'm sure some undesirables had taken notice.

Then Tim said, "Sure I'll go with you, I wasn't planning on living past 20 anyway."

Then thinking out loud, I said, "Should we bring anything with us?"

"What do you mean?" said Tim.

"You know like a hammer, or a knife or something?" I said.

"John, it's not like either one of us are what you would call skilled street fighters, what good would it do?" Tim responded.

So the Wednesday before Thanksgiving after supper I asked Dad if I could borrow the Lincoln to go visit my new pal Tim.

The Lincoln was Dad's company car and he rarely let me use it. Mother's Buick Rivera was totally off limits. Mom had recently gotten a brand new 1965 Buick Riviera and it was without a doubt one of the most elegant cars General Motors had ever designed. The idea was for the Buick Rivera to compete with the now upscale luxury of the Ford Thunderbird.

I picked up Tim and cautiously drove to St. Marks, trying to be as inconspicuous as a shiny Lincoln Town Car can be in the slummiest, most dilapidated part of St. Paul.

Minnesota November nights are all the same, cold, windy, dark, and depressing.

"She said to park in the back of the church lot, farthest away from the back door," murmured Tim.

"Lets keep the car doors locked," I said.

"Good idea, if a bunch of Flat Rats start jumping on the car just slam it in reverse. Who cares if we crunch over a few of them," countered Tim. As if I wasn't going to do that anyway!

"What time did she say to meet her?" I asked for probably the third time.

"7:30" said Tim, "let's give it a few more minutes, then bang out of here."

I was just about ready to start the car, when the back door of the church flew open. About twenty girls all about 15 or 16 years old poured out, laughing and chattering as fast as they could. They turned left around the corner of the church and disappeared up the street.

"OK John that's enough, let's roll out of here, somethings gotta be up," said Tim.

"Your right Tim," now more scared than ever.

I was just putting my hand on the ignition key when Tim said, "Wait a sec, that's her."

From the corner street light I could see a dark figure scampering as fast as she could to the car.

Tim popped his lock, opened the door and Ricky Robinette's foxy sister slapped her perfect ass into the front seat. Tim furtively looking around jumped in the back.

I looked at her and said, "Where are we going?"

"We're not going anywhere," and motioning to Tim in the back seat said, "what's he doing here?"

"Huh!" Was my reply.

Now getting angry, Miss Robinette said, "What's he doing here? He can't watch," she ripped.

"Ah, ok, ah, huh!" was my only answer.

"I said he can't watch," she said.

Now turning to Tim she snapped, "Get out."

Tim, far more aware of what was happening than me, sighed and said, "John, give me a cigarette."

I handed my pack of Tareytons and lighter to Tim and he slipped out of the car, walking away in the dark.

Silence! More Silence!

I suppose there are people who have had easy first experiences. Unruffled, smooth, joyful, without guilt, shame or complications. Never met one!

"My name is Saundra, I needed to see you again, John."

"Hi Saundra," I said inching my left side deeper into my door handle.

Saundra looked ahead, took a deep breath and then said. "John, I can't get pregnant." She started inching closer to me her left thigh now against mine.

"OK, that's nice, me neither," I said without thinking.

"No, you don't understand," Saundra said. "There's not enough food in the house now. What's more the Stock Yards are closing soon and Dad will be out of work. Just as well, he comes home every-day stinking of guts and blood. No wonder he's always mad."

I didn't know what to say so I didn't say anything.

"So look John, I can't get pregnant," she said again, this time more firmly.

"Ah huh, me neither," I whispered.

The slap on my right shoulder was hard and sharp not playful at all. Maybe everything about this girl was hard and sharp.

"You rich boy's think everything is a joke, that you can make fun of all of us," she said.

"I'm not rich," I countered.

Saundra stopped a moment and looked around Dad's lavish Lincoln.

Sliding further into me she wrapped her left arm around my neck, I could feel her finger nails touching my throat.

"Beverly says if I do this I won't get pregnant," said Saundra.

"Who's Beverly?"

"She's my best friend."

"How does she know?"

"Because she's pregnant."

"Beverly's pregnant?"

"Yes, I just said so, look that was really nice what you did for my twin brother."

"Ricky and you are twins?"

"Yes, I just said so, and what you did was the nicest thing anyone's ever done for me."

I could feel Saundra moving her small, yet undeveloped breasts into my right ribcage.

"What did I do?"

"You know." She took another quick glance around.

"John we have to hurry, we have to make it fast, and I've never done it before."

With that she slid her right hand up my inner leg and started to unzip my fly. *"My dick, penis, cock, Johnson, (who came up with Johnson?) immediately felt like it was hitting against my Dad's steering wheel."*

I have long legs anyway but I powered the seat back further, unsnapped my pants buckle. Out came guess who! Saundra's eyes widened and then with great resolve dove down. I trembled, she trembled, she found my right hand and moved to the the base of my Dick. I stroked, Saundra sucked. She dove further, and at approximately 7:58 PM

Wednesday November 22nd 1967, in my fathers luxury company car, "THE HILLS CAME ALIVE WITH THE SOUND OF MUSIC."

Time slowed, Saundra came up, eyes wide, mouth full. Saundra started fighting with the passenger door. I must have hit the automatic door lock during the action. I reached over with my long arms and flipped the door handle. Saundra banged it open with her head and started spitting, coughing, gagging out my sperm, all the time screaming that she was going to kill Beverly. A minute later she came back up, slamming the door shut.

"That bitch, I'll get her, if she wasn't pregnant I'd kill her," Saundra snapped out.

I sat there confused with my throbbing cock still out.

Saundra went on, "She told me that it didn't taste that bad, and that I needed to take as much as I could, that big liar!"

I tried being supportive, "Maybe it's something that you need to get used to."

She whacked me again on the shoulder, again sharp and hard.

"Do you have any tissues?" she asked.

I reached over and opened the glove box, Mother always had tissues on hand.

"Do you have some gum or mints?" she asked.

I reached in my pocket and pulled out my last stick of Double Mint.

Saundra took some deep breaths, then said, "Thanks again for not hurting my brother, we're now even." Then looking at my joystick said, "You can put that away now."

"I've never had it out in front of a girl before, it's kind of exciting," I replied, putting it away and zipping up.

Again with the sharp whack in the shoulder. Maybe hitting people is something they do a lot of in this part of St. Paul.

Carefully unwrapping the gum, she politely started chewing.

I asked, "What are you doing at church on a school night?"

"This is a young girls class," she said. "Sister Mary Katherine is teaching us how to be responsible, virtuous young girls."

We paused to think about this a second.

I then said, "I guess this town could use a lot more Sister Mary Katherines."

Saundra started to half cry, half laugh.

Gathering herself together she said, "I have to run."

"So you did this because I didn't hurt Ricky?" I asked.

She just nodded.

"Hmmm, how about if your brother and I get into more fights? You know, like once a night. I'll make sure he always wins," I joked.

She started to cry, and laugh some more. I put my right arm around her but she broke free and jumped out of the car, dashing away.

I put my head back and then she was back knocking on the passenger door of my Dad's Lincoln.

I powered the window down and she looked in, "I suppose now you're going to tell all your rich friends at that toney school of yours that there's a slutty Low Town girl down in the Flats that gives sloppy blowjobs?"

"Ah, is that what you want?" I questioned.

"What I want is for you to get your Daddy's fancy car out of my neighborhood before somebody sees you," she said.

She tore off, I just saw a whisp of her hair fly past the corner of the church. I leaned back in the car collecting myself when my new friend Tim nearly gave me a heart attack. Tapping on my window he said, "John, can I come in now? It's getting really cold out here."

Not wanting him to step in the remnants of John Williams first sexual experience I backed up and Tim hopped in.

"You OK John? You look kinda nervous, you need me to drive?" asked Tim.

"I think I'll be alright, just need something to settle me down that's all," I said.

"Maybe a few beers would help, drive us over to Rice Street I'll see what I can do," answered Tim.

I had no idea what Tim was up to, but considering my present state of mind I wasn't going to argue. Rice Street is where the people who can't make it in the Flats live. Low rent flop houses, dive bars and discount liquor stores seem be the popular businesses. Rice Street is also known as "Derelict Drive."

Passing a particularly depressing liquor store Tim said, "Let's try this one. Pull over to the side, and park near the back." Parking in the dark wasn't a problem on Rice Street because a lot of the street lights were out anyway. After watching one unfortunate after another slumping into the disgusting old liquor store, Tim bolted out of the car saying, "This guy looks good."

A dirty, defeated looking guy in an old weathered coat, with a few days beard and long uncombed hair, slouched over to Tim motioning from the corner of the store. Tim offered him one of my Tareytons that the guy put in his pocket. I saw Tim pass him something and then Tim zipped back to the car hopping in. "Wait here, when we make the switch meet me at the end of the street," Tim said.

A few minutes later out skulked Mr. Excitement and started walking toward our car. Tim quickly got out and started moving to our buyer. The handoff was smooth, Tim slipped him another five dollar bill the guy handed the beer to Tim. Neither of them ever breaking stride. '*Maybe this is how those CIA spy guys pass information on the streets of Europe,*' I thought. I started the car and met Tim at the end of the street. Jumping in he said, "Let's try the Bluffs, nobody is ever there this time of the year."

About thirty minutes later I pulled into an empty ice caked parking lot and killed the engine. Tim popped a couple cans of Grain Belt Beer and handed me one. A lot of people in Minnesota drank Grain Belt Beer. The motto around the state was, "Pabst Blue Ribbon Beer, The Beer That Made Milwaukee Famous, Grain Belt Beer, The Beer That Made Milwaukee Jealous." Cute!

As we both started on our second Grain Belt, Tim asked me a question, "So, why did you throw the fight?"

"What?" was my quiet and evasive response.

"You know, last week, why did you take the dive?"

"I didn't take a dive," I lied. "No, ...and why do you care?"

"Well, it's just that I lost a lot of money on you, that's all," responded Tim.

I nearly spit up my Grain Belt, "You what!"

"Ya, I hung around West Seventh Street last week. Let it be known that I was willing to take some action on your fight. I ended up getting three-to-one. I lost 60 bucks, but I should have, I mean, I could have won a hundred and eighty."

"Gee, I'm really sorry Tim, that's a lot of money," I said.

"Nothing for you to be sorry about, after all, you said you didn't take a dive," Tim quietly replied.

I changed the subject to what was going on at Cretin High and we finished our third beer. I then drove Tim home.

As I slowly cruised back to my parents house I thought about the nights events. First sexual experience with someone other than myself. First time I'd broke the law by helping buy illegal alcoholic beverages. First time I drank alcoholic beverages with someone other than myself, and first time I ever met someone who had total faith in me.

What a night!

8.

NOBODY WINS 73% AND LIVES

Tuesday Jan 11th, 1977, 5 Days before Super Bowl 10

I got up early that day around noon. Tim was just putting lunch on: Cheddar chutney toasted sandwiches on rye, with Tim's homemade chicken vegetable soup. I never really knew how or why Tim was so good at this kind of thing. Tim didn't like canned soup, (he thought it was lousy) so he would cook his own from scratch. Amazing!

"Did you read the article about Maui last night?" Tim asked.

"Yes, I took it to bed with me, it was either your article or a beautiful girl. I opted for your story, very interesting, but I have a few questions," I countered.

Tim looked in and waved me to continue.

"OK, here's what you're thinking we should do. Give up our Bloomington Pleasure Palace," I swept my hand around in an expansive manner. "Say good bye to all our friends. Sell the Brown

Bomber, cum stains and all. Go off someplace six times zones away, where we don't have jobs and don't know anyone. Hope that we get lucky and get hired during this horrible recession. And ohh, that we might like the place. Is that it?" I said.

"John, you got it. But there's more, things just might be getting hot here," said Tim. "As you know I've been making more football bets than ever this season, and as you also know, we've been really lucky this year."

Tim and I had pooled our resources for years now betting sports, mostly football. Tim would do the bulk of the research. On Saturday afternoon, after I'd finally gotten up he would take me through what we were going to put our hard earned money down on. I once asked Tim, "Why we never bet on college teams?" Tim told me, "Way too many teams, way too many coaching changes, way too many players." Made sense to me!

Our Saturday afternoon meeting would sound something like this:

"Ok, John, here's what I think we should do this week, I've narrowed it down to three games I like," Tim began.

"Giants/Dolphins, game in New York. Giants defense is one of the best in the league. Dolphins got away with a lot of stuff last week in New Orleans but now they're up against a real defense. Weather in New York is going to be cold, windy and rainy. I see the Dolphins quarterback blowing on his throwing hand to stay warm while he stares into that hard east coast rain looking at a great New York defense, Giants by 10.

Bears/Seahawks, Bears won last week up in Green Bay and that was a monster win for them. Now they go on the road all the way out to Seattle. Really hard for Chicago not to have a let down game after beating the Packers. I see plenty of scoring in this game, and a Seahawk victory by 7 or more points.

Finally, Redskins/Eagles in D.C., always a bruising match-up. Both teams need a win badly and both teams are much better defensively than offensively. The big difference is the Skins played a tough game on Monday night and that gives them one less day to heal up. I see the Eagles winning at the end of a low scoring game by a field goal.

What do you think?"

My normal response would be something like, "Gee Tim, I think you're right on all three games. Sounds good, how much do you want me to throw in?" Not really understanding half of what my friend had said.

"John, over the course of this season we've won at a 73 per cent clip, that's unreal. The bookies in this area must be getting wind of where the money is flowing and a lot of it's been flowing our way," Tim said.

"You think we've made some enemies?" I asked.

"I don't know, however, I don't much like the smell around here lately," said Tim.

"What do you mean, smell, what smell?" I asked.

This was not unusual for Tim, I secretly referred to it as, "Little mans paranoia." Out there on the edges of life were threats and dangers that I never saw, but somehow Tim felt them. Very Spooky!

Tim quickly spoke, "Like I said last night, now's a good time for a change. We're both still young, 'if you consider mid-to-late-twenties young', and most of what we do is either illegal or close to it. The sports gambling we do, the poker game we play, the escort service we started, your occasional coke habit, it all adds up to trouble."

Tim could see me thinking, something I rarely did, "Tell me more," I said.

Tim continued, "Then there was the big fight several weeks ago at the bar. There was something about that brawl that didn't seem right. Besides, you could have been killed. I think it is time to bang out of here."

"Ah Tim, that was just another Packer/Viking game, you know that tempers run hot over that game, always have," I countered.

9.

FISTS, FIGHTS, AND A FOGGY HEAD

About seven weeks before the Packers had come to Metropolitan stadium to play our Vikes. This had been going on since Vince Lombardi and Norm Van Brocklin were coaching back in the early 60s. Maybe there's bigger rivalry games in the NFL but this is a big one. Every time the Pack and the Vikes meet there's fights, in the stands, streets, parking lots and bars.

Naturally, because Maxwell's was the number one sports bar in the Twin Cities every one that didn't have tickets to the game tried to get in. The place was jammed, purple and white, green and gold. To make matters worse the NFL decided to make this a Sunday night game so everyone was really lubricated up by kickoff at 7:00 PM.

Steve Lynch, head bouncer had put on extra staff. Boomer, and his little/big brother Einer had volunteered to help. There was still going to be some fights, but hopefully things wouldn't get too crazy.

Everything was fine until midway through the fourth quarter. I never really found out how or why it started. I had just come back from a quick smoke break when the bottles, fists, and people started flying. Crazy, was there anyone who wasn't swinging?

It was like there was a mass of green and gold fighting the purple and white, it was everywhere. I looked around the mayhem for Boomer and the other bouncers but couldn't see them. Did they all go on break at once? It was then that I spotted head bouncer Steve Lynch trapped with two Packer fans holding him down and three more moving in on him. I knew that if Lynch was taken out there was no chance for order to be restored. I never liked 'psycho Steve', but he was our only hope. The rule was very firm and clear, you could not leave your bar station under any circumstances with your money drawer in the register. If you did you faced immediate expulsion.

Tim was working night audit and smartly decided to lockout all the bar stations when the fighting got out-of-hand. Tim was thinking that this could be some kind of ruse to steal the cash drawers on one of the busiest nights of the year, but he was four bar stations away.

I looked back at Lynch who was now going down and then saw Big Einer with six to eight Packer fans swarming over him. I looked again for Boomer and the other bouncers, still no sight of them. I had no choice. I punched out my cash drawer, slammed the lid shut. Put it on the floor and with everything I had slid it down the bar alley to Tim. On busy nights like this there's always puddles of booze, water and mix on the floor. I watched the steel cash draw zoom down and bang into Tims ankles. He turned around startled and mad. I mouthed 'lock me out' and did a throat slit with my hands.

Tim gave me a quick thumbs-up.

Grabbing a bottle of long neck scotch from the rail, I threw myself over the bar and fought my way to Lynch. A sharp left smash took out one of the two guys holding Steve down. I then turned and with my ridiculously long arms, violently waved the scotch bottle at the heads of any Packer fans wanting to get in on the action. My plan was to give Steve enough time to get up and stand with me against the wave of Green and Gold.

Wrong! Lynch was up in no time but instead of barricading himself with me all I saw was Nazi Steve Lynch, karate and judo master, Viet Nam Vet Marine fly past me into a gang of Packer fans. My eyes then moved to my right where I saw Big Einer down with guys kicking in his head. I slipped through a crack of Packer fans and threw myself on Big Einer's upper body.

I took a few kicks, and then looked up from the floor to finally see Boomer in the entry way. I shook my head at him, just as somebody stomped me on the back of my scull. Everything slowed, I saw Boomer pick up a bar stool and wave its over his head like some kind of Teutonic Warrior. I saw the purple mascot on the carpet of the bar. Nothing!

'This one should be OK, at least he's not as bad as the others. Just make sure he gets a ride home. No driving until tomorrow. If he starts getting sick take him into Emergency at Hennepin County Hospital," said the medic.

"John, we can go home now. Can you get up?" asked Tim.

Things got spotty for the next few hours. I was sitting across from Tim in our Bloomington Pleasure Palace, as he was recanting the night's festivities.

"One drink John, just one, then turn in," said Tim.

"What happened after I got taken out?" I asked.

"It was wild, everybody including the staff started fighting. I was lucky to get the cash drawers out of there, and locked up in the vault," said Tim.

"Are Steve and Einer OK?"

"Einer! They took him in an ambulance, but I hear he is okay. Lynch, boy oh boy, I hope he didn't kill anyone," sighed Tim.

"What do you mean?"

"After you saved Steve, he went psycho, I mean it was scary. Some of us had always wondered if Lynch was everything he advertised himself as. Nobody's wondering now," Tim said.

"Huh?"

Tim continued, "Steve went totally berserk, one big Packer guy thought he could take Lynch. Steve did some kind of wild cart wheeling kick and nearly knocked the poor guys head off. Then the guys stupid buddy wanted a piece of Steve so he rushed him. Lynch did a springing jump kick and caught the guy full in the throat. I doubt that guy will ever talk right again. That was just the beginning, I had to rush the drawers out, but they told me that it took three cops to pry that bar stool from Boomer. He chased half of Wisconsin around the bar beating them with it."

"Is that it?" I asked, finishing my Manhattan.

"No, everyone wants to thank you for saving the bar," said Tim.

"Huh?"

"If you hadn't freed Steve and protected Einer I don't know what would have happened, the place would have been torn up, maybe closed," Tim finished.

Tuesday Jan 11th, 1977 5 Days before Super Bowl 10

"Fine, but why Maui? It's so far away?" I asked.

"Why not Maui? It's growing, it's warm, it's clean, John think! I'm talking beaches, babes and bikini's," Tim said.

This alliteration was another speech characteristic of Tim's. Not only would he sometimes assume other accents like the upper class British, or the down south negro, "Booooy yoah white boooyys shure does plays a power-full game of poker."

His most amusing one was the Northern Minnesota Scandinavian, "Ya sure don't ya know, we don't have no good jobs up here on da range, yo know. Da mines day all closed, for shure."

But when excited his words would often roll into alteration, one time after a Vikings win I heard him shout out, "Vikings defense, ferocious, fantastic, befuddled their fumbling Falcon foes." Unbelievable!

"So how much are we up, you say we've won a lot, what is a lot?" I asked.

Tim got up and went to his room, pulling out a brief case he tossed three heavy manila envelopes on the table.

"Plenty" responded Tim.

Tim had me count it. He wanted me to see with my own eyes what he had been talking about. When I was done I looked up at him with near shock, "Tim, we got over seven thousand dollars here," I said.

10.

HE SHOOTS, HE SCORES,
NOW WHERE'S THE GIRLS?

Cretin lunch room Nov. 27 1967

"Hey Tim, I got a problem, maybe you can help," I started.

"Nice of you to ask how my Thanksgiving break was; how was yours?" he said.

I continued, "Give me a break here. My parents came down and had another one of those rec-room talks with me. You know sometimes I wish they would just put my meals on the top step. Anyway, the basketball coach talked to them last week and he wants me to go out for the team. I told them I'd tried it two years ago and that I was no good. They gave me the old, 'try, try, again' stuff, the same old 'winners never quit, quitters never win' noise. I said, 'OK I'll never win!' They didn't think I was funny. They say, "I need to experience being part of a team." "Ugh!"

Tim responded, "The coach wants you on the team because you're so tall. He's hoping you can rebound and block shots. I think he's wrong."

"Great, so you don't think I can play either, would you talk to the coach?" I asked.

"John," Tim said with no small annoyance, "I can't tell the school basketball coach who he should have on the team or how to do his job."

"Ya, I guess not," I said.

"But I really think there's only one position on the court you could play," stated Tim.

"What's that?" I asked with suspicion.

"So let's break it down John, are you quick enough, to dribble, steal, drive and pass like a guard?" asked Tim.

"No," was my obvious and honest reply.

"Do you have the heft to bang near the basket, to rip rebounds, fire outlet passes, block shots and intimidate penetrators?" asked Tim.

"No," came out of my mouth again.

"So that means there is only one place left on the team for you to play," stated Tim.

"The bench?" I said hopefully.

"Highly amusing," was Tim's dry response.

"Dang, I thought I had that one, OK where?" I asked.

"Outside Forward," responded Tim.

"What's an Outside Forward? Does that mean I get to be outside the building during the game?" I asked.

"Someone's not taking this seriously," said Tim finishing off his gourmet Cretin High lunch.

"Outside Forward! What does the Outside Forward do?" I asked.

"He shoots, he scores, a lot," answered Tim.

"Tell me more," I asked.

"The Outside Forward plays, well outside, away from the basket, always looking for a 'kick out pass' so he can take a jump shot usually from the midpoint range," said the all-knowing Tim.

"What's a midpoint range?" I asked confused as ever.

"Anywhere from 15 to 22 feet from the basket, shouldn't be hard for you to develop a jump shot," he said.

"What makes you think I can develop a jump shot?" I asked.

"Are you kidding," smirked Tim, "with your long arms, and long fingers you wouldn't even have to jump much. You'd be impossible to block, and you have good eyesight."

So the next week we asked the janitors to open the gym and let us use about ten basketballs. Tim marked off what he considered a midpoint range and I would shoot for hours. Tim would work me from various distances and positions and even guard me at times making me shoot over him. Strangely, Tim was right, with all my length I didn't have to jump much, and with Tim's coaching I became a real deadeye.

What was even better was that with my huge hands I didn't have to put the ball on the floor. Tim said so many guys have to dribble first to get a rhythm and then shoot.

I could just take a pass and go straight up with it, swish, swish, swish.

So although I still had little to no interest in sports I made the Cretin Basketball team. Naturally, I spent most of the time on the bench which was good by me for two reasons. One, I didn't have to play, which I didn't want to anyway. Secondly, this gave me a far better line-of-sight view to the jumps, swirls, and spins of both our good looking cheerleader squad and the opposing teams.

Summer came and our parents decided that two healthy High School students should have summer jobs. My folks had joined St. Paul's swankiest Country Club about four years previously and Tim's parents had been members there for years. The Town And Country Golf Club, located on the bluffs of the Mississippi River, was first laid out by a Scotsman who wandered down from Canada in 1888. By 1895 the course was one of the finest in the country, and is today one of the oldest courses still on its original setting. This is the power brokers Country Club of St. Paul. The T. and C. has a long history of deal making, posh retirement parties

and elite, elegant, refined weddings for the debu-
tantes of St. Paul. Mr. Langford and Mr. Williams
chatted up the Club President and the week after
school was out we were both working at T. and C. I
lucked out and was hired to be a starter. What that
meant was I stood near the first tee, checked golfers
in, made sure they had a clean golf cart, scorecards,
pencils, beverages, and anything else they wanted,
and wished them a fine round of golf. Tim worked
in the kitchen and bar area supplying cooks, and
bartenders with whatever they needed, and helping
with cleanup. In the evenings we both doubled as
car parkers. We even had a special T. and C. uniform including hat. It was our job to help elegantly
dressed ladies out of their expensive cars, take the
keys from Mr. Bigshot, and safely drive it to the
parking lot. Then after the dance, wedding, party,
drive it back to the front of the club, help the now
wine and cocktail infused lady into her car, and
wish Mr. Bigshot a very good evening. Great job
for two seventeen year olds, and T. And C. opened
the course on Mondays from 8:00 AM to 1:00 PM
to let the staff play free. Great summer gig!

II.

PUNT, CATCH AND FLATULENCE:

Mid August 1968

Briinnng! "Is John available?"

"Yes, this is John, can I help you?" I replied.

"John, this is Coach Gramme of Cretin High, I need a word with you."

"Uh…Oh." Back then seventeen year old boys in the midwest did not say no to people in authority, and Coach Gramme was the head football coach of one of the most expensive and prestigious prep schools in the midwest.

As always I made sure Tim was with me when I met with Coach Gramme in August of 1968. Coach Gramme welcomed me into his office and thanked me for bringing Langford because he had a job for him too. Both Tim and I looked at each other confused.

Coach Gramme went into his serious Coach voice "Special Teams is an important part of any football program, and we are pretty thin right now at a few positions. John with your length and height I think you could learn to be a good punter. As you know our punt team was fairly average last season, (I didn't know, or care). What's more our punter graduated last year so I'd like you to do it. Now Langford we have another problem on our team that I think you could help with. Last season we lost a close game because of problems with the field goal and extra point team, so I'd like you to be this years' holder."

Neither of these are glamour positions on any football team, in fact holder might be worse than punter.

Suited up, sitting at the end of the bench, one of the Assistant coaches would tap me on the shoulder and tell me to get ready whenever our team was faced with a third down and long. I would get up, stretch out my leg, and run out on the field to bang one as far as possible. I was then supposed to dash down the field and help out with the tackle. Luckily for me my services were never needed. By the time I loped down the field our blood thirsty tacklers had already slammed the ball carrier to the turf. Of all the positions on the field it was one of the safest, and my parents were so proud that their wimp son was on the powerful Cretin Football team. Rah!

Tim had bigger problems. Being a holder for field goals and extra points may sound easy but try it on a late October early November Minnesota night. With the Canadian wind whirling down the field and the snow and ice in your eyes, the ball zips into your hands like a frozen missile. The holders job is to signal the snapper, catch the ball, quickly put it down at the angle your kicker wants it and make sure the laces are facing out. The first practice session Tim knelt down with the scared kicker three steps behind him to catch the snap. The long snapper was a monstrously hefty sophomore kid who did not appreciate his role, and was sure that he should be starting on the line instead of being relegated to special teams. Tim put his hands out and the hulking underclassman sailed the football over his head. The second snap totally missed the mark as well. It was here that Tim calmly called the three of them together. With the big snapper looking down at him and the reluctant, nervous kicker fidgeting behind him Tim began. "OK you two here's the deal. If we don't get this right everyone on the team and in the school is going to blame us. They're all going to say the same thing, 'The snap was bad, the hold was wrong, the kicker screwed up again' do we want that?" There was a small pause and then the big snapper banged a friendly punch on Tim' shoulder and said, "Hell no I don't want that!" That's all it took, typical Tim, keep it short, don't make it offensive. Move on! Our senior season we only lost one game, and it wasn't because of any lapses on special teams.

Now for the game we lost that cost the team the conference championship. Cretin Highs head defensive coach was a short, powerfully built guy by the name of Robert Thorguard. Defensive Coach Thorguard had played his football in the day of leather helmets and the flying wedge. Coach Thorguard was a dedicated history teacher, ("Class read chapter 7, work the problems at the back of the chapter, leave them on my desk and don't ask me any stupid questions"). Coach Thorguard also worked real hard monitoring study hall and refereeing intramural basketball games. During a football game Coach Thorguard would take a wide stance, put on a grim face and fart at the poor bench players. It was the sixth game of the season against St. Thomas Academy, our arch rivals, that changed the career for Coach Thorguard for the worse. Two minutes into the fourth quarter with Cretin trailing by 7 points the Tommies had the ball on their own 48 yard line third and three. The Tommies broke huddle and went into a strange looking 'I' formation with the quarterback under center, the halfback directly behind him and the fullback behind the halfback. Out of nowhere Tim Langford jumped to his feet, ran to the sideline and started screaming at the Cretin defense to "Not take the fake to the right! The play was going to the left." Coach Thorguard woke up and grabbed Tim, telling him to "Shut up." Tim wrestled free and hollered that the Tommies quarterback was going to "Fake to the right and roll back over the left guard and tackle."

Some of the Cretin players on the field gave a confused look to the sidelines as Coach Thorguard tried to put Tim in a headlock. Tim broke away again and continued to yell at the our middle linebacker to not "Bite on the fake to the right." The Tommie quarterback took the snap and just like Tim had said took two steps to the right faking the handoff to the halfback while the big Tommie fullback blew through the left guard/tackle slot clearing a path for their quarterback who spun around, tucked the ball into his midsection and following his fullback gained seven yards for a St. Thomas first down. Game, set, match! Now here's where all hell broke loose on the Cretin sideline. Coach Thorguard ordered Tim back to the bench, but the normally calm, thoughtful Tim was now in full rage. Getting right into Coach Thorguard's face roaring about how he was the dumbest guy in football and how the Tommies had been running the same play on third-and-short forever. Thorguard's eyes got wide and for a second I thought he might slug Tim. It was here that Coach Gramme, knowing that I was Tim's best friend, told me to get between the two. Just as I approached them Coach Thorguard was rearing back his fist, Tim blurted out to him, "One call from my Dad and the only job you'll have at Cretin is pushing a broom fatso." That stopped Thorguard in his tracks and I could see fear on his face. Cretin was not any normal high school. Not only were the parents paying top dollar for their kids' education but it was the endowments that kept the school in big bucks. If Tim went to "Corporate Big-Time Mr. Langford" and complained about a coach, Tim's Dad just might put in a call to the athletic director.

What this meant was many years after Old Mr. Langford had gone to that, "Big Corporate Boardroom In The Sky." Mrs. Langford, now a 95 year old widow residing in a luxury assisted living facility in Naples, Florida, would still be wheeled over to her desk once a year by an undoubtedly pregnant Hispanic Nursing Assistant. Carefully taking out Mrs. Langford's check book the Nursing Assistant would help Mrs. Langford write a nice big check with many zeros to good old Cretin High, the school that had done such a wonderful job of educating her only child. This is how it was done! Cretin needed those never ending endowment checks. It did not need a lazy history teacher and an incompetent, flatulent defensive coach.

The next week Coach Gramme asked Tim to come into his office. "Young man I want to thank you for your contribution to our team. However, Coach Thorguard has been with us for many years and I would like it if you would say something to put this matter behind us."

So before we went out to practice that afternoon Tim went to the locker room chalk board and said,

"Look, we all want the same thing, we all want to win! There isn't anyone in this room I'm not cheering for." With that all the players and coaches looked over to Coach Thorguard who snorted out an acknowledgment and that was it.

But it wasn't. First, all the players and coaches were really impressed with Tim's knowledge and attitude. Secondly, things started to spiral down for Coach Thorguard. The next season Thorguard was demoted to assistant special team coach in charge of field goals and extra points.

Unnoticed by Thorguard, the Detroit Lions' new Cypriot kicker Gero Yepremiam recently debuted soccer style field goal kicking. On a swirling windy day in old Metropolitan Stadium Yepremian had single-handedly beaten the Minnesota Vikings by nailing a new NFL record six field goals. Normally the big open air Metropolitan Stadium in Bloomington Minnesota was nearly impossible to kick in. This new method of kicking made quite an impression on all the young kickers in the midwest. So the next season when Coach Thorguard lowered his heft, bad knees and all, down to take a snap he turned to his new fuzzy faced kicker and said, "OK kid, line up and let's see you hit one." The kid took two steps to the left and soccer kicked it through the goal posts, dead center. Coach Thorguard looked back at the young boy and said, "Look kid, that's not how we do it here. That's just a fade, now kick it straight on like Pat Summerall did for the New York Giants." Again, Coach Thorguard with much effort lowered himself into the holders position and again the young kid took two quick steps to the left and soccer blasted the football right through the goal posts. Coach Thorguard climbed up, took off his whistle and slouched off the field muttering something about, "I don't coach soccer." The game had passed him by.

Basketball season came and I made the team again, however, as a senior and as the best shot on the team a lot more was expected of me. With my can't miss mid-range jumper I'd incorporated a running base line hook shot that was impossible to stop. For some reason I could hook with either hand. Flying to my left or right I would swoop the ball over my head and let it backspin off my fingers. Smooth! Swish!

Defensively I still had work to do, but luckily for me we played a sagging zone so I wasn't over matched in one-on-one situations against quicker players. We were half way through the season of my senior year when I noticed something in the mirror of the gym locker room. At first I thought it was the locker room lighting, then I took a closer look. My face had changed, the acne issue I'd had since seventh grade was gone. My face was clear, and there was more, I'd stopped tripping over everything. What's more, I was actually starting muscle out in the chest and shoulders. Finally, my unruly black hair seemed to lay in place. John Williams body was maturing!

12.

COLLEGE, RELIGION, AND CHARLTON HESTON:

Tim skipped his senior year spring session at Cretin to take some early courses at Macalester College. Mac is a highly rated academic small school in St. Paul, one of the top colleges in the midwest. I knew I didn't have the grades to follow Tim so I was planning on enrolling at the University of Minnesota of maybe a State College. It was then that I got a letter from St. Olaf, a small college in southern Minnesota. Dad and Mom were both really excited when they heard that St. Olaf had contacted me. Both said that it was a great school that would open doors to various grad programs. What's more, St. Olaf wanted me on their basketball team. I was sure I didn't have major college basketball talent but the coaching staff at St. Olaf were positive I could help them. From the beginning I wasn't sure I was a fit for a school like St. Olaf. First they didn't allow students to have cars, and

I loved my car. As a reward for turning seventeen my parents bought me a Pontiac GTO. Secondly, they didn't allow smoking or even have a cigarette machine on campus. Finally, they had some weird rule that the coeds had to be in their dorm rooms at 9:00 PM on class days and 10:00 PM on weekends. Screw that!

The campus buildings all were built out of gray stone on a large hill over looking Northfield a small farming town. At first I thought this must have been much like Helen went to at Troy when she bolted Greece because she couldn't get any decent dates. Right from the beginning it was clear that I would make the basketball team. But what was strange was that very few of the student body cared a hoot about their sports teams. Music, art, theater were the glory activities at St. Olaf. Worse the party scene consisted of campfires, sing-a-longs & polka dancing. I had gone through a long dry spell but finally one of the basketball cheerleaders agreed to go to a movie with me at the Grand Theater in glamorous Northfield. We took the Northfield Taxi to the theater and I headed my new girl up to the back of the balcony away from curious eyes. Carol Anderson was from Edina, a very upscale burb of Minneapolis and her Dad was a Dentist. I almost cared!

Charlton Heston was starring in the movie El Cid. It didn't take me long to grow bored with the Heston hacking his way through Spain, and my hands started moving and the dentists daughter started squirming. In the upper reaches of this dark old theater I started kissing her, then moved my hands to her tummy moving up to her left breast. Blocking me with her left forearm I quickly moved overland and approached my desired destination in a southern tract. Kissing her with more enthusiasm I firmly massaged her left breast and then moved my infantry down her body to invade her valley of sin. Still kissing her, (you have to keep kissing them guys, rule one, make them feel like you care), it was here that the cheery cheerleader crossed her legs throwing my forces into a minor retreat. *What experienced commander hasn't defeated this defensive tactic?* It was now a Naval War. I slid my sub down under her inner thigh and fired off a quick sharp squeeze. Carol yelped and this released her tension and I shot my hand up to the confluence of her legs. Williams keep firing! Massage, Massage, Massage, Rub, Rub, "John No!" "John Please" "John Not Here." Still kissing her I gripped the top of her head with my left hand and softly said, "Let's go get a room." Carol started to shake her head no, but my left hand forced her head up and down. We both got up, just as Charlton Heston finished slaying about half of the Spanish Moors.

Another ride from a Northfield taxi driver who seemed to think we needed to know that this job supplemented his real income as a school bus driver and pizza delivery guy. College City Motor Inn was on the northern part of sprawling Northfield. I got Carol out of the taxi and told her to wait outside as I approached the tiny motel office. Behind the counter sat an old bearded guy who looked like he'd been in Northfield when the James, Younger Gang came through to rob the First National Bank. The sign on the door said rooms available $18.95 a night. I slid the guy a twenty, he looked at me and asked, "Are you a college guy? I'm not supposed to rent to college kids." I flipped another twenty at him and he slid me a key saying, "Just don't make any noise or I'll kick you out."

I grabbed Carol by the arm and raced her down to my luxury motel room. Leading her inside I knew that sex is a lot like football, it's a game of momentum. You have to keep the ball moving to the goal line, keep your defense off the field, make first downs, and above all score, score, score.

I stripped off my shirt, shoes, pants, and went to work on Carol. "John slow down, John we're moving too fast, John we need to talk first." Carol struggled to say. Kiss, kiss, kiss, feel, feel, feel, finally we were both on the bed - she in her bra and panties, me in my tighty whities when she firmly put up her hands and yelled, "Stop."

"OK Carol, what can I do to make you happy?" *"Remember guys, you have to make it all about them!"*

Carol was on the verge of tears, *"Aren't they always on the verge of tears at a time like this?"*

She took a long sigh, "John, I don't want you to think badly of me, I'm really a very liberal person."

I immediately thought, *'OK, you're liberal, I'm liberal, so why are we stopping?'*

Haltingly now she began, "John, ah, is it really true what the other players say about you on the basketball team?"

"Ya it's true, but I'm trying to get better defensively."

Great. Done. I took off my shorts and made a move on her.

Again with the hands in front of her and her eyes closed trying not to look at the now naked John with his naked Johnson. Carol gave a nervous sigh and seemed to summon up some big inner thought, "No, I mean about the other thing?" said Carol.

"Oh you mean about me being slow in transition, well it's certainly something I'm working on. But I think over time I'll be one of the best players on the team and maybe in the league."

Still with her eyes closed, "Oh no, no, John, are you really a ...Catholic?"

"Huh!" What is this?" was my only thought.

Haltingly now Carol said, "Some of the guys on the team told me there's a rumor that you know, you might be, a, ah, ...Catholic? They refer to you as the 'Shooting Mackerel Snapper'," she finished.

I sat back against the motel wall, "Well my parents raised me to be a Catholic, and I went to a Catholic Military School," I said.

Carol let out a quick gasp, "It's true! Oh, John, we have to go right away, everyone at St. Olaf will call me a, a, 'Catholic Loving Slut'."

Now you might think that something like that would hurt, but it didn't, because I just didn't care.

Carol started quickly putting on her cloths and called up to the front desk to have Mr. Personality call her a cab. Talking fast now Carol said, "Listen John, get dressed and hurry. I'll have the driver drop me off at the entrance to school at the end of St. Olaf Avenue. You take the other route on Highway 19 and walk up the hill. Please don't think that I'm some kind of conservative square. Like I said, I'm really a very liberal person. But what would my friends and parents think if they ever knew that I'd been with a Catholic?"

The same multi-talented driver picked us up and said, "Wow, you two work fast."

Ten minutes later I was smoking a cigarette off of Highway 19 two hundred yards from school. Not only did I feel weird, but little old Carol Anderson seemed to get all religious after I gave that slug at the motel forty bucks of my money. I finally slumped into my dorm room and asked my roommate a question. Punky Iverson was a seldom used, talent-limited, third string point guard on the team, but a decent guy.

"Punky am I the only Catholic on the team?" I asked.

"Gee John, I thought you knew. I think you're the only Catholic in the school," he said.

"Well then why did they want me here at St. Olaf and on the team?" I asked.

"Gee John, (evidently 'Gee' was a popular word in Punky's vocabulary,) you don't pay attention much."

"Pay attention to what?" was my confused reply.

"St. Olaf is like most colleges now. They're trying to liberalize the school. John Kennedy was elected President seven years ago and he was a Catholic. You know, like what the University of Minnesota did just three years ago when they recruited those two black players?" Punky said.

"Huh!" was my one syllable reply.

In 1964 the University Of Minnesota Basketball team was one of the last major colleges to recruit black players.

"St. Olaf is a conservative Lutheran college, but it wanted to get with the times, so they recruited you, a Catholic. This was a big step, you're the token," said Punky.

I finished out the semester and transferred to St. Cloud State College in Central Minnesota. St. Cloud State was famous for two things, parties and more parties. At last a college environment I could deal with.

I dedicated myself to catching up on some serious college fun. Two semesters later, after many empty beer kegs, bourbon bottles, bags of Mexican Gold, along with a considerable number of used condoms I found myself back in St. Paul sleeping on Tim's couch, with no job, no money, and no girl.

13.

OPTIONS: SAY WHAT? SPRING 1969

"What am I going to do Tim? My next stop could be Vietnam, that doesn't sound like much fun," I questioned.

"It isn't," was Tim's unsympathetic response, "what were you thinking of?"

"My grades started to slide and then they sunk.

College isn't for everyone, and I guess it's not for me," I said.

Tim stared at me, "I think you have six to ten days before you get your draft notice, we better start planning."

"Planning! Planning for what?" I asked.

"Well, what branch of service you want to go into of course," said Tim.

"Tim you know me: I'm a lover not a fighter. I'm not a warrior; I'm a womanizer, a boozer and not a battler," I quickly said.

"Very amusing, tell that to your draft board! It won't get you far. By the way, you're going to go to

Vietnam, cuz the smart guys volunteered for Germany months ago. Deutschland is full," Tim said.

"So what should I do?" I asked.

"There's always Canada, some guys are doing that," Tim said.

"Forget Canada, it's cold enough in Minnesota what's next," I asked.

"You would get a two year deferment if you went into the Peace Corps," responded Tim.

"Sounds good, what does the Peace Corps do?" I asked.

"It helps with all kinds of things in Third World Countries, education, health, agriculture, construction projects…" Tim said.

"Wait minute, wait a minute, what do you mean a Third World Country? What exactly is a Third World Country, and why are we sending people there?" I questioned.

"OK John, the Peace Corps is designed to help poor people in poor countries. The idea is to develop better relations by helping these folks attain a higher standard of living. Trust me, John, it's a good thing," Tim said.

"What countries? Where? Doing what?" I asked with growing suspicion.

"John, the Peace Corps is not in London, England, Paris, France or Sydney, Australia, if that's what you're thinking. They don't need help at any of those places," said Tim.

"So where would I go?" I asked.

"Probably some violent, corrupt, poverty stricken hell-hole in Africa with no running water, or a disease ridden dump in South America," Tim said brightly.

I jumped out my chair, "I thought you were my friend! You're sending me to Africa to get harpooned by some crazed spear chucker, or down to South America to be devoured by bugs and flies?" I roared.

"John you're running out of options, and time is limited," said Tim.

I slumped back into my chair, "I don't even know where Vietnam is, and from what I hear they don't even play golf there. Who cares about a shit country that doesn't even tee-it-up?" I whined.

Tim took a deep sigh, "Well there is one other way out," he said.

"There is! Does it keep me from getting shot in Nam?" I asked.

"Yes," said Tim.

"Does it keep me from freezing my ass off in Canada?" I questioned.

"Yes," Tim said.

"Do I have to go to Africa where they crap in the river and chase Zebras, or worse to South America and get some jungle disease nobody has ever heard of?" I asked.

"No" replied Tim.

"Really! What! Give! Tell me," I hollered.

"No, I don't think I'll tell you," said Tim.

"What! You know a way to keep me out of the rice patties and you won't tell me?" I questioned.

"John you're not going to like it, and anything you don't like you don't do," Tim said firmly.

Unfortunately Tim was right. The first 18 years of my life were all about order and regimentation. Catholics have to go to church, midwest boys had to do what their parents, and teachers tell them to do. Military School students better "Fall in!"

Evidently none of that stuck with me for long. What's more my safety net had ripped a big hole in it. Dad and Mother had both retired, sold the nice house, and moved to a golf course community in Florida. Before they left they felt the need to give me some heartfelt advice. Mother began, "John, my son," there she did it again, "Your Father and I have tried with you, but it's time now for you to learn from your mistakes. We feel that the best course of action is for you to have your own life; and take care of yourself the best that you can."

Hmmm, I didn't like this at all. I tried to get them to take me with them to the beaches, and golf courses of the sunshine state. But they just gave me more of the old, "Stand on your two feet, man-up, carry the ball by yourself," stuff.

"Tim at least give me a hint, I might be able to live with it," I asked.

Tim gave me his exasperated look, finally he spoke.

"John, pack your suitcase, you're going on a bus ride."

I threw my bag in Tim's Plymouth and got in.

"Where are we going?" I asked.

"Down to the Federal Building," replied Tim.

After walking down one corridor after another of the massive Federal Building Tim finally stopped me at a junction.

"Ok John, what's it going to be?"

"What's what going to be?" was my dumbfounded reply.

"Your choice, left is Coast Guard, right is VISTA," Tim said.

"What's VISTA?" I asked.

"Volunteer In Service To America. Sounds like you're going to help reduce poverty in America, and you get a one year draft deferment. I'll help you fill out the paperwork," said Tim.

"Where will they send me?" I asked Tim

"Oh, some swell place like the Appalachian Coal Country, or an inner city Ghetto. But who knows, maybe you'll luck out and be assigned to an Indian Reservation out in that lovely Dakota Plains Country," said Tim.

It was here he mimicked a bow and arrow and voiced, "Zing, Zing, Zing."

"You're not being serious Tim, do you really mean this?" I asked.

Tim stopped and grinned at me, "Your choice John, Da Nang, or Detroit! Saigon or South Dakota! Hanoi or Houston!" There he goes with that annoying alliteration lingo.

14.

THAT TODDLIN' TOWN: 1971

Three hours later I was on a bus to inner city Chicago.

Tim had sent me off with his usual amusing sarcasm.

"Honestly John, I had no idea you were such a concerned American! I applaud you! You're an inspiration. Just one thing, when the Ghetto erupts, and the rioting is raging, try to duck down, you tall white boys make easy targets. See you in a year."

I was sent to a poverty ridden development in Chicago, to help rebuild houses. Most of us were really nothing more than carpentry helpers.

"Williams measure this wall."

"Williams bring me the level and sawhorse."

"Williams paint this bathroom."

But Chicago was a real blast for me. Real nightclubs, great bars, Bears, Bulls, Blackhawks.

I had gone to all white schools, in all white St. Paul, in German, Scandinavian Minnesota. Big surprise! Chicago was different.

What better town to first experience racial and cultural discord than 1971 Chicago.

What amazed me about inner city Chicago was the way they viewed basketball. In St. Paul and Minneapolis people cared about and followed basketball. In ChiTown it was some kind of religion. There were all kinds of city leagues with fantastic players, most of them black. When they saw me play at a shoot-a-round I was asked to join a team.

This was a totally different kind of basketball than I had ever played. Eye scratching, bone crashing, balls-to-the-walls basketball. Every loose ball was contested, every rebound fought for, every shot challenged. I became a much more aggressive, hustling player. As the only white guy on the team I once again found myself in the "token" mode. Surprisingly most of the guys I played with didn't care about that racial stuff. They just cared about basketball and staying ahead of the bill collectors. All my teammates had low paying menial jobs that barely kept them going. Basketball was their escape from the drudgery of pushing a broom, driving a cab, or throwing bags at O'Hare. Maybe that's why they all played so hard. I'm sure that most of them felt that if they could have gotten a better draw in life they would be starting on some major college team. With a bright future in the NBA ahead of them, riding in Cadillacs, smoking Cubans and dating beauty queens.

Chicago was good me, bright lights, big city, great clubs, basketball, all in the service of my country. I must admit that there are times when I get a small twinge of guilt thinking of the guys who were fighting in Southeast Asia while I partied and played in Chicago, but it usually passes quickly.

15.

BOOGIE, BARS, AND BROADS: SPRING 1973

A year and-a-half later, the Viet Nam War was winding down. The draft had been eliminated and I was back in St. Paul on Tim's couch. I was a 23 year old guy with no job, no money, no girl, and an aging Pontiac GTO. Tim had graduated from college with a degree in business just as the economy was diving into the tank. Not to be deterred Tim went out knocking on doors and came back to his apartment one afternoon and told me to get ready to go to an interview that evening. "Interview! You mean like for a job?" I guessed. Tim patiently began, "John, I know this is hard for you but things like food, bourbon, and illicit drugs cost money. You're going to have to get a job."

"But Tim it's the spring, golf season is just beginning, couldn't this whole job thing wait until, like, October?" I pleaded.

"John, go get cleaned up, and pretend like you know how to be a bartender," Tim said firmly.

Tim had applied, interviewed and immediately been hired by a new restaurant boogie bar in Richfield a suburb of Minneapolis as a business manager in charge of payroll, and accounts payable. Perfect first job for a young business major.

When Tim had been interviewed he asked about other career opportunities in this new addition to the Twin Cities bar and restaurant scene. Tim was told that they were hiring for experienced bar staff. Tim volunteered that he knew a reliable, dedicated, highly motivated young man who had spent a lot of time in bars. He was one-fourth right.

16.

MAXWELL'S RESTAURANT AND BOOGIE BAR, RICHFIELD MINNESOTA SPRING 1973

Tim swung open the massive door to the new Maxwell's Restaurant with the handle that was secured to the buttocks of a Viking Quarterback that graced the front door. He was caught in the act of passing to a receiver downfield in the end zone. If the picture had been snapped two seconds later it would have shown the touchdown. But as it was, it was left to the imagination whether there would be a score on the play or not. Appropriate. The hallway ran the length of the building and separated the banquet rooms from the bar and dining areas to the right. Floor to ceiling photos of football action plastered the walls between short stretches of deep red wall paper. This place was huge, with eight bartender stations, plus three service bar stations for the banquet and restaurant. A big stage for the various bands that would blast away overlooking a large dance floor. The bar area alone could seat over two hundred thirsty, lusty, lonely souls. I couldn't believe such a large restaurant and entertainment complex was being built during the middle of an economic recession.

I was introduced around to the management staff who all were glad to have me working for them. I then got fitted for my purple and white Maxwell's Bartenders jersey, purple number 43, dark purple pants. It was here that I met some of my new coworkers and what a wild bunch they were. Taco Tom, dark black guy with shiny bald head was head chef and Boomer Mattson white guy about my age was Assistant manager. Both ex-cons, both about six feet tall and about 240 pounds, both recent graduates of St. Cloud State Reformatory. I never knew what Taco Tom did to earn his three year hitch at Granite. But I did find out that Boomer, after many violent criminal escapades, was sentenced to Granite for three to five. This was due to him beating up an off duty cop who didn't think it was funny when Boomer tried to steal his vintage Corvette. Poor sport! When short of bouncers Boomer would step up to the plate but he's really not supposed to be doing that kind of work considering his past tendencies toward violence. Boomer got his name from the way he would fight. Due to Boomer Mattson's short, but bulky, powerful body, Boomer would simply take a run at his foe and blast them with his powerful shoulders, much like a pulling guard teeing up a defensive back. Boom! Fight over!

How did two criminals, both repeat offenders get to work at the Twin Cities latest addition to the fine dining and boogie bar scene? Remember, Granite really is a "reformatory prison." St. Cloud State Prison is your last stop before a life of "hard time." On your first day in Granite every con is given a job. Taco Tom was sent to the kitchen, Boomer was sent to the dining hall. Tom would cook, Boomer would set up, tear down, and clean. One summer day between lunch and dinner they both stepped out on a three step concrete patio overlooking the prison yard, leaned against the rail and took a smoke break. A black con and white con casually taking a smoke break together talking about what a lousy season the Minnesota Twins baseball team was having was not a normal occurrence in any prison in America. Many prisoners stopped playing basketball or talking and took notice. Many did not like what they were seeing. Tough shit! This was during the racial hatred riots of the 60s, and 70s. The Arian Brotherhood was not high on the Christmas Card list of the Bloods and the Crips. Unbeknownst to anyone, a couple of Assistant Wardens and Prison Guards had also been watching Boomer and Taco Tom. So one morning the Chief Warden called both of them to his office.

The Warden made it short, "Look, you two seem to work well together, and the kitchen and dining hall operation has never been better. Here's the deal. I need to have an answer now. If you two want to go to culinary and restaurant management school there's a trade school about ten miles from here that teaches that stuff. The restaurant business is growing and there seems to be no end to it. The program is about 14 months long, we'll drive you there and pick you up. The fact that a white and black con have been working effectively together without trying to stab each other is a first for this prison. If you guys succeed at this school you'll be setting a great example of what two guys from different ethnic and racial backgrounds can accomplish. One thing, if you cause any trouble at that school, get smart with the instructors or steal anything you'll both be shoveling out the prison yard this winter. Do you know how cold that yard gets in the winter? Now what's your answer?"

So both Taco Tom and Boomer went to school. Tom studied to be a chef and Boomer to be a restaurant and bar manager. They both succeeded and now were gainfully employed at the latest glamorous hot dining and entertainment establishment on the I-494 strip.

Other than trading some top shelf scotch for an occasional quality steak dinner I didn't know Tom very well. Large black man, quiet man, stoic man. But Boomer and I had become good friends, partied together, played poker together and went into the escort security business together. Boomer's family was in the moving and trucking business. Boomer was the oldest of four siblings and seemed to do most of the talking. The youngest one was Big Einer, a huge guy, maybe 310 pounds, possible more, about six feet, two inches. Sandwiched between the two was Gretchen, a tall, stunning, blond, blue-eyed beauty who had graduated from college with a degree in business. Finally, there was Little Carl. Little Carl was a bit strange for my taste, and I never felt comfortable around him. How comfortable can you be when the guy is always flipping open this strange looking Philippine knife? Carl would sit there at our poker games continually flipping this vicious looking blade open. The blade was like something out of an old-time movie, where you see the mustachioed barber run a straight razor over the big shot's face. Little Carl had gotten this pearl handled beauty from some Viet Nam Vet who'd owed him something. Whatever!

Little Carl was well, very little, scrawny, slight. Little Carl looked funny positioned at family photos between the loud, large, gregarious Boomer, the still larger, quiet, distant Big Einer, and their tall, glamorous, educated Gretchen. As a boy Little Carl had various nutritional issues. Ricketts or something. What's worse for Little Carl is that because of his health condition his face never filled out, he looked perpetually drawn and sallow. So with his small frame, Little Carl had gotten a bad deal, naturally this made him mean as hell. As if it wasn't bad enough to be called Little Carl, at times someone, usually Boomer, would refer to Carl as, "Runt," Carl Mattson hated being called "Runt."

As a teenage boy, to prove his worth, Carl made the mistake of stealing things, lots of things. This unfortunate habit got him a nine month pull at the Red Wing Minnesota Detention Home for Wayward Boys. This was where the the State Of Minnesota placed the "groovy juvie" boys until they learned their lesson. Naturally his older brother Boomer was a former inmate, who had graduated to Granite. Red Wing is an idyllic little town in southern Minnesota along the Mississippi River Valley. However, this was not a good place for someone of Little Carl's size or demeanor. Carl had always been able to run his mouth whenever and wherever he wanted knowing that his two huge brothers were there to back him up. This turned into a big problem when he was sentenced to Red Wing because his brothers were a hundred miles away. Needless to say, Little Carl got the crap beat out of him a lot which only reinforced his sadistic attitude.

But Carl had learned one thing in prison that he was proud of. Because of his diminutive size and temperamental behavior, the warden decided to separate him from the other inmates. He assigned Carl to the business office. It was here that Carl learned how to do bookkeeping, filing, report writing, and record keeping. Little Carl had excelled at this Detention Center assignment so completely that some of the staff were actually sorry to see him complete his sentence. Little Carl had found his nitch! Just before he was to take the shuttle van to the Red Wing Bus Station for his trip back to Minneapolis the warden had him report to his office. "OK Mattson, I'm going to give it to you straight. First, you can continue in your life of stupid ass crime and follow your idiot brother to Granite. Or you can shape up and straighten out. Secondly, you have proven to everyone on this staff that you have the ability and intelligence to succeed. It's totally up to you, but one thing, nobody is going to cut you any favors at Granite." With that the warden got out of his chair, came around his desk, shook Carl Mattson's hand and thanked him for all his hard work. Little Carl had no intention of ever going to Granite.

Another staff member was Steve Lynch the head bouncer, a complete dickhead! If there was a Minnesota Bad Ass Hall Of Fame he would be a charter member. Of course I would never say that to his face because he might kill me. Check that, he would kill me. Ex-Marine MP, oops, there are no ex-marines. I suppose it was because we were exact opposites that Lynch and I didn't like each other. Steve was disciplined, exacting, regimented, didn't smoke, and rarely drank, hated drugs and the problems they caused. It was important to Lynch that Maxwell's succeed, he was making good money and needed the dough. Steve was ambitious, taking courses at the University to eventually get out of the bar security business and become a Pharmacist. Steve had a steady girlfriend, never strayed and was planning on marrying soon. I was none of these things and had no intention of ever becoming any of them. I lived to party and have a good time.

Although Lynch was only about 5'11" and 180 pounds there was never any doubt who was in charge. He would regularly have meetings before the bar area was open for lunch with the other bouncers and put them through drills, demonstrating various kicks, holds, thrusts, including escape maneuvers. The bouncers would come in early and push the tables and chairs away and Lynch would take over.

"OK what do you do if some drunk puts you in back choke hold, four things? Steve demanded.

The bouncers would in unison recite the maneuvers and then perform them. "A. Foot stomp, B. Back slug to the crotch, C. Double back elbow thrust, D. Slide the attackers forearm to your face and bite hard with incisors."

Lynch: "What is the first thing you do when encountering a hostile situation, and why is it important?"

The bouncers in unison would reply, "Deflate and defuse, because you don't know how drunk or crazy the perpetrator is."

Lynch, "When defusing a hostile situation what is your first thought?"

The bouncers in unison again, "Your own body language and position, must not appear to be threatening. Remain controlled but alert."

Lynch, "What is our first, second and third priority?"

The bouncers, "The security of the customers, staff and property including money."

One day during this drill Lynch pulled a good one on the bouncers. Lynch asked: "How to you handle an irate, drunken, woman?"

Lynch would have stumped me on this one, frankly he would have stumped me on all of them.

The bouncers weren't expecting this one. Blank faces!

Lynch, "Now let's think about this a minute. How many of you have ever seen a woman fight fair?"

The bouncers started laughing.

"Right, never!" Steve replied. "This puts you at a double disadvantage. She's going to kick you in the balls, tear at your face with her nails, or bite your nose. You don't get to do any of that. Of course if you grab her in the wrong place she's going to scream rape. So what do you do?" With that in walked Sue Abbott one of our pretty, perky, young cocktail servers in her street cloths, slacks, blouse, and casual shoes.

"Thank you for coming in Sue. Sue has volunteered to be our irate, drunken female customer."

Sue smiled shyly, and nodded to the gang.

"Now Sue I want you to come at me with everything you have," Lynch said.

With that Sweet Sue flashed her nails, snarled her mouth, let out an ear piercing shriek and charged Lynch. He immediately went low grabbing her around her knees while smoothly throwing her over his right shoulder. With Sue pounding on his back he slid over to a wall, flipped her off of him, and in one quick move turned her around holding her face to the wall and bracing her legs so she couldn't back kick him.

They obviously had rehearsed this but it was still really impressive.

Steve continued, "If she's over your shoulder all she can do is pound on your back and that's not going to hurt guys your size. When you hold her against the wall remember: Your hands are on her shoulders and your right leg braces against her legs. Thank you, Sue."

The bouncers, cleaners and busboys who had all stopped to watch broke out in applause.

Finally, how do we always end this meeting. The bouncers in unison now, "Always ask for backup."

"That's right, before the situation deteriorates further you always ask a bartender, busboy, cocktail server, whoever to go get another bouncer for backup." Gesturing to the side, Lynch pointed to Mary, 'Merry' Smith, the head cocktail waitress. "Merry is here so we can be sure all staff will cooperate with the backup plan. Good work men, that's it for today." Lynch and I didn't like each other, but I had to admit he knew his stuff.

Mary 'Merry' Smith was a smack talking, chip-on-the-shoulder, hard eyed, head cocktail waitress. Her blue eyes, long brown hair, and trim body were all still looking good as she approached the 35 year mark. Merry was a good sort. She was also chief babysitter for her charges who would listen to their problems in an easy way that belied the fact she had her own troubles. Pregnant at 15 and then again at 19 by different guys who never came back, she worked as hard as possible to keep her kids fed and clothed.

"Oh Merry, he never called, he never called, he told me it was more than just a physical thing. But he never called, when am I going to meet a real guy?"

"Now, Mindy, Carla, Amber I'm sure there's a good man out there just waiting to hookup with a sweet girl like you, and when you meet him you're going to give him all your love. Just one thing, you don't need to ever tell him about all those other guys. Even when you're both 95 years old in rocking chairs don't ever talk about all the Bobs, Joes and Franks you've done. That's just none of his business."

17.

CHANGE OR DIE: SUMMER 1975

My first encounter with Steve Lynch started off badly and everything between us went down from there. It was about two years after Maxwell's had opened on a Friday night, about closing time. As always on a Friday night I was planning on sprinting out of Maxwell's and making tracks to a late night party that had promising prospects of plenty of lonely girls, loud tunes, and copious amounts of alcoholic beverages. In short, what I always did on weekend nights. Lynch approached my bar station and in a loud voice to carry over the blasting band.

"Meet me in the business office after you clean up your station." Not, "Could you meet me?" Or "Give me a few minutes of your time when your shift is finished."

Just a direct order. I replied, "Can't, got a party, maybe some other time."

Lynch shot back, "Twenty minutes, business office!"

"Lynch, I didn't know I reported to you!" I fired back at him. "Williams there's lots of things you don't know, eighteen minutes, be there," snarled Lynch.

Naturally I had no intention of missing that party for his stupid meeting. What's more, "Nazi Steve" wasn't the owner, head bartender, or the food and beverage manager so I owed him nothing.

Thirty minutes later I was just reaching for the exit door when I heard his voice, "Williams, now."

So I slumped to the back of the building and stomped into the office, to be greeted by Tim, Boomer, Merry Smith, and a few of the other members of Maxwell's management staff. The first thing I did was fire up a Marlboro and blow a stream of smoke in Lynch's direction, knowing that this would tick him off.

Glaring at me Lynch said, "I don't suppose you could put that poisonous thing out for a five minutes." With that I sent another big flat blast of smoke at him. My goal was to piss him off just short of him hurting me. I knew in a fight Lynch could kill me.

"John, I'm making some changes at Maxwell's and I would like your help." The statement was directed at me from Micky Maxwell, owner of Maxwell's, and many other businesses in the midwest. Maxwell was a former NFL wide receiver famous for never dropping a pass. I had only met

Maxwell once. Because of his various business enterprises, and the charity foundation he ran, he rarely was at Maxwell's. Maxwell was a very large man, dressed well, perfectly groomed, if you hadn't known he'd been a professional athlete you would just think he was another conservative businessman. The striking thing about Maxwell wasn't his size, or manner, it was his hands. You couldn't help looking at Maxwell's amazingly large hands, even larger than mine. No wonder he never dropped a pass. Catching a football to Maxwell would be like a normal guy catching a paper cup.

I sat up straight. Maxwell continued, "I have reviewed the work that this team has done since opening and I'm impressed with much of what you guys have accomplished. Langford, your accounting is seamless and accurate, you're a natural for this kind of work. Lynch, your training and experience has been invaluable, and Tom the city sanitation inspectors give your kitchen top marks so there's plenty of good things happening here. However, although we're making money I think the bottom line could be improved. Way too many guys coming in here sitting on their two dollar beer all night, taking up space, trying to get lucky and then stiffing the bartender."

Unfortunately this was true, and a lot of us had commented about it. The big spenders and corporate lunch and dinner crowd was slowly disappearing from us.

Maxwell continued, "There are twenty two drinking and dining establishments on the I-494 strip. We have to get better to survive. I've decided we're going to upgrade the whole place. Higher quality food and better decor in the restaurant including a jazz pianist. Top shelf booze in the rail at all the bar stations. I want sexier outfits for the cocktail servers, uniforms for the car valets and coat check girls. In short, I want this place to be the go-to place for dining and entertainment in the entire midwest. Any comments?"

Nobody said anything so I finally spoke up, "Ah Mr. Maxwell. …."

Maxwell cut me off, "Mickey, not Mr. Maxwell, just Mickey, I'm just a former football player who got lucky in business."

"*Five minutes with Mickey Maxwell and you knew he'd never manufactured an ounce of bullshit in his life.*"

"Mickey, then what you want us to be is the next Charlie's Exceptional," I said.

Chins shot up, eyes widens, mouths went open from the group. There was a reverenced moment of silence.

Boomer and Tom looked at each other and smiled.

Merry Smith blurted out, "John's right, you want us to be like Charlie's place."

For 31 years Charlie's Exceptional had ruled supreme as the power restaurant of Minneapolis. The wood paneled walls were lined with autographed photos of every major athlete, politician and business heavyweight that ever came to town. On a campaign stop, President Nixon recently ate there. In a business that saw staff come and go constantly, the employees at Charlie's were dedicated and loyal. Management was famous for returning that loyalty to everyone who proudly worked at the most iconic restaurant in the Midwest.

Wives who never would consider joining their husbands on business trips anywhere else would beg to be part of a swing through Minneapolis just to spend an evening being graciously fawned over by the courteous, professionally trained staff at Charlie's. The original bartender created a famous cocktail called The President, a mixture of gin, lemon and orange juice with a slight touch of grenadine. Tunes of Sinatra, Como, Crosby and Peggy Lee would be heard as you entered the lobby, to be warmly welcomed by a finely groomed Security greeter. To say you dined at Charlie's was to say, "you made it."

"So where do we begin?" asked Boomer.

I took the reins, "We begin where the customer begins, right at the front door. Steve, we all know that you do a good job training your bouncers and because of it there's rarely any problems. But you have to get them to look sharper and act better. Many of them are wearing the same sports coat that they wore to their high school prom, and those hair cuts! Shined shoes and a friendly presentation, straighten those ties, widen those smiles, get the gum out of their mouths and the cigarette's off their lips. If we're going to class this place up, the bouncers need to make the leap from knuckle draggers to security greeters."

There was an uncomfortable pause. Then to my surprise, Lynch spoke.

"You make some good points, John. I'll get on it, by the end of the month my guys will have a whole different look, and a much more professional attitude," said Lynch.

'Well now that was a shock, I thought he might belt me.'

"What about advertising, if we're changing the public has to know about it," said Merry.

Tim now took the lead, "You're right, Merry, let John and me handle that."

"*Huh?*" Was my immediate thought.

"John and l will right up a commercial and take it to one of the advertising companies. It will be playing on all the local TV stations in a few weeks," said Tim.

"Huh? We will? Tim sure has a lot of faith in us."

With that the meeting broke and Tim and I slouched into the Brown Bomber, "We're going to come up with some kind of advertising campaign?"

Tim responded, "Don't worry John, you'll think of something, you always do."

"Huh?"

18.

HOORAY FOR HOLLYWOOD:

"You Did It, You Earned It, You Made It, You Belong at Maxwell's!"

Sinatra's, "Here's to the winners," plays softly in the background.

The stylishly dressed couple get out of their conservative brown Buick Park Avenue and are greeted by the uniformed valet who helps the lady out and runs around to take the keys from her husband. At the door is the impressive looking Security Greeter, who welcomes them and chats with as they are ushered down the hall to the restaurant. As they pass the entrance to the discotheque the husband looks in and is spied by a sexily dressed young cocktail server with a tray full of drinks and a chest full of tits. She smiles and nods to him. Catching up to his wife and the Greeter, they are passed on to Boomer the big jovial host who robustly shakes the husband's hand, pats his shoulders and gets them seated. Next shot is the couple enjoying a wonderful meal as the wine steward presents them with a bottle. Finally, the dessert tray is passed before them but they both demur. Leaving the restaurant Boomer is there to gently take the lady's hand in his two big paws and again pounds the husbands back sharing a bit of manly banter. Walking down the hall the husband again lags behind his wife gazing into the disco as a pretty cocktail server with a perfect tight butt smiles back to him, coyly nodding at him over her bare shoulder. Now we see the wife's long, elegant arm reach out and playfully grab the husband dragging him forward. The Security Greeter opens the door for the couple as their Buick slowly rolls in front of them.

"You Did It, You Earned It, You Made It, You Belong at Maxwell's!"

Not a major motion picture but it played on all the local stations and got the job done. Within a few weeks the big shooters and heavy corporate expense accounts were back. Maxwell's became the number one destination for dining and disco in the Twin Cities.

19.

SEX, DRUGS, AND THE ROLE THAT LIGHT PLAYS IN PHOTOSYNTHESIS

If girls are made of sugar and spice, why do they taste like sardines?

Why did I like working at Maxwell's, back in the 70s? Decent money, snappy outfit, good benefits, naw… it was the girls. It's always the girls!

"Look, I have to go."

"Don't go…call in sick"

"I can't, my Mother wants me to take her shopping."

"Last night you told me your Mother had moved to Florida."

"I did? Well then I best get going it's a long way to the Sunshine State."

"Well, I'm not letting you go," she announced.

"Oh yeah? How are you goin to stop me?"

"I've hidden your socks."

"Oh, you've hidden my socks have you?"

"I most certainly have."

"How old are you, not counting tomorrow?"

"Tell you what, I'll let you leave if you kiss me."

"OK, here."

"Not there."

"Where then?"

I'll give you a hint, start at my navel and go about six inches due south.

The girl's name is Cathy, or Donna, or Mary or Sandy or maybe I've forgotten it. That happens sometimes. She has a chest full of boobs or great legs or fantastic eyes, hair and lips, or maybe she's just aggressive, cause I'm shy in a pushy sort of way. She's probably divorced, with one to three kids, and me with my stiff mustache are trying to get out of her apartment, condo, townhouse with as little hassle as possible, but she doesn't understand. Maybe she feels rejected or a touch guilty about trying to copulate her way into the, "Guinness Book Of World Records" the night before.

Her kids are up now. Little Donny, Chet, David, Alice, Ben, Tommy, Mary, Darren, Rhoda, Spot, Rover, or Prince.

"How many kids do you have?"

"Two, and a dog."

"Well, it seems like more, and while we're on the subject I'm leaving."

The temperature outside is near zero. It's December in Minnesota, and I'm on my way home without my socks.

The gusting wind scooped a handful of loose snow from the hard pavement and threw the small pellets against my bare ankles. I jerked the door open of the Toronado and jumped behind the wheel.

Yes, as a bartender at a large boogie bar you meet a lot of girls. I could write a book about them. Maybe I am!

Someone once asked me who the fastest girl I ever met was. I had to think for a minute, but then it came to me. Cindy Carol Coleman, Miss 3Cs, 'Have Tits Will Travel.'

It was a Thursday night about a year ago and Maxwell's, in she bounces with a halter top on in the middle of December. Ounce for pound she was 5'2" of the wildest stacked geography I had ever seen. Shoulder length blond hair, with a hint of curl, and sea blue eyes, aimed directly at me.

"Can I talk you into something?" I asked.

"I want to take you home and put you under my Christmas tree where I will slowly unwrap you," she answered.

"That sounds a little suggestive," I considered with unerring perception.

"What time do you get off?" she asked.

"About five minutes after I get to your place," I answered.

"Not that," she smiled. "I mean what time can you leave work?"

"About one. I'll have the other bartenders clean up for me so I can leave right at closing time."

"Say what time is it, 12 o'clock? What time is it Ben? Do you have the time sir? Bob, I think your watch is running a little slow. I'm sorry sir, but it's five to one and if you want a round of drinks you'll have to get them from another bartender."

"Cindy lets go! I'll get my coat and punch out and it'll be one o'clock. Where are you parked, you came with a girlfriend and she left five hours ago. Where do you live?" I asked, helping her into the brown bomber.

"About thirty minutes from here in St. Paul," she said as her eyes momentarily glistened, reflecting the neon purple football.

We cruised down the freeway ramp and started for St. Paul. Now, I don't want to say Cindy was sitting close to me, but she was as much behind the steering wheel as I was. First she kissed my ear, then licked it, then ate it.

Obviously hungry, she followed the same procedure on my neck and chest, opening the zipper on my number 43 jersey with her teeth. Continuing the southerly course, she crossed the equator and easily negotiated my fly in the same manner as the shirt zipper.

What's this coming out to greet her, the old one iron, the joy stick, yes my cock was pretending to be the IDS Tower. 3Cs went to work. Chomp, slurp, yum and a few other sounds I can't spell were the audio portion of the track.

Now while all this was going on, for those who don't remember I'm zooming down the freeway exhibiting less than my usual driving expertise.

We end the narrative here and pick up again with Miss 3Cs muttering: "Is this what sex at 60 is like?"

"Don't talk with your mouth full."

"How many hands do you need to drive?" she purred.

"One for sure," I answered.

"Then would you mind massaging my breasts with your other hand?" she asked.

So where am I now, and why am I losing my place? Oh yeah! She's all over me, and I'm all over her, and the car is all over the highway.

We finally pulled into the Concord Apartments on Concord Avenue. How original!

These kind of apartment complexes seem to be growing by themselves. Underground parking, phony lobby, (vinyl furniture that no one ever uses, plastic flowers that nobody ever smells, and a security system that everyone always beats.) Indoor swimming pool, sauna, and workout room that no one ever uses but always shows to visitors. Sunken living room, fireplace, tiny kitchen, and of course a small balcony overlooking a busy highway.

"Care for a drink?" she asked.

"What, and lose all my inhibitions?" We both laughed. She had brandy. I like brandy. We drank brandy.

"Are you going to spend the night?"

"I'll tell you in the morning. Where's the bedroom?"

"Here," she took my hand and led me into the dark bedroom.

All I could think of was, "John's going to get it, John's going to get it!" The bed was easy enough to find. I did a quarter gainer into the sack and waited. The only sound was my breathing. I could sense 3C standing over me.

"Click, Click," this couldn't be my zipper unzipping, my belt unbelted and my pants de-panted.

"How about a nice Cindy Carol Coleman All American blow job?" she asked.

What it means to be an American by John Williams. Long live America the beautiful, its rolling hills, majestic wheat fields, flowing rivers. Keep going Cindy I'm not there yet. President Ford, Hugh Hefner, Casey Stengel and AWWWWW WOOOOW thank you Cindy!

When the tribute ended I treated Cindy with the same hospitality she had bestowed on me. The remainder of the night was your basic bumps and grinds, ups and downs, ins and outs. She couldn't get enough, I couldn't get enough. Doing it was a hell of a lot better than writing about it.

What more can I say, I left her apartment about noon the next day and she moved to Denver the following week. You people in Denver be advised, the Cindy Carol Coleman All American blow job is in town.

I bumped through the swinging doors into the restaurant and was on my way to the bar when I noticed a couple sitting near the salad bar.

"I should know those people, at least the girl," I thought. She glanced up, but returned to her French onion soup with what I read as a slight bit of recognition. I dismissed the episode and entered the dimly lit bar area.

"Hi Dave, Joe, Jim, Terry, Carl, Joni, Vicki," I greeted the other bartenders and waitresses. I didn't notice if they were all there. Of course they're all there. It's 5:10. They're always here at 5:10. The same faces, the same jokes, the same drinks, the same conversations. Liars poker, the numbers game.

"Get Carl a drink."

"I'll get this round."

"Tell that cheap son-of-a-bitch to buy me a drink."

"When's the house gunna buy one?"

"The Vikes have looked good this year."

I don't have to pay attention because all my responses are taped. "Yes. No. Pretty good. Not bad." Etc. Tell them what they want to hear. By 7:00 PM they'll all be going home, and their wives will have to contend with them.

Tonight is Monday. Not much business. Time goes pretty slow. I sipped a little orange juice and talked to the waitresses.

The couple I had noticed in the dining room negotiated two bar stools.

"Can I help you with something?" I asked.

"Yes, I'll have a Kahlua on the rocks and Cindy, what would you like?"

"I'll have a Drambuie on the rocks."

"Cindy Anderson, yes another Cindy, that's who it is," I thought.

"C..C. Rider. My god she's married. I haven't seen her for two years. She cut her hair and I bet she wears contacts."

I finished pouring the drinks and returned. Her husband had gone to the mens room.

"How's it going Cindy?" I asked.

"Fine."

"Are you happy?"

"I'm married."

"Nice guy?"

"He's got money."

"Nice talking to you Cindy."

Girls are most reluctant about letting on to their husbands that they ever knew a male before they got married.

(That's right Jack, she never liked guys, she was a lesbian, but you turned her back).

"Oh darling you're really the only guy that ever mattered to me, those other guys were all jerks. Besides, I never really did anything with them, just blow jobs. Honest. You're the first one, and ah ah, oh but, I still cheer for the Chicago Bears, including their coaching staff."

"This is only my second time, really, there was only one guy before you, and we only did it once, in his parents place, before going to church, is that a bad thing?"

"It was just one of those wild weekends on the beach, I can't believe I let myself go. I still can't drink a Mai Tai without feeling guilty."

"It was a gray, cold, November night, I was lonely, he was lonely, OK, OK, they were lonely."

"Look I was broke, the mechanics all agreed that I needed a new carburetor. What was I supposed to pay them with, blood?"

"Cut me some slack Bob, do you know what it's like to be the only girl in town wearing the same coat four winters in row?"

"I come from a broken home, it was the 60s, I was reaching out and finding myself."

Stories! We've all heard them. There is something about girls, they somehow think their hymen grows back the minute they say, "I Do."

Cindy Anderson, built like a Mama Celeste pizza. Everything you like and plenty of it. I noticed Cindy the first time she came in. Shoulder length blond hair, 5' 6", great figure, if you like pizza, striking facial features (try saying that fast five times), and black horned glasses. She looked like a teacher with those glasses and she was.

All I wanted to do was join her class, but the timing was never quite right. Finally she needed a ride home one night and I went to the head of the class.

As we crunched through the frozen parking lot she told me that, "Her parents divorced when she was three. That she was raised my an elderly grandmother. Married at 18, divorced by 20, and now was thinking of relocating to New Mexico to teach at a poor hispanic community." *Oh boy, sounds swell!*

We drove in silence for about 10 minutes. "I live here," she finally said, pointing at a row of apartment buildings on the east side of Nicollet Avenue.

"If you promise not to touch me, I'll invite you in," Cindy said.

"Big deal," I thought, *"taking Helen Keller home is not my idea of a good time."* We stepped up three flights of stairs in a modest apartment building. She let us in and disappeared into the bathroom. Not a word had been spoken since the car. I sat on her couch with the air of a man who had waited on a couch before.

"Let's see," I thought, *"two semi-comfortable chairs, a couch, two end tables, three lamps, and a small dining*

room set. This has to be the 1500 group from the furni-ture barn." A petit stereo to match the petit TV and the slight aroma of popcorn completed the picture.

"Well, I think I'll be going," I said. (silence)

"Did you hear me?" I tried again, "I better go."

The bathroom door opened and out walked Cindy in a blue nightgown cut just above two dark eyes that stared at me. I didn't know fabric could be that sheer. Cindy's slender, naked body was a sight to behold, and I wanted to hold every inch of it. If I hadn't been sitting down, I would have been sitting down. (Say something funny John, break out of your nervousness.)

"Who do you think will win the pennant this year?" (She sat next to me.) "Personally, I think the Twins are out of it." (OK, that was dumb).

The silence was driving me crazy. She looked at me briefly, as if she were thinking about something. Still not speaking, Cindy produced a small mirror and a tiny bag of white powder from one of the end tables. She precisely spread four thin lines of the powder on the mirror.

"Do you have a dollar bill?" she asked.

"I have a five and some change," I answered (that was really dumb too).

She took the five and rolled it up like a straw, and proceeded to inhale two lines of the powder. Cindy handed the mirror to me. My two lines disappeared and soon I had the feeling that this wasn't all bad. A slight flush accompanied by a mild speed lift and a mellow high.

The warm shower head pulsated on my naked body as Cindy stroked my cock. Pulsate, pulsate, stroke, stroke, stroke, finally my knees started to give and I blasted all over Cindy-the-teacher. Gasping for air in the steamy bathroom I reached for her shoulders, but Cindy backed up saying, "Remember, no touching the teacher."

Cindy reached past me, turning off the valve, I mumbled something about my grade point and she giggled. Bracing against the shower wall I asked her, "If she played baseball? Cindy, you've got a hell of an arm." Again she giggled.

Yes, sometimes when I take my daily shower I think of Cindy and her amazing fast ball.

"Could I have a drink?"

"What?"

"Could I have a drink?"

"Sure, why didn't you say something?"

"I have been for the last five minutes, are you bartenders all on dope?"

"No, we just put up with 'em."

I can't understand why he walked away. I must have forgotten to say, "Can I help you, sir?"

The band started with its usual easy listening set at 8:45. They do this for the people still dining. The help takes a nap during this set. At about 10 o'clock, the band begins to rock and roll, get down, get funky…boogie. They get loud. All the bartenders and waitresses know how to read lips, as we can't seem to hear anything from this point on except, "Here's a quarter for your trouble."

Even as the band increased the volume, I could see little hope for a busy or sex filled evening. I tried going back to the daydreams, but the colors seemed to go dry. Then up near the dance floor was Sally Cassel, complete with escort.

To the girl in my life who possessed the largest set of breasts, the biggest boobies, the naughtiest knockers, ol' jumbo jugs herself, "The envelope please, oh she'll be so happy. And the winner is Sally Cassel." Cue, "Thanks for the Mammaries."

She was also dumb, she once asked if a shrimp cocktail was an ice cream drink made with creme-de-shrimp. I said, "Yes" and walked away.

I never paid much attention to her. I'm not attracted to girls as large as Sally because I feel when a female reaches 200 pounds she becomes a place. And Sally was a place I had no wish to visit, at least most of the time.

It was a Saturday night about a year and a half ago, one of the few I got off so I decided to celebrate.

I hit a few of the hotel bars, but somewhere between a Christian Brothers and soda and a Beefeaters martini, I missed supper. By 10 o'clock

I was at Maxwell's with my mind playing taps and the ol' body on automatic.

"Excuse me Sally, but is this chair taken?" I asked her.

"Why don't you ask the fellow sitting in it?" Sally replied.

"Sir, is this chair taken, and before you answer that question you'll consider that I'm 6' 4" tall and know all the baddest people in here tonight. It's not taken? Well, I'll just sit down here before someone else grabs it."

"That wasn't very nice," Sally said.

"You mean a guy gives his chair up to a perfect stranger and you don't think that's nice?" I questioned.

"That's not what I meant John."

"Sally, can I totally level with you?"

"Yes John."

"Really Sally, I would like to confide in you."

"Yes John."

"The other night I was home changing the water in my aquarium and from out of nowhere came an impure thought about you."

"About me, John?"

"Not exactly you, Sally, it was your tits, your left tit to be precise. I've always liked that side of your body, why do you think I chose this chair to sit in?"

"John, are you leading up to something?"

"I might be if nothing better comes in."

"How many drinks have you had?" she asked.

"Let's not talk about me, I've always had kind of a …oh, how do I say it…kind of a dirty thing for you. Or, to say it more romantically, I've always wanted to jump-on-your-bones. Say you'll be mine or the semen will back up into my brain causing me to do outrageous things and be late for work tomorrow."

"Are you being serious, John?"

"About what?"

"About taking me home and jumping by bones."

"Boy, have you got an imagination."

I remember people buying me drinks, having six drinks in front of me at one time. I remember drinking two of them: the first one and the sixth one. I remember a short car ride, a flight of stairs, an apartment, a bedroom, and a dream with Captain Ahab, a harpoon and a fight to the death with Moby Dick, massive doses of blubber being Moby's only defense.

Morning, moaning, more moaning, I had never noticed before how close the two words sounded.

"Good morning John."

"Good morning Moby said Captain Ahab."

"Sally, can I pretend this never happened?"

"No you can't."

She'll never buy this but here goes: "How about if I leave but get your number and call you later?"

"That'll be fine." (She bought it) "Here you go. Now you can call me any time. Promise?"

"Yes."

"You're really going to call?"

"Of course I will."

"You promise?"

"You've gone through this before, I'm leaving."

Naturally, I never called her, but Sally took it pretty well and only hated me.

She and her new flame got up to dance, she seemed thinner now.

"Thank you Sally, and thank you Melville."

20.

IF INFLATION IS OUT OF CONTROL, WHY IS MY DICK NOT GETTING BIGGER

A DAY IN THE LIFE.

Now that I've covered the best part about bartending at a large boogie bar in the mid-70s, which if you were *paying* attention was the girls we meet. I should include a few small paragraphs about the bad part.

Day bartenders are a different breed than their night time counterparts. They're usually married and older, more stable sorts. Many work Monday through Friday with hours like a real job. They don't have as many customers as the night crew, so a large part of their job is making sure the bar is well stocked with everything that will be needed later in that evening. I doubt that I could ever be a full time day bartender, in fact I only take a day shift if really pressed.

Time for a small test:

What is the worst, the absolutely worst small group of customers that a bartender and cocktail waitress deal with?

A. A gang of drugged out, knife wielding, jive talking, bar trashing, black gang members.
B. A group of middle managers that are sure that their company in on the verge of downsizing and know that any day now they will be out of a job.
C. A group of recently divorced men who have met to share sob stories about how their ex-wives lawyers are a bunch of stone cold, arm twisting, blood sucking shysters.
D. Four middle aged housewives that decided to meet at Maxwell's for lunch.

If you said "D" you are 100% correct.

Ladies. Four ladies chatting away. Whhhiiirrrr, clank, my mind tossed out the stereotype.

"Let's meet for lunch Myrtle, Ethel, Martha."

"Wonderful, thrilling, fantastic."

"I hear the chef salad at Maxwell's is amazing."

"Lovely, fabulous, I can't wait."

At the end of the meal they had split up the bill and then Martha, or was it Myrtle had gotten a naughty twinkle in her eyes.

"Let's have a drink at the bar."

(After the legal limit of two minutes hesitation: "I have to bake a cake. Harry's bringing some business associates home for dinner. I really should get back to the blood bank," they all agree, but just for one drink).

When they finally decide where all four of them should sit, and, as the cocktail waitress approaches, one of them will undoubtedly get up and announce that she needs to visit the ladies room.

"Would anyone like to join me?"

Now this is something that has always confused all men of all cultures. What is the deal with women going to the restroom together? If a man asked his pals if they would like to go to the men's room with him he would get some really strange looks, might even get punched. What do woman do for each other in the ladies room, cheer each other on?

"Come on Dorothy, push harder, it's coming, I can see it, go Dorothy, go."

So back at the table, the conversation is like this, "What are you going to have?" they ask back and forth as the poor waitress, who's been all through this before, stands by.

When the "I don't know's," and the "no, I think I'll have a…"instead's," die down, the waitress pad reads: "II GH, I PKS, I GT." Translated that means two grasshoppers, one pink squirrel, and a gin and tonic.

Collecting the money for the drinks takes at least as long as balancing the National debt. Each pays separately and in change, small change, of course theres no tip for the waitress or bartender.

Women! Women alone, that is, don't normally come in the bar in the afternoon. But when they do, they're about as popular as the Black Panthers at a Klan rally.

21.

CAR TROUBLE AND ACTING LESSONS

There are not a lot of what you would call tender moments in the bar business, especially during an economic recession. Everybody is struggling to keep the bills paid, and their head above water. Naturally the employees with kids have it the hardest.

Terry Jacobson is a tall, good looking part time bartender. I don't know Terry real well. Terry majored in Acting and Theater Arts at the University and has been in various theater productions and radio and TV commercials around the Twin Cities. Like most of these media people getting work is a constant issue, and as often times happens the actor has to pay the bills somehow. So working in the restaurant business is quick money.

Another thing about Terry is that he likes a good practical joke. Joni Milton is a hard working cocktail waitress that is not what you might call bright. In fact, if her IQ was three points lower she could probably be outmaneuvered by a bowl of cold oatmeal. Secretly other employees have wondered if

Joni was dumber than Hush Puppies. However, Joni does have some physical characteristics that would make the proverbial wet noodle stand at attention.

Unfortunately Joni is also gullible, she could be talked into betting against Perry Mason in the re-runs. Joni was having trouble with her car near Maxwell's one day and stopped in to ask one of the bartenders what to do about it. Terry was working and listened as she described the symptoms of her car's troubles. Terry thought for a moment when she was finished.

"Sounds like it needs to be wound up, Joni," Terry finally told her.

"Oh, c'mon Terry, cars don't need to be wound up," Joni replied.

"They sure do, about once a year. I just wound mine up last week," Terry earnestly said.

"I've never heard of that before," Joni replied, evidently slightly confused.

"Go out and look in your glove compartment. There's usually a small pouch with a key in it somewhere in there," Terry said with a straight face. "Then open the hood and look for a place the key will fit. The different car manufacturers put the wind-up spot in different places. I've got a Ford, theirs is right next to the radiator. But you've got a Chevy, I don't know where they put theirs. If you can't find the key or the wind-up spot, go to a gas station. They'll give you a new key and wind it up for about a dollar."

So Joni went to her gas station and explained to the mechanics her car symptoms and asked them to wind up her car. By the time Joni caught onto the joke and roared out of the station, the guys were on their knees laughing.

The next day both Joni and Terry were working when Joni stormed over to him, "I'm never speaking to you again, Terry," she shouted at him.

A few minutes later Joni went over to Terry's station and said, "I need napkins."

"What?"

"I need napkins, you tall mean jerk."

"Cocktail or sanitary?" Terry calmly replied.

Now Joni was seething, "I'll get them from someone else."

Terry immediately took a few long quick strides around his service station bar and roped his long arms around Joni who melted into his chest. They both started laughing.

"I'm sorry Joni, I was wrong, let's be friends."

I later asked Terry how he seemed to always be able to sell his nonsense.

Terry smiled and said, "John, you can't force it, when playing a role or advertising a product you can't push it too hard. Thoughtful, earnest, calm, and sincere. You may be selling sand in the desert, or gorilla poop in Africa, but always make your target think that you are the most heartfelt guy in the room."

Little did I know that Terry's one minute acting lesson to me was going to pay huge dividends in a few weeks.

22.

LIES, LINES, AND TOTAL WHOPPERS

The lions share of the guys coming into Maxwell's discothèque looking for a stray piece don't fit either the drunk or big spender molds. Most are just horny with a few bucks in their pockets, like me. But I do have one advantage over your basic hustler off the street: I've heard most of the lines and I've seen which work best.

If all the buffers, killing time lines, nervous fillers, and all around bullshit were left out of the first conversation between a man and a woman at boogie bars across this great country. If only key questions and comments were left in, the dialog on a typical Friday night would be something like this:

"Hi, my name is John. Could I buy you a drink? (Initial contact is made, you've shown that you have a few bucks in your wallet, and are not a total loser.)

"Sure, I'll have a gimlet." (That's good. It's a strong drink, shows she's not afraid to get a buzz on, and you won't have to buy her singles all night long.)

Ask her what she does for a living? Remember, it's all about her.

"I'm a stewardess." (Bingo, you've hit the jack-off pot. Make a reservation at the Budgetel. A stewardess, waitress, bank teller, etc. are all fun jobs. She probably does it to meet people. Look for jobs with people contact.)

"How does a handsome stud like me get into your pants?"

"I already have one asshole in there. What do I need another one for?"

(Strike last remark. You moved too fast. Never show vanity. If you're really interested in this girl, play her for about an hour, try this.)

"What do you like to do?" (Phrase it just that way. It's all about her! You may even get a coy little smile that says, "What I really like to do best is screw the eyes out of little white boys like yourself." But she probably won't say it.)

"I like to swim, ski, and play tennis." (That's a pretty standard answer. You haven't learned much, but she didn't poke you in the eye with a swizzle stick. If she goes on, however, particularly into less feminine sports, golf, hockey, avid football fan, that's good. She's into physical contact sports.)

"Would you like to dance?" (You almost have to ask, even if you waddle around the floor like a pregnant warthog in a swamp.)

"I'd love too, do you bump?"

"Only if someone bumps me first." (Wait til two or three fast ones have gone by, it's likely you'll hit a fast dance followed by a slow number. See how she responds to you during the slow one. How close she is. If she grabs your joint or not. How she looks into your eyes, wait a minute, hold the phone. There will be no grabbing of joints on the dance floor. Try two or three dances, and always leave after the slow tune. It protects the mood. She's just left your arms. Order another drink, you'll both be thirsty and, dare you think it, hot.)

"Are you married?" (It has to be asked, although the most subtle approach possible is best.)

"I couldn't help noticing your wedding ring. Does that mean you're just here looking for a one-night stand?" (Not overly smooth I'd say.)

"I don't suppose a sleazy looking girl like you is married, is she?" (If you're on this track, you're going in the wrong direction.)

"Why isn't a great looking girl like you married?" (Not bad. If she is, it's up to you. I'd leave. Certainly her husband is an animal with hair all over his body. If he catches you, they'll have to remove the floorboards before you can get up.) If she say's she's never been married, pass go and collect $200. If she's divorced, proceed with caution, she's got a ex out there somewhere. Ex-husbands! What can be said about them that hasn't already been said about the plague, air pollution, nuclear war, and Wayne

Newton. A sign should be required apparel for pre-viously married women: "Beware of ex-husbands."

"Look, I'd like to talk to you but the band's so loud. Let's go get some breakfast, are you hungry?"

"Well, I'd like to but I drove my girlfriend and we live 70 miles from here." (This business of a girlfriend means she's looking for a way out. Get her phone number on flash paper and leave, or:)

"Tell her to take a cab."

Cut to the 24 hour restaurant across the street.

"You mentioned you were hungry. What would you like?"

"A cup of coffee."

"Two coffees, please." (Here's where the heavy pitch is made.)

"You like music? You do?" (What a shock.)

"You like skiing? What kind of skiing?"

"You know, in the winter."

"That would be snow skiing."

"Right." (Lucky guess.)

"What else do you like?"

"Weightlifting."

"You lift weights?"

"No silly, I like to watch guys lift weights."

"You know what let's do?"

"No, what?"

"Let's go over to my place, listen to some great music. I'll show you my skis, and you can feel my muscles."

(Cut to my place. The Bloomington Pleasure Palace, known for its great stereo system, well stocked bar and king-sized bed.)

"How about a drink as long as I've already made two? Let's see, a brandy and water for me and a gimlet for you."

"A beer mug full?"

"I only have two clean glasses. Besides, it will save trips to the kitchen for refills. How about some music?"

"I'm getting drunk," she theorizes.

"You know, you're lovely and I think I'm going to kiss you hard on the lips." (*Shit. You've been watching too much afternoon television. Don't say anything. She just told you she was helpless, didn't she? Kiss her gently first. Think of her as a bad carburetor: It'll kill if you give it too much gas at first. Now, ease it into second. Go for third. Slide! You were almost called out, but she wants it as bad as you do. Remember, more girls have been talked out of going to bed than have been talked into the sack. Congratulations! You've got it made. Maybe she wasn't the best, but when you're old and shriveled, you'll look back and say what all old men say, "The worst I ever had was great."*)

23.

IT'S A GAME OF INCHES

"How about a little poker tonight, John?"

"That's sounds good, Boomer, who's goin' to play?"

"Mark Fletcher from Edward's and Russ. Mark wants to play at his place right after work. Big Einer and Little Carl will be there."

"Sounds great! Tim can't make it, he's busy handicapping this week's NFL games. Say, can you ask Carl to not bring that vicious looking little knife of his?"

"John relax, Little Carl is harmless."

Hmmmmm!

I played poker with Boomer and his brothers along with some of the other bartenders on the strip maybe once every couple weeks. Friendly stakes, at a friendly game. Sometimes we'd have enough guys for two eight player tables. Great way to de-stress, and catch up with everything at all the bars and restaurants on the I-494 strip. After a couple of hours someone would invariably suggest a raise in the stakes and that was fine. I'd been doing really well at this game the last couple of months and with all the cash Timmy had been winning for us betting football I was feeling flush.

Most games would be fun with the usual banter about girls, sports, and work. Pizzas would be ordered, and a case of beer would disappear.

Boomer's suggestions of a game came at the right time. I had tomorrow off and I'd been trying to think of something to do after work tonight. I no doubt would have preferred an encitingly endowed young lady to wiggle up to the bar and say:

"I'm taking applications for a mutual masturbation program. Would you like to come over to my place tonight and audition?" But it didn't look like that was going to happen tonight.

But I hadn't completely given up thoughts of the fairer sex for the night. It was still early, only a little after seven, and if something foxy did stroll in, I could always plead horniness to the other fellows and cancel out of the game. They wouldn't like that, but what the hell, they'd do it to me just as fast.

My eyes snagged a blond head of hair attached to a fine looking body as it bounced into the bar area. She moved straight to my station and sat down.

"Can I help you?"

"Yes," she smiled, "I'd like a Black Russian."

"Sure thing," said John, wishing it were a sure thing.

"*Not too bad,*" I thought. "*Not too bad at all. I think I'd rather play poke-her than poker tonight.*"

"Would you like something else?" I asked, delivering the drink.

"Oh not right now, thanks," she mouthed slowly, her eyes holding mine.

"*Poke her,*" said the bulge in John's pants.

Just to keep things moving between me and Ms. Tonight, I kept smiling and nodding to her.

"Nice weather, for December, I offered on my next pass by her.

"Yes, it is." She was still smiling and nobody else had moved in on her yet, but there was no sense taking chances.

I mixed another Black Russian and slid it toward her.

"Where's this from?" she asked.

"Oh, old number 43 thought you were looking a little undernourished," I said.

She looked at my number 43 jersey.

"Thanks." She gave another shy smile and looked down at the drink.

I went by her again, ""Are you going to be around for awhile later tonight?" I asked.

"Oh, I don't know, I'm here with a girlfriend, but I probably will be. Why?"

(It's fourth down and a yard to go, hang onto your Grain Belt Beer, this could be the play of the game. The Vikings are down by four points. They have to go for it. A field goal won't do 'em any good and there's less than a minute to play. The Viking break out of the huddle. They're lining up, there's the snap from center…and…)

"Why? I'll tell you why, I want to get you drunk and screw your wheels off," I thought.

"No, I better not say that."

"Oh, I thought maybe I could buy you breakfast after I get off," I said.

"That'd be nice, but I'll have to see what my girlfriend wants to do," replied Ms. Tonight.

"I can give you a ride home after," I said, hoping to be persuasive. "Keep me posted, will ya?"

"For sure," she smiled.

(…it's a handoff to the fullback…he hesitates… now he slants off-tackle…he makes a yard and he's hit by the middle linebacker and dropped…stand by folks, they're going to have to measure to see if he got the necessary yardage…)

It wasn't what you'd call a sure thing, but then it wasn't a, "No" either.

"Oh, I hope, I hope, I hope," came the the tiny voice from John's scrotum. The juices were beginning to flow. My outlook was brightening.

(…they're bringing the chain onto the field… from up in our booth, it's hard to tell if he made it…they're straightening the chain, 80 thousand fans are on their feet here at Soldier Field in Chicago, and we will be right back after this message from our local station…)

I hummed around the bar, picking up a few drink orders stopping to chat with Ms. Tonight.

Another girl sat next to my blond.

"This must be the girlfriend," I thought.

(…they're putting the chain down and…)

"She wants to go to Edward's," she said, indicating her girlfriend.

"Are you going to be there for awhile?" I asked.

(…it looks from here like he didn't make it… here's the referee's indication…)

"Ya, I'm sure we will be," said Ms. Tonight.

"I can get off at midnight and meet you there," I offered.

"OK," she said, "are you coming for sure?"

I gave her the big shy smile now, with a little fawning head nod, "For sure."

"See you at Edwards, a little after midnight then. Don't be late." She slid her perfect butt off the stool and headed for the exit.

(…right after a few words from our sponsor…)

There's a 50-50 chance she'll be there at midnight. At least those are the odds I've been running on this type of deal. However, there are other elements to take into consideration. First she's better than average looking. Has slightly bigger than average boobs. Her butt is at least an 8 maybe a 9, and I haven't been laid since Sunday night.

(....We're experiencing trouble with our network feed, ladies and gentleman. As soon as it's repaired we'll continue coverage of the game...please stand by...)

"Boomer, I'm not going to be able to play poker tonight," I said.

"How come?" Boomer grunted.

"I just remembered I've got a date tonight," I said.

"You know the new rule, don't ya?" he asked.

"What new rule?"

"If you say you're going to play and then cancel out, you've got to pay $20.00 toward beer for the next game," said Boomer.

"I never heard of that rule," I countered.

"We made it last week when Terry dropped out. If you don't pay your black-balled from playing anymore," Boomer said it like he meant it.

I wrote out a check for Boomer, putting a, "For blow job" in the memo line.

I walked into Edward's a few minutes after 12 o'clock. No Ms. Tonight. I checked the peanut bar, the disco downstairs, the phone booths, and the men's room. She was not to be seen.

I sadly came back to the peanut bar and ordered a dry Beefeaters martini.

I finished my drink, and still no Ms. Tonight to be seen. I headed for my car, thinking that, "*At least I had a nice bottle of brandy at home waiting for me.*"

(…we're sorry for the delay of the game, folks, but play on the field was stopped while we corrected the technical difficulties…the official's were just measuring for a first down…the marker is down…)

I mixed myself four fingers of brandy and splashed in a tad of ginger ale. Flipping on the late show, I crossed the room and flopped in the easy chair.

"Briinnnng." I jumped, spilling a healthy slug of the brandy down my shirt. It was only the phone.

"Hello?"

"Hi, is this John, the bartender?"

"Yes, can I help you?"

"Oh hi John, this is Ashley, we met tonight at Maxwell's and I was supposed to meet you at Edwards."

"Ah ya."

"Well my girlfriend decided that she didn't like Edwards, so we went back to Maxwell's but we must have missed you, sorry."

"Oh, ya, I guess so."

(…that was close, but the Vikings just made the first down and have new life….Viking first down on the Bears 22 yard line, eighteen seconds to play…., 22 yards in 18 seconds…can the Vikings do it?… Tarkenton takes the snap from center, fakes a give to Foreman, rolls right, he's looking down field…)

"Well anyway John, I felt bad about missing you. So I asked one of the other bartenders for your phone number," said Ms. Tonight, I mean Ashley.

(...Tarkenton looks trapped, he scrambles left, buys some time, the fullback is open over the middle and he makes the catch for a nine yard pick-up.... but that play burned a lot of time off the clock...)

"Look John, if you want I could give you my address and you could come over for a little late night snack," said Ms. Tonight.

"Oh and what a late night snack it would be, I can taste her, I mean it, now. John Williams, once again pulling victory from the jaws of defeat."

(...last play of the game folks, and what a game it has been....back and forth, back and forth, both teams look exhausted...the Vikings break huddle.... Tarkenton under center,....drops back to pass...the Bears rush is on him...he looks right but everyone is covered....Tarkenton steps up in the pocket.... THE TIGHT END IS WIDE OPEN IN THE BACK END ZONE...TARKETON SEES HIM AND LET'S IT GO....)

"Sounds great, I'll be right over, where do you live?" I said.

I'm hearing crying in the background of Ms. Tonight's phone.

"Oh no, I'm sorry John, you must think terribly of me. My roommate just got dumped by her boyfriend this week and she's just a mess. I have to go console her, let's get together another time. Bye."

(...the pass is in the air...at the last second the Bears defensive back recovered and batted it away... this game is over..and the Bears sideline players have stormed the field.)

"Buzz give us a recap of this great game."

"Yes, it truly was a great game and what a tough loss for the Vikings, and in particular their punter, number 43 John Williams. I bet he feels really bad now, terrible, horrible, a complete fuck-up, what a dumb-ass. I bet he's going to do what he always does at a time like this. Get drunk, go to bed alone, and like the complete loser he is, jerk off to the memory of the girl that got away."

24.

HAMBURGERS, LONELINESS, AND EXTRA HASH BROWNS

Wednesday 1977, Five days before the Super Bowl.

"Briiiinnnng."

"Hello?"

"Hello, John?"

"Ya?"

"This is Joe Schmidt…we went to High School together, remember?"

"Ahh, OK!"

"You do remember me, don't you?"

"Ahh kinda, I mean, I remember High School."

"I sat three rows from you in Biology class. I always cheered extra loud whenever you were on the basketball court. Remember me now?"

"Look what time is it?" I asked.

"11:45 in the morning, I figured you'd be up by now."

"Actually I was still sleeping."

"Well look John, since we know each other so well I thought I better call you. See I talked to Jim Shelly the other night …remember him from Math class? He said he ran into you bartending out at Maxwell's."

"Ya, I guess, I must have seen him."

"Well you won't believe this, but I'm selling condominiums now, and Jim said you sounded pretty well settled. I thought you might be in the market," Joe said.

"Ah, look I don't think so, Joe…"

"Trust me John, I'm trying to do you a favor here. The market is really heating up. Now is the time to get in! I wouldn't be calling you if I didn't think you needed my help," Joe responded.

"Look, ah, aren't interest rates awfully high now?" I questioned.

"See, that's the John Williams I remember. You always were really smart. But I can do something about these high interest rates, and I'll even give you a discount on my commission, just because we've known each other so long."

"Well it's like this, Maxwells is closing and won't be reopening until spring, so I can't make any plans right now…"

"Don't let a little thing like not having a job get in the way of your financial success. You're my friend and I want to help you. We'll work it out, I'll get it done, nows the time…"

Click.

I flopped back in bed staring at the ceiling, *"I'm not good at change. I'm barely good at routine, and now I was looking at a world of change. My job, my rented townhouse, my car, my social life was all going to change."*

"What is Tim thinking? Maui Hawaii? What does he know? This requires serious rational reasoning on my part. I wish I could pay someone to do it for me.

Lunch time, Tim's at work so that means I have to go out.

"What fun it is to eat alone?" I thought, slamming the car door and walking toward the restaurant entrance, the smash of cold wind snapping in my face.

It isn't all that easy eating alone, I should know. I only eat at home when I've exhausted all other possibilities. The rest of the time I eat out, either with someone or, as often happens, alone.

"Just you?" asks the hostess.

"Well since you're all alone I'll seat you right here in this tiny booth, right next to the front door so every time someone comes in or out you'll be refreshed by the polar air, you don't need to thank me."

People stare more when you're eating alone it seems. It makes me uneasy. I try to make it look like I'm waiting for somebody, or that I'm eating alone out of choice.

"I've got lots of friends. I'm a very popular guy. I'm just sitting here by myself 'cause I enjoy eating in silence."

I slid into the seat and hid behind the menu. I know it by heart. I know all the menus in this part of town by heart. But it's something to read, even if it's for the 132nd time.

"Have you decided, John?" The waitress knows me by name. That means extra hash browns.

"Ya Sue, I'll have the hamburger royal dinner, hash browns, blue cheese dressing, and a large skim milk."

"How do you want your hamburger?"

"All 12 cents worth of meat and she wants to know how I want it done. Oh, I'd like the outside browned ever so gently, so as not to bruise the delicate heart of the patty, which should remain moist, and only slightly warmed, to conserve the natural juices which represent the true flavor which the cow died for."

"You want it medium, like usual, right?"

"That'll be fine, thanks Sue."

"What to do, what to do. I've read the ingredients on the catsup bottle twice. Here come the milk, I can drink it cold now or warm with the meal."

"Hummmmm." *"I shouldn't hum, it looks simple. Don't stare at strangers, they'll think you're strange. Tapping on the table is out. Fumble with the salt and pepper shakers, consider who might be the next president and if there's a God."*

The meal arrives, and I start in on it.

"What is Tim thinking? What does he know? Always Mr. Logical, always looking down the road,

thinking ahead. Why Hawaii? Sure it was warm, but so are lot of places. He mentioned something a few days ago about Maui. It was expensive, expensive to get there, expensive to live there. So that must be it. Tim is thinking of getting in on a beachfront real estate boom in Maui. We're going to buy a place, and start flipping. Tim has always said that 'money follows money.' Whatever that means! With his business degree Tim won't have any problem getting a good job, and just like he did for me at Maxwell's he'll fold me in too.

Who knows, maybe there will be some older, rich, divorced or widowed lady who would like a tall, good looking bartender for a very close personal friend. Maybe even marriage. A guy doesn't have to marry into poverty, or even the middle class.

'Money follows money!' According to Tim, Maui is an expensive place to live, that means there's a lot of financially comfortable people there with plenty more in the future.

There I'll be, working some luxury hotel beachfront bar wearing white khaki shorts, sport sandals, a floral shirt with the warm Maui sun on my neck, a soft pacific breeze in my face, and big tipping tourists all smiling and grooving to the Hawaiian beat."

"Are you finished?" said the waitress. I jolted back to the south Minneapolis coffee shop I was sitting in.

"Ah, ya, thanks,"

"Overtip the waitress, pay the bill, tell them it was great."

The cold metal of the door handle penetrated my bare hand as I opened the Toronado's door. I swish the snow off, scrap some ice off the windshield and kick the clogs of slush off the fenders. When I start the car I feel the blow of cold until the mill warms.

"Timmy my friend you are a genius. It's time for us to go."

Flipping on the car radio, I hear the two big stories of the week: The Vikings in the Super Bowl this Sunday and the size of the Siberian Express that's going to be followed by a deep Arctic Air Mass. Tuesday morning I'm going to be on a flight to Hawaii.

Vikings and Steelers in the Super Bowl. The Purple Gang defense against the Steel Curtain. Tim has been researching the game for days.

25.

NOT JUST ANY SUBURBAN MOM

Summer 1976

Maxwells Fine Dining was doing well and the new-look Security procedures and appearance was a big reason for the turn-around. Not only had I helped write the acclaimed commercial I also coordinated the new uniform. Winter the Security staff would wear dark purple sports coat, crisp white shirt, dark pants, shoes and ties. Under the breast pocket of the sports coat in red stitching was "Security". In the summer it was a gold coat, white shirt, brown pants and gold tie. Blue stitching for "Security." Perfect hair cuts, with ingratiating smiles. Gone were the disheveled, sloppy looking thugs.

This seemed to change the whole tone of the operation: Far fewer fights, much better dressed clientele with more money to spend. Even the Brothers seemed to behave better when they came to Maxwells.

It was a late July morning that Mary "Merry" Smith called me and asked me to lunch. This was a little strange I thought, *"Why lunch and why Mary Smith?"* As head cocktail waitress and mother of two I would think that she would have better things to do than meet me for lunch.

I asked Tim if he wanted to join us, and he said, "Sure."

We met in the parking lot of the Charter House Restaurant in Mendota Heights. Nice place, swell view of the Mississippi River.

"Could we have a very private table in the back?" Mary asked the hostess.

"What? Are you two joined at the hip?" teased Mary about Tim's presence.

We all ordered and went through a little small talk about work, her kids, blah blah.

Finally after finishing our salads Mary leaned forward and in a hush voice said, "Guys, I think I need your help."

"Why? And with what?" was my only thought.

"John, Tim, you know I don't have just two kids, I have three. My youngest is in a facility, I never talk about it."

"Okay!" I replied.

"It costs me a fortune and I still have to take care of my other two kids."

"Okay! But what about your ex-es, don't they help?" I dumbly asked.

"Oh John, please! I collect dead-beat-dads like you do bourbon bottles," was Mary's typical sardonic reply.

"Huh."

"So how do you think I pay all the bills, certainly not on my waitress salary?"

"Do you need some help? Tim and I have some money saved, we could give you some," I volunteered.

"No John, I don't need your money, I make enough, it's how I make it that I need to talk to you about," Mary whispered.

"I'm sorry Mary, I'm confused," I said.

"John, I'm going to just say it, but try and understand, I'm a Madam."

"Huh?"

"You're not that surprised are you Tim?" Mary said.

"Not really," Tim thoughtfully replied.

"Yes, I have an escort service. It's how I make my real money. I waitress just to hide my income from my …service," Mary confessed.

"Okay!"

"Look John, try to get this, you single guys don't have a care or responsibility to anyone but yourselves. Other people, especially girls, are not so lucky," Mary continued.

"Ah huh."

"This recession is hard on everyone, kids need new cloths, rent needs to get paid, cars need service and food prices aren't going down out there," Mary lectured.

"Yaaa!"

"I have about fourteen girls working for me, you know some of them, we only do out-call, we only do hotels."

"Wait a minute, I know some of them?" I asked.

"Sure," Mary then ticked off some of the names of her charges that I knew, including three that worked at Maxwells. My mouth fell open.

"You mean…?"

"Yes."

"Not that nice, sweet…?"

"Yes."

"Surely not….?"

"She's one of my best girls, a real producer."

"No!!!"

"Guys, it's like this, times are bad, do you know anyone out there that's not scratching for a buck?" Mary asked.

Mary had us on that one, unemployment, inflation, food prices and gas were all going through the roof.

President Ford kept talking about wearing WIN buttons, Whip Inflation Now. Didn't seem to be working.

Tim took over, "So what exactly is the reason for this meeting?"

Mary began, "I'm getting to that Mr. Accounting Wiz. In the last couple of months I've had some real problems, and these problems seem to be getting worse."

Both Tim and I leaned in.

"My girls are getting abused, knocked around, ganged up on, humiliated, and stiffed. Just this past week one of them was thrown out of the hotel room naked, her cloths ripped up, her purse trashed and thrown down the hallway. There she was naked, bruised, broke and abused. I could tell you other stories but you get the idea. Besides, I have to get home soon. The phone usually starts ringing around happy hour. Guys get a few drinks in them and start looking for comfort and companionship," Mary finished.

"Well thanks for the cheerful information Mary, but I can't think of anything we can do about it," I said.

"Oh I don't know about that John," Tim interjected.

Mary looked at Tim and grinned a little smile, "Always a step ahead aren't you Langford."

Tim grinned back, I was totally lost.

"I'll talk it over with the guys Mary, you're in a tough spot, let's meet at our place in two days," said Tim.

"Thanks Tim, you're a sharp guy, thanks for listening John, see you in 48 hours," Mary finished.

We all got up and walked out of the Charter House. Settling into the Brown Bomber I turned to Tim, "What did I miss back there?" Tim smiled and said, "Everything."

26.

THE CLASSIEST HOOKERS
IN THE TWIN CITIES

Two Days Later:

Everybody was there, Boomer, Nazi Steve Lynch and four of his best Security members, Tim, me, and of course Mary "Merry" Smith.

Drinks were poured, chips, dips, and pretzels bowls passed around.

Tim began, "I've talked privately with most of you about the dilemma Mary has with her escort service. Mary has made it clear that if this situation continues she's out of business. No girl can do that job, if she has to worry about physical, sexual, or financial consequences."

Everybody's head in the room nodded.

Tim continued, "There isn't a major city out there that doesn't have many agencies like Mary's. Here in the Twin Cities there are at least a dozen escort services of all sizes. But just like the Security operation at Maxwell's that Lynch, John and I started, we want to be the sharpest and the best.

This is a business like any other, there are only so many clients out there. Like at Maxwells, we want the ones with the most money. In short we're going for the gold."

Everyone started clapping.

"Those guys with $40.00 dollars in their pocket looking for a quick blowjob in the back seat of their shitty old car are not our clients," Tim said.

Now even louder clapping.

"You've all heard me say it, 'money follows money'. Word gets out that we have the best looking, best dressed, most engaging girls out there, in a safe, secure environment we can charge whatever we want," Tim stated.

Still louder clapping, and a few of the guys jumped to their feet.

"Now this is where you guys come in, just like at Maxwells," Tim continued.

"First, we're only looking for really big guys, intimidatingly big, offensive lineman big. This isn't a job for some moderately sized guy who knows fifty ways to kill you. Steve will do all the training, we're all responsible for recruiting. You see somebody you think fits talk to them," Tim finished.

Steve replied, "I hear you Tim, and you're right, we're not here to hurt our own customers."

Then Tim turned to me and gave me the floor.

I began, "This is going to be short, and clean. Remember, Mary's crew only does out-call at hotels. No parties, no private homes, mostly on the I-494 strip, and near the airport. Primarily these guys are from out of town here on business or to catch a sporting event. We see them at Maxwells all the time."

"Our Security Officer goes to the hotel room and knocks on the door. No, we do not meet anyone in the bar, restaurant, or in the parking lot, strictly in the hotel room where we can control everything."

"He shakes the hand of the client firmly, but not so hard to make him whack off left handed for a week. The Security Officer asks to come in and talk with the client. If the client says no, that's it, we pull out right away, and take the girl home. We're not taking any chances."

"If the client lets us in we thank him and do an immediate security sweep of the room. The days of three guys hiding in the closet and and then jumping on one of Mary's girls is over."

All the heads in the rooms nodded in confirmation.

I went on, "You sit with the client and chat him up. Where's he from? What teams does he follow? How's work? You're developing a quick rapport, two guys rapping about life. No guilt, no shame, no stress, guy stuff. Now you tell him that everything looks OK, he's our kind of guy. A guy's guy. Tell him you'll be back. A few minutes later you bring her up and both enter the room. Just like with the Security Officers, Mary has agreed with us that all the girls will be looking great. Coiffed to the max, dressed to the nines. This is the best looking girl he's ever had. He'll pay anything to be with her. His car payment will have to lapse for a month. That new coat he promised his chubby wife back in Des Moines, forget it! He can't believe his good luck. He's made a friend in you, and now he is going to score the girl of his dreams."

"You shake his hand again, a little harder this time and tell him you'll be back in an hour, and that tipping is not required but appreciated. One last thing, you tell him he pays you now. This will be confusing for some of them. Just tell him that in the past there have been some problems. I'm sure you're not that kind of guy, but the rule is you pay me now."

"Why does the Security Officer take the money? Easy, the days of Mary's girls getting their purse ripped open and their money stolen are over."

All the heads nodded again.

I continued, "Finally, all of Mary's girls are enrolling in a four week massage class, and all the Security Officers will be enrolled in a five night Basic Life Support Class."

"There's no law against a guy getting a rub-down in his hotel room from a massage therapist, and there's no law that says a trained Security Officer can't make sure she's safe. What with all the gang violence, street crime and robberies that are going on in this city what we're doing is dead last on the list of things for the cops to worry about."

"One hour later you knock on the door and collect the girl. You give him this, I held up a small packet of business cards. Thank him, and shake his hand."

Thus was born:

North Star Security LLC

27.

BIG GAMES, BIG CONCERTS AND BIG PROBLEMS

Seven weeks later around 2:30 PM I was busy sitting in an easy chair, smoking, sipping coffee and thumbing through a Penthouse Magazine while Tim vacuumed our Bloomington Pleasure Palace when the phone rang.

Tim turned off the vacuum and I leaned over and answered the phone, nearly getting my left ear blown off. Mary Smith was roaring through the lines at full throttle. I tried to calm her down, but quickly passed the receiver to Tim.

"Mary please, what is the problem?" Tim implored.

"I'll tell you the problem, you two smart ass college boys have ruined my life," she screamed.

"Mary dear, you're obviously agitated, and disconcerted, let's relax a minute and try relieve a volatile situation," Tim said.

This only seemed to upset Mary more, "Would you stop using all those big Grad School words. I'm a waitress and a Madam, not one of your phony professors."

Tim surrendered and passed the phone back to me.

"Mary this is John, ..."

"Williams are you so damn dense that you think I don't know your voice on the phone, put Mister IQ back on the line," Mary snarled.

I tried to pass the phone back to Tim, he was afraid to take it, and waved me off.

I got back on, "Mary where are you?"

"I'm at home, hiding, exhausted, and sleep deprived, and it's all your fault," Mary cried.

"We'll be right over," I said.

Tim had already put away the vacuum and was reaching for the car keys.

Twenty minutes later we cautiously approached Mary's front door, ready to run if she hadn't calmed down.

Mary looked like hell, dragged out, and beaten down, "It started about three weeks after you revamped the whole process with my girls. Now it just gets bigger every week and there's no way that I can keep up. Sure, I'm making more money than ever, much more. But I don't have any time for my two kids at home and I haven't been to the institution to see my Down Syndrome child in a month."

After sitting in Mary's kitchen for twenty minutes it was obvious what needed to be done. But who could help? Tim was busy running Maxwell's business office, and I had no administrative experience. Besides, I was tending bar at night, and needed six hours a day to sit on my ass and do nothing anyway.

Then she turned to Tim and snarled, "OK, Finance Fart, how am I suppose to shield this money from the IRS, and by the way, I know zip about investing."

Tim tried a professional detached approach.

"Mary, first let's look at the positives," Tim stammered.

Mary was staring daggers at both of us.

Tim continued, "Since we changed things have there been any problems? No. Are you making more money than ever? Yes. Are your girls making more money and in a much safer environment? Yes. I think that's quite an accomplishment," Tim said congratulating us all.

Mary shot back, "OK, from now on you take my kids to soccer practice, piano lessons and little league. You two clowns can move in tomorrow."

"Mary we'll get you some help, I think Boomer's brother's might be a good fit," Tim said.

"Don't know the guys, but send them over quick, I can't continue like this," Mary sighed.

It was becoming clear that Tim's and my plan to upgrade Mary's escort service had been a complete success. Maybe a little too successful. If a guy wanted the company of a strikingly attractive young

girl, well groomed, friendly, in a safe, controlled situation he would pay top dollar for it. More to the
point, word had spread fast both locally and with
the out of town crowd. Minneapolis was a great
place to get a great looking girl with no problems.
No problems! Nobody was going to sneak up on
you, bang you over the head and steal your wallet
while you had your pants around your ankles in a
dark alley. No more hanging around a boring hotel
bar eyeing every girl that came in hoping that one
might be willing to give a visiting salesman a bit
of a thrill. No more casually prowling around the
hotel parking lot, while smoking a cigarette looking
for a girl to roll down her window and invite you
into her backseat. Just call this number and the best
looking girl you've ever been with shows up with a
protective Security Officer and a smile on her face.
Done!

All of a sudden it became very popular among
various business types to schedule a meeting or
conference in South Minneapolis. Many salesman
insisted that their managers just didn't understand
how important the Greater Twin Cities area was to
the future of their company.

Not only had business gone through the roof,
Mary had another good/bad problem. Girls talk,
and now she was getting requests for interviews
from a lot of girls. Girls who wanted to look great,

feel good, make great money and above all, be safe and protected.

Little Carl Mattson was somewhat reluctant at first. One brush with the prison system had cured him of ever wanting more. Then Mary laid out the money part of it and Carl decided that helping this over worked, dedicated single Mother of three was the honorable thing to do. Besides, with the layers of legal obstacles we'd put in place he felt he was safe. As far as he was concerned he was helping run a Security company for vulnerable young professional massage therapists. A principled, righteous cause.

Since completing his time at Red Wing Reformatory Carl Mattson had lived an exemplary life. Running the business office for his Fathers moving company and going to school. Because Carl had been such a stand out prisoner at Red Wing Reform School he had qualified for an, "After release" education program. In Little Carl's case he was taking correspondence accounting and finance courses. All he had to do was show the parole board that he was staying out of trouble and progressing in his classes and they left him alone. Of course, the cost of these business courses was on the tax-payers of the State Of Minnesota. Now, five years years after finishing his sentence at Red Wing Reformatory Carl Mattson was a trained accoun-tant. In fact, the parole board was so impressed with his progress they asked Carl to talk to other reform school graduates about how to turn their lives around. Amazing!

After reviewing the Escort Service processes Carl made one needed adjustment. Carl knew that eventually there would be some dickhead, probably with enough alcohol in him to think he was tough, that would try and push-some-boundaries.

Little Carl had planned for this and had his Security Officer's prepared. Sure enough, one night just as one of the burly Officers was leaving a hotel room after escorting a girl into the room and receiving the money from the client, the guy turned to the Officer and says: "Just out of curiosity, what would you do if I did something you didn't like?"

The now iron faced Officer asked, "Do what?"

The wiseass replied,"I don't know, let's just say I got a little rough with her."

The Officer smiled a crooked smile, "First let me say that I'm sure you would never even consider getting a 'a little rough' with one of our ladies. But if you were to make that unfortunate mistake three things would happen. One, I would go downstairs and put this quarter in a pay phone and in ten minutes three guys just like me would come to this hotel. "Two, . . now the Officer opened his wallet and took out a fifty dollar bill. "I would tell the supervisor of this hotel to give me a pass key and take this fifty dollars. Three, you would spend the next month getting your face put back together."

Very needless to say, the wiseass with the stupid question made sure that his, 'lady of the evening' departed his hotel room in the very same condition she had entered.

Problem solved!

The first thing Carl did was open a small office in Burnsville, a south Minneapolis suburb. Then Carl hired an assistant, who needed a job and could keep her mouth shut. Also he had me design uniforms for all the Security Officers. White shirts, dark ties, conservative brown pants and coats with SECURITY in deep blue stitching under the breast pocket.

As for Big Einer his role would only be that of a driver. Big Einer was neither quick of mind or foot. Brother Boomer had a family and was erratic and selfish. Some day Gretchen the sister would be married with her own family. It was always understood that Little Carl would take care of Big Einer.

At a time when the economy was sliding further into the tank, and unemployment numbers were nearing levels not seen since the great depression, North Star Security was actually recruiting staff.

The now exhausted Mary Smith was only to glad to part with all of the administrative issues with running her escort service. Carl took over everything except the recruiting and interviewing new escorts. Mary knew what she wanted in her girls and that was fine with Carl.

So that was the structure of North Star Security. Mary recruited the girls, everyone else enlisted the Security Officers. Every Officer would spend a few days with Steve Lynch preparing for any and all problems, Carl ran the Office.

Within a few months under Carl Mattson's quiet, exacting leadership North Star Security was growing at a steady rate. Then late one afternoon as Carl was finishing up for the day he got a nervous call from one of his Security Officers.

"Look Mr. Mattson, I think we need to talk."

"About what?" Carl replied.

"Well, yesterday I did double duty at the Crescent Motor Lodge, you know the place?" said the tense Security Officer.

A double duty meant that the Security Officer took one girl to that hotel and then an hour later had to bring in another one for a different client.

"Ya, sure, you guys are there all the time, what's the problem?" asked Carl.

"The hotel manager asked me to come into his office for coffee," stuttered the Officer.

"You didn't go did you?" replied Carl.

"Well, ya, I did, and this is what the manager wants," said the Officer.

Carl braced himself for bad news. *"The manager had found out what's going on and is going to the cops. Or he wants in on the action. Or he's going to shake us down for money,"* he thought.

The officer on the phone went on, "He wants to hire us."

"For what?" asked Carl.

"He said that when we're around his hotel there's no problems. People behave themselves. No fights, no arguments, no theft, he said that everybody acts better and is generally nicer when we're on property. He says he wants to meet with you," exclaimed the Officer.

"This sounds like trouble, this sounds like a set up," Carl said.

"Well, you know Mr. Mattson that's what I thought at first too. But then this hotel manager told me some more stuff.

He said he was at a luncheon with a bunch of the other managers and supervisors of hotels on the 494 strip and near the airport, and they all say the same thing."

Carl let his Officer go on.

"Anyway, what this guy wants is for us to patrol his hotel property on weekends, you know Friday, Saturday and Sundays. He said those are the nights there's often trouble. After the NFL, NHL, and big college sporting events are over people get wild. Also when there's rock concerts and big shows in town people get drunk and get crazy. Fights in the parking lot, theft, property damage, pawing the cocktail waitresses, threatening the bartenders, skipping out on the bill. He said that all the hotel owners and managers are fed up with all the trouble and want our help," said the Officer.

Carl let this sink in for a few seconds.

"Let me ask you something, did he sound sincere or was this just some line of crap?" Carl asked.

"He said he wants to set up a meeting with you and some of the other hotel bosses as soon as possible," the Officer gasped.

Carl took quite a long time to respond.

"OK, I'll meet with them, but I get to pick the place. I'm still not convinced that this isn't bullshit," said Carl.

A few days later Carl, a few of his Security Officers, and about fifteen supervisors and managers of south Minneapolis hotels met in the banquet room of Maxwells.

Boomer had made arrangements for a light lunch and double checked that there were no cops snooping around.

The hotel bosses laid it out for Carl, and his Security Officers. What they liked was the way that Carls guys handled themselves. Non-threatening, smooth, yet powerful and confident. Also the way they looked, clean, sharp, and professional. They actually added class to their operations.

"On weekends we're calling the cops all the time," said a weary manager.

Another one piped up, "What we need is for your guys to be on display, in the lobby, strolling through the restaurant and bar, cruising the parking lot, checking entrances. I'm sure that well over half of our problems would go away if we could just have your men visible to everyone."

"Nobody is expecting your Officers to hurt anyone, we don't want that. If it comes to anything physical, just have our staff call the cops," said another manager.

Finally, a very well dressed manager spoke. He ran one of the larger more expensive chain hotels near the airport.

"Mr. Mattson, what my contemporaries are saying is that it is considerably more cost effective to prevent a problem than fix a problem. What goes on in the hotel rooms is something we can't control. However, your staff could benefit our operation in so many ways. Would you at least let us contract with your company on a trial basis?"

Carl Mattson was fast building a viable, dynamic Security business.

28.

MY SUMMER OF LOVE

It was early July of 1977, I'd been working at Maxwell's for about four years, and most everything was going well. Tim cleaned up at the regular poker games and I was showing a short profit. The Security Business that we helped start was going great, and we got a small check every month from it. Word had spread fast: If you need something protected call North Star Security! Not just hotels but religious ceremonies, formal dinner parties, weddings, graduations, gala Country Club events just call North Star. The Security Officers would show up looking sharp, chat people up, put everyone at ease, quietly roam around doing Security sweeps all without intimidating or embarrassing anyone. Professional!

Football season would be starting soon and hopefully our luck, meaning Tim's research, would pay off with another winning season. Tim's ability to analyze and handicap Pro Football was amazing. Every NFL season Tim would increase the amount wagered, and every season we cashed in for more money. Fabulous! Finally Maxwells was doing fantastic and we all got a small raise, and better tips. Tim and I were flush.

It was a Tuesday, Wednesday, or Thursday, it doesn't matter. In walked a good friend, Russ, with a fox on his arm. He said hello, and introduced me to Judy. After an exchange of small talk, Judy turned to me.

"I've got a friend I bet would love to meet you," she said.

"If she's anything like you, when can I meet her?" I responded.

"Here's her phone number. Give her a call." She jotted the number on a cocktail napkin and handed it to me. Russ and Judy left shortly after. The next day I called the number.

"*She sounds very nice,*" I remember thinking when she answered. *But then, so do telephone operators and I've never met one that was good looking. Oops! How come my phone just went dead? All right, phone operators are all great looking. That's better.*"

I made a date with Kristen for the following Monday night. On that afternoon after 18 holes of golf, I was kidnapped and forced to drink way too many cocktails in the clubhouse with two friends. I was too drunk to call her and not drunk enough to go. Tuesday morning I wrote her off. I don't like blind dates anyway. Good looking girls don't hang around with other good good looking girls, that would be competition. Losers go on blind dates.

A week passed. I was working a service bar at Maxwell's. No customers, just waitresses. I could hear Paul Zeller in the bar. He had a very distinctive laugh, inhaling deeply as the sound came out. Paul Zeller loved life. Paul Zeller loved beautiful woman. Paul Zeller loved money. Lots of money. Zeller was one of the Twin Cities biggest bookies. I had heard that a lot of the areas gambling money was funneled through Zeller and then on to bigger cities. He always had a great looking lady on his arm, and tonight was no exception. He also had his good friend, close associate, and general bad ass partner Andy The Axe Kople with him. Because Zeller, who was not a big man, always had lots of money on him, he always brought along this charming fellow Andy Kople. Some men are big, some men are huge, some men are mountains, Andy The Axe Kople was an Everest. Andy Kople could always be counted on for protection, but also provided another service for Zeller. If some unfortunate guy had a few bad weeks and gotten behind paying Zeller, Andy The Axe would have a meeting with the poor guy. Most of the time one meeting with Andy Kople would be enough for the woeful gambler to sell his wife's jewelry, or cash in his kids college fund. In fact, I never heard of anyone needing a second meeting with Kople for fear of losing many weeks of employment due to various serious injuries. Tim and I had bet with Zeller many times so he came around the corner of the service bar and said hello.

I returned the greeting, but couldn't take my eyes off the girl with him. She was gorgeous, piled 69 inches high. Lush waves of swirling brown hair surrounded a pair of glistening hazel eyes. Generous curves from ankle to neck completed the picture. I was impressed.

"Who's your girlfriend, Zel?" I asked when I was able to yank my tongue off the bar surface.

"John, I think you know each other. She asked if a John Williams worked here, so I thought I'd show her what a John Williams looks like." Zeller evidently read the shock registered on my face. He smiled, the girl smiled, what my facial expression was can only be guessed at.

"John, this is Kristin Anne Bennett," The roof caved in on the bar, breaking bottles, furniture, and stunning me. My blind date!

"How are you, John?" she opened.

"Listen, about last week…" I tried.

"It doesn't matter, I can tell you simply don't like aggressive women with big smiles," she warmly said.

"I…I…I…blither, blither, stutter," she turned and walked away with Zeller.

In a matter of seconds after getting home that night, I was tearing through the pile of papers on my dresser. I found the number. About two weeks later, I finally arranged a date.

Kristen was sick with a cold that night and only looked sensational. If she'd been 100 percent together, I don't think I could have talked to her. Rare beauty affects me that way, which is wonderful if you're trying to make an impression. A normally adequate vocabulary turns into one of less than 500 words.

She wanted to stay in. I soon found out that as a model, sometime actress and spokesperson she went out all the time. Best shows, fifty yard line seats, finest restaurants, she said that it got tiresome.

I thought for a second, *"Interesting, Kristen is easily one of the most attractive looking girls in the state, always going to the best of everything, but finds it tiresome."*

We were interrupted constantly by the phone. Big surprise, she was popular. Watching her move to the telephone was more entertaining than a volleyball game at a nude beach.

After what seemed like the hundredth call of the night, she unplugged the phone. She looked upset.

"Who was that, Kristen?" I asked, *as if it were any of my business.*

"Oh, just my ex-husband calling to tell me what a failure I am at being a mother," she sighed.

"Huh!"

"He said he'll be bringing Darren back to me tomorrow afternoon," she said.

Exasperated now, "OK John, I was 17 years old, a small town girl from Austin, this guy comes through town. He's good looking, talks slick, drives a sports car. I can get in his Thunderbird or I can marry the grain elevator assistant manager. Our son, Darren whose seven, splits time with us," she said.

"Austin Texas, or Austin Minnesota?" I asked.

"Austin, Minnesota, the Spam capital of the world. My dad was a canning machinist. The next time you open a can of spam you can thank dad for keeping it fresh," Kristen declared.

"Why did you want to leave Austin, Minnesota?"

"Because I didn't want to spend the rest of my life living in a town where a great night out consisted of drinking 3-2 beer at the bowling alley, and getting excited over the new popcorn machine at the local Drive In," Kristin confessed.

"Why the divorce? Or am I going too fast?" I asked.

"No, it doesn't matter, I wasn't good enough for him," she waved.

"Huh!" was my only thought.

Kristen sighed and began, "John I'm just a small town girl from rural Minnesota. Never went to college, didn't even finish high school. Jack's career took off, hospital equipment sales, he does great. It's fast becoming a very different business situation out there. He meets with professional woman. Female Doctors, Lab Techs, Administrators, Pharmacists, it's becoming a professional woman's world. Now Jack is stuck with no college, high school drop out, susie-cream-cheese me. We go to company entertainment functions and I may be the best looking woman there, but I'm also the least accomplished. He was embarrassed to be with me. Honestly, I don't know what's going to happen to me in a few years."

"Why do you say that?" I questioned.

"John, modeling and acting, or whatever you call what I do . . It was here that she assumed a character, "Nerdy paste for a smarter, more intelligent smile!" she crooned.

Wow, the girl has a sense of humor too, I thought.

"Soon I'll be thirty, what happens to girls like me when the face starts wrinkling and the boobs start sagging? And they will, there's no escaping it," she snapped.

"I can just see myself in five years as a grocery cashier, sore feet and aching back, when someone says, "hey weren't you the spokes-lady for nerdy teeth?" Kristen finished.

We ended up talking for hours, mostly about what we both wanted. Relaxed, trusting, comfortable kinship, void of drama and suspense. Two bottles of wine disappeared.

From the first night I was with Kristen I was in love with her.

We did everything together, including silly, stupid things like smuggling hero sandwiches into the movie theaters.

My life was so hassle-free, maybe a M.R., meaningful relationship, would get me off my butt and into the real world again.

We kissed a lot. Made love every time we touched. God, it was great to feel like that about someone.

We may deny it to ourselves but everyone has a check list of what they want in a spouse, lover, or life partner. With Kristen I could toss the list out, she nailed them all. Tall, slender, gorgeous skin, funny, irreverent, spontaneous, and sexually fearless. I could continue the list but why bother.

What a summer! Surprisingly, I bonded with her 7 year old son. Took him to the range and gave him golf lessons. Camping at a state park, where, like all good Minnesotans, we hiked, fished and swatted mosquitoes. Kristen knew lots of important people in town. At a Twins baseball game after easing into our seats I noticed that fans would turn to look at the beautiful super model girl, her son and the tall, dark friend. After the first inning a Twins official came down and asked if we would like to see the game from a private box. Beauty and glamour opens doors!

What amazed me about Kristen was her confidence in any situation. We had been invited to a formal dinner party at the Interlachen Country Club on a mid August evening. Kristen had done some advertising work for an implement manufacturer, making small tractor mowers look sexy and fun.

The minute we entered the cocktail reception I found out what it was like for Kristen every time she went to anything like this. Everyone in the room, both men and woman stopped and stared at her. You could see the desire and lust in the men, and, in the woman, jealousy and envy. But more to the point, in the woman you also detected shame and fear. Fear that Kristen could steal any man in the room.

Then Kristen would pull the most interesting and enlightened maneuver. She would not chat up the men, some who would have gladly gathered a chair, passed her a tissue, or handed her a drink, just to be near such loveliness.

She would smoothly introduce herself to the ladies, all of them older than her. She would listen to them, smile, nod and be respectful. Within minutes they would be gently laughing together, warmly communicating. Soon the rest of the woman would be wanting to take turns being with the most elegant, enticing, alluring young woman in the room. By the time dessert, coffee and cognacs were served she had won over even the most unattractive woman at the club. Before leaving she gathered many of the ladies in her long hands and thanked them all for being so nice to a small town girl like her.

One of the men had a busboy run to his car to fetch his camera. There was Kristen in the middle, towering over all the other ladies, her long arms controlling them, as they shouldered close to her for the photo.

On the way home I asked her how she knew what to do and how she did it? Her answer was so spot-on.

"It was about four years ago at something like this, I guess I made a bit of a fool of myself," she said.

"What?"

"I really had no experience at social functions, and it evidently showed, because after the dinner a very nice lady about fifty to sixty years old asked me to have a private drink with her," Kristen said.

"Together we sat there as everyone danced and talked enjoying our cocktail. Finally, this lady leans into me and quietly says, 'Little girl, years ago I was just like you, from wall to wall I had all the men in my purse. No challenge there. Now go get the woman to like you, aim for the most spiteful, catty, vindictive ones. Charm them and the room is yours.' "

That summer my whole party scene changed. No more late night backyard kegs in a dilapidated part of town. No more goosing squealing girls at 3:00 in the morning after a night of cheap bourbon and bad weed. No more waking up in some unknown crash house to the smell of full ashtrays, broken furniture and bleary eyed party mates.

Kristen was in the Cessna set, with firm plans to soon elevate herself to the jet set. I definitely wanted to be in on her ride.

29.

GOLF, CELEBRITIES AND JURISPRUDENCE

No matter what we were doing, Kristen and I had a great time doing it. I recall some of the parties we went to, one in particular. It was after the Wally's Celebrity Golf Tournament. A Minneapolis bar owner with a big heart organized a charity tournament about six years ago. I think the money raised went to kids with congenital heart issues. There were big name golfers, movie and TV celebrities from out of town, as well as most of the local media people in it. It had quickly become one of the events that the local business and political heavyweights circled on their calendar. Minnesota summers are short, every weekend counts, but this was an event that anyone who was anyone had to be seen at. Kristen's modeling and advertising agency was involved, with Kris out front of everything. Greeting the celebrities, introducing them to the locals, posing for pictures, flying around in a golf cart making sure everyone was happy. After the golf there was a big dinner party with dancing and Kristen was everywhere getting the big stars seated with the little stars. Of course once the band started playing she was up swaying with one guy after another until her legs were ready to buckle.

Just as the dinner entrees were served the Governor came dashing in, frantically apologizing for missing the golf, but oh so glad to finally be here to see everyone. The Guv jumped on the stage and grabbed the microphone from the singer saying, "I just have to get this out before leaving for another function. For those of you who have so tirelessly given your money, your energy and your time for this marvelous event I can't thank you enough. For those of you who have traveled so far to our beautiful state and magnanimously arranged your busy schedules to support this wonderful cause, I can't thank you enough. (Now sounding exhausted, rubbing his hand through his hair), Finally, for the senior volunteers who organized and worked so diligently to make this important event a success, would you all stand up."

With that Kristen and a few other people stood up from their chairs. Naturally everyone started thunderously applauding.

The Guv was wrapping it up now, "For everyone in this room from wherever you are, you truly do represent what is right about our state, you truly are 'Minnesota nice', I wish I had time to shake hands with everyone of you."

With that he hopped off the stage and damn near shook hands with everyone before bolting out of the club.

Naturally there were scores of parties that night, Kris and I headed to a big one at the exclusive Palm Plaza Townhomes west of Minneapolis. A TV security system passed us into an already crowded party room. A long table of cold cuts and dips lined one wall of the room, while three bartenders stood ready to get any libation we wanted on the opposite wall. A jazz trio provided background music from a tucked-away spot in the corner. A great ritzy affair.

I recognized a lot of the athletes and local TV and radio personalities. Kristen slid her arm through mine and marched me over to meet the host, Ira Silverman. I guessed about 40 years old, 5-6, maybe 170, Silverman was a lawyer and a good one. I'd heard his firm was becoming a real force in the legal landscape of the midwest. He didn't put much pressure in the handshake, didn't need to prove anything, I liked that.

"So this is the tall stud you've been shaken, huh Kristen?"

I noticed Silverman's free hand had found Kristen's back and smoothly slid down her butt. Kristen just smiled and laughed. I didn't much care for his paw action but Kristen was being a good sport about it so I kept my mouth shut.

Most of the people at the party were wealthy or famous or both. They talked about things that didn't interest me, the stock market, capital gains, tax shelters. I was bored.

It was then that Kristen whispered to me, "John, you want to get loaded? Ira's got some snow, pure."

"Sure," I answered.

We followed Silverman to the bathroom, wow, I'd never been in a biffy like this. Palatial would not describe it. I never would have dreamed of putting a chandelier in a bathroom. It even had some kind of heated matted or carpeted floor so that when you stepped out of your award winning designed roman shower your little tootsie toes wouldn't get chilly. Nice!

"This is clever," I thought, "no one will ever notice a tall guy, a power lawyer and a super model going to the bathroom together." (We're not going to snort coke folks, we're going to gang-bang Kristen.)

Once inside the powder room Silverman produced the promised coke from a film canister. I took a small pinch and spread it on my gums. It numbed them instantly.

"And now," Silverman said, pulling another canister from his pocket. "a little something extra for my special friends." I didn't know what it was, and

I still don't. Ira spread the mixture in three lines on a round hand mirror. It looked like washing machine soap with bleach crystals added. He rolled a dollar bill and inhaled one line and passed the mirror to Kristen and then me.

Wham, my head filled with boiling water, a cannon blasted off somewhere between my eyes. I couldn't feel my legs let alone my feet. Kristen forcefully pushed me against the wall of the roman shower, practically tearing my clothes off, and then turned the valves on hot. I drifted near the ceiling, dodging through clouds, banking in now on final approach. I couldn't get the landing gear down, the rain pounded my fuselage, poor visibility, short run-way, this pilot is in trouble. I saw Kristen standing in front of me mumbling something about, "You're big John, you understand these things."

Rolling with the tide I saw Silverman behind Kristen his hands caressing her boobs, I saw her move her hands to his, pressing them even harder on her breasts. I felt her lips fly to mine in a crashing kiss. I heard her say, "Big John is a Big Boy."

By now Silverman had his pants down and his joint out. Sitting on the shower bench Kristen went to work on mine. Breathe John, keep breathing, was my first thought. "Where are the landing lights, my navigational aides are out, my copilot is unconscious. Mayday! Mayday!"

Somewhere lightening was streaking across the bathroom. I jolted forward to see Kristen hurriedly taking the rest of her clothes off. Was that a marching band that just went by, or Teddy Roosevelt on a horse? Kristen was kneeling in front of the power lawyer performing an oral bar exam. I felt Kristen's free hand grasp my testicles, her nails stinging my balls. She sprang up and came at me biting my neck, and shoulders. Sitting on me her back to me, reverse cowgirl style, she forced my cock in her and turned to take Ira back in her mouth. Her hips bucked and galloped her head surged, I kept trying to focus on breathing. Kristy's head snapped up and I felt her body quaking as I fired my last blast. Ira had finished on Kristen's tits and was slumped against the far shower wall gasping.

Finally, I was able to touchdown, and smoothly taxi to the gate. The shower was off, the clothes were on, the hair was straight.

"Yes Mrs. Silverman, we found Ira's medication just in time. Thank goodness John knows CPR, that was a close one. I would never tell another woman how to handle her man. But there are a lot of good people counting on your husband. We all know that Ira is a driven, tireless, power lawyer. But you need to reign him in sometimes. It's your job to see that he doesn't work himself to death. John, this has been exhausting, I need you to take me home," said Kristen.

Ira gulping air now, "Thank you John, if you ever need a legal consultation please feel free to come by the office, I'll assign my best associate to you."

Driving back to Kristen's place was difficult both physically and emotionally. I was still feeling the effects of whatever Ira gave us. Kristen was mindlessly humming a tune. Then seemed to notice my feelings. She laid her hand on my shoulder and moved in and kissed my neck. Purring now, "John, it's not easy, but things have to be done," she said.

"Huh!"

She smoothly continued, while warmly breathing on my neck. "It was Ira that saved me. Without Ira and his Law firm I would have lost my son. That vicious, mean ex-husband of mine was trying to convince the judge that I wasn't fit to be a mother. That my lifestyle was erratic and detrimental to Darrens development. Outrageous!"

"Huh!."

30.

BARBECUE, INVADERS, AND MARY TYLER MOORE:

August 1977

Boomer called us all to a meeting late one night in August at Batts Barbecue. Batts was a south Minneapolis all night sandwich shop off Cedar Ave.

Batts was one of those rare places that could make Porky's in St. Paul look like a fine dining establishment.

Batts only had one item on the menu, in fact it didn't have menus. Everybody got a monstrously large, sloppy, pork sandwich, on kaiser roll, with an enormous plastic bowl of fries and chopped onion rings. That was it.

Another thing about Batts, there was no service. In fact, in some ways, there was literally less than no service.

You picked up your own sandwich that was slid out on the counter on a paper plate. Took your combo fries, and rings to your battered up booth. Grabbed a pitcher and went to the beer tap to get your Grain Belt. No flatware, no dishes, no menus, no service, one sandwich, one side, one kind of beer. The owner was a dangerous looking old blue haired lady who would sit at the entrance scowling and hissing at everybody. A bum off the street or the mayor of Minneapolis were all treated with the same amount of contempt, and disdain. As you walked through the front door she'd set her cigarette down, slowly look at the seating area and snarl, "booth four, or booth six." I never knew why this lady was always in such a bad mood. I think she was left the place by a deceased husband whom she hated. A dark, cold, grim place. But if you wanted a great barbecue pork sandwich this was the best place in town.

Little Carl, Big Einer, a couple of Security Officers, me and Tim met Boomer about 2:00 AM.

Boomer began, "Thanks for coming. Here's the deal, two things. First, you all know Zeller the bookie. Well he wants in on part of North Star Security. Says he can help us expand the business to other cities and states. He laid it all out for me. Said we're missing the big picture. He wants North Star in Duluth, Milwaukee, maybe even Chicago. He said he knows a lot of people in those places and that with his contacts we can grow North Star faster with bigger profits. Zeller says that if we give him half of North Star he could double maybe triple it in size in a year. After that there's no telling how big North Star could be. Zellers a sharp guy, and I don't want us to miss this opportunity to expand."

"Secondly, I think it's time to run Mary Tyler Moore out of town."

We all sat there in total dumbfounded, stunned silence. Even Tim, who could find humor in almost anything had no idea what Boomer Mattson was talking about.

Boomer continued, "Zeller says we have to think big, real big, and that he's the only one in town that can help us reach our dreams. Zeller told me that it's not for nothing he's the biggest bookie in the Twin Cities and with him at the controls, the Security business could be huge. Now, soon as they put up that statue of Mary Tyler Moore, or Mary Richards or whatever that lady calls herself we'll steal it. Are you with me?"

In the past Boomer had spoken out about his hatred of the Mary Tyler Moore show. But like ninety per cent of what Boomer said nobody paid any attention. Mary Tyler Moore had a very popular television show about an independent minded single woman living in Minneapolis. The show depicted this intelligent, successful young lady living alone, finding career and social fulfillment without having a husband or kids. Boomer had gotten the idea that this was some kind of subversive

anti-family, anti-America, anti-heterosexual program dreamed up by a bunch of low life, Hollywood
homos to ruin our society as we know it. Boomer
could rant forever on this strange topic. He was
sure that if enough young girls saw this attractive,
accomplished, Mary Richards as their role model
that Western Civilization would fall on its ass.

In no small way the Mary Tyler Moore show had
brought a considerable amount of good publicity
to the Twin Cites. Thus the city fathers were considering the idea of erecting a small statue of Mary
Richard tossing her little hat in the Minnesota winter down on the Nicollet Mall. Boomer thought that
soon as the statue went up we should knock it down
and throw it in one of Minnesota's many lakes. Like
I said, most of the time we would just ignore whatever came out of Boomer Mattson's mouth, knowing that it was harmless, and usually crazy. But this
business of bringing Zeller into the Security business
was a different matter. Not a good one!

That night as Carl and Big Einer were driving
home Einer, who rarely spoke, looked over at Carl
and said, "Little brother we got a big problem."

31.

BRANDY, SPORTS, AND EX-HUSBAND'S:

Wednesday Night 6:30 PM, October 1977

I had the night off, and Kristen was out of town on a shoot. So I was relaxing at Edwards slowly sipping brandy and talking sports with the bartenders. I was in a great mood. Love with a strikingly good looking girl could do that to any man. But even more, Tim was doing great with his NFL betting and North Star Security was getting bigger and better every month. Tagging Little Carl Mattson to run North Star Security was a great move by Tim. Carl Mattson was a natural business manager, he probably would be good at any business. It was then I felt a light tap on my right shoulder

"Excuse me, are you John the bartender from Maxwells?"

The guy looked like any other businessman who was finished for the day and was ready to have a drink before going home. About six feet, maybe

180, nicely dressed, blue tie, white shirt, dark suit, slightly tired eyes.

"One and the same, what can I do for you?" I buoyantly responded.

Sticking out his right hand, "Ya John, my name is Jack, Kristen's husband, may sit down?"

I immediately noticed that he didn't refer to himself as Kristen's ex-husband.

My back went up, and I could feel both my defense and anger gears engage.

Jack sat down next to me, signaled the bartender, pointed at my drink, indicating that he would have what I was drinking and to get me another one. The bartender nodded his head up and went to work on our cocktails.

"So where's the slut this week?" Jack asked.

I could feel my temper throttle accelerate.

"If you're referring to Kristen, the love of my life, she's in Atlanta shooting a commercial. Oh, and I don't like you or your comments about her," I replied.

"Atlanta, huh! Even I didn't know that tramp screwed in the Confederacy," said Jack.

I slammed my hand on the bar, turned to Jack and said. "Listen man, you say one more thing like that and I'll …."

The bartender brought over our drinks and leaned into my left ear, "John, you know better than anyone we can't have that kind of behavior in the bar. If this guy's pushing your buttons just walk away."

Now I felt embarrassed, of course the bartender was right.

Jack spoke up, "Look John, sorry to upset you, I still have some deep scars from that whore, I mean girl. There, is that better? I've done some checking about you, people say you're a good guy."

"Really, what else do people say about me?" I sneered.

"That you're kind of funny, a little flaky, but a nice guy, which is why I came here to warn you about that bitch.

John, you sell liquor and beer, I sell medical supplies, this doesn't need to get ugly."

My jaw tightened.

"Say, who's watching Darren right now?" I asked.

Jack stopped a minute and stared at me. Pausing he took a slow, careful sip of his drink.

"You really are a nice guy, you care about my son," Jack thoughtfully said.

Looking away for a second I heard him mutter.

"This could be worse than I thought."

Coming back to me Jack said, "My Mother is serving him dinner now, I have to get going. I just wanted to warn you about that slut, I mean Kristen, she could get you hurt."

With that Jack slipped a ten spot out of his elegant wallet and laid it on the bar, signaled a thanks to the bartender and was gone.

All I could think of was, "*What a loser, that clown thinks he's going to turn me away from the best looking, best acting, best screwing, best ... well, everything girl I've ever been with. Swing and a miss, Jack old boy.*"

32.

THE AXE, THE ARM AND WHERE'S MARY'S HAT?

Poker Night, Late October 1977

The game was just about to break up, as always Tim was the big winner, I had another short profit, Little Carl had done OK, the rest of the guys had lost or about broken even.

Before we left a couple of the guys asked Tim to give them some thoughts on this weekends NFL games. Tim didn't give out information for free so he would just reply that he, "Hadn't had time to look things over yet, but would get back to them." Which he wouldn't do. Tim felt that why should he do anybody any favors like that. Do lawyers give free advice, or investment counselors, or anybody? To Tim this was the same kind of thing. More and more I could feel that some of the guys were jealous of Tim's success at Maxwell's and with his gambling. Tough shit!

Then Boomer asked Tim and I to stick around a second, he had something he wanted to talk about.

"Listen, you two know how the game is played so maybe you could help me," Boomer began.

Neither Tim or I had any idea what this was about.

"Remember when I told you that Zeller the bookie and his pal Andy The Axe want to be part of North Star Security?" we both nodded.

"Well Zeller means business. He says if we don't give him half of North Star he'll start his own Security Company. He also made it really clear that he knows ways of getting to our, I mean, Mary's girls. Why don't we just let him have say, 25 per cent. That way he can grow North Star faster, we get more money, and none of the girls get hurt. Zeller says he's losing patience with us. On Monday he's sending Andy 'The Axe' over to have a discussion with my brother Little Carl. Look I don't want to see Carl get hurt. Maybe you two could talk some sense into Carl and Einer?"

Tim and I let this digest without making a comment.

Boomer continued, "Now here's the other thing. It looks like that statue of Mary Tyler Moore is going up in the spring. Mary Richards, tossing her hat right down on Nicollet Mall. I get sick thinking about that no husband, no kids, big shot career pain-in-the-ass lady. Now remember we were going to steal the statue and dump it in a lake? I don't like that idea anymore. So I thought that we'd go down on Nicollet Mall some night around three in the morning when nobody but a bunch of drunken Indians are there and knock off her arm. No arm, no fucking hat. Then I got to thinking, what I really want to do is just knock off Mary's hat. It's the hat, that's the symbol. It's all about Mary's hat. How she tossed it in the air. What she was saying was, 'the hell with family and responsibility.'"

Tim and I could not believe this.

As always, Boomer went on. "You get it guys? It's all about the hat. We have to knock the hat off her hand, that's it. Without her hat, Mary's nothing. People will show up some spring morning and there will be Mary Richards without her hat. Just her hand, giving a Nazi salute. We could even put a little sign at her feet that says, Heil Hitler, is that funny or what?"

That night on the way home Tim and I had nothing to say.

The next day I woke up late and trudged into the Bloomington Pleasure Palace kitchen for coffee and a smoke. Tim was pouring over various sports magazines and newspapers trying to get a read on the betting line.

"What do you think Tim, should we try and get Little Carl and Big Einer to give up part of North Star to Zeller and the Axe?" I asked.

Tim's reply was about what I had expected, "John, I think we should at least let Carl and Einer know that Andy The Axe is on the way, that's really all we can do."

I picked up the phone and dialed North Star.

33.

MERCURYS, MEXICO,
AND MARGARITAS:

Mid November 1977

I was over at Kristen's house playing a game of football strategy with Darren.

"OK Darren, you're the coach. It's fourth and one, from the opponents 23rd yard line, your team is trailing by three points, with less than a minute to play. Sixty thousand fans are on their feet yelling for you to go for it. What is your call and why?"

"I think I'd kick the field goal and try to win in overtime? My field goal team has been very effective this season, and if I go for it and fail the game is lost. Also, my opponent has a good run defense, especially on big plays," Darren said.

"Good call, I know it's only one yard, the crowd is going to be roaring for you to go for it, but it's your job and your team. That's it for now, do you want to go to the gym and shoot hoops with me this Saturday?" I asked.

"I can't, Mom is going to Acapulco and Dad is taking me to the hockey game," Darren replied.

"What?"

"Dad's taking me to the hockey game this Saturday," said Darren.

"No, where is your Mother going?"

"Acapulco, it's some place in Mexico, sounds yucky. I hope Mom doesn't get sick," Darren said.

I knew that it wasn't unusual for Kristen to be asked to accompany major business or political big shots on trips. Being seen with a knock-out girl never hurt anyone's career. But I didn't think she had accepted any of these luxury trips since we'd been together.

I quietly strolled into the kitchen where Kristen was doing the lunch dishes. I smoothly approached her from behind and slid my big hands up her side and cupped her breasts. She giggled and looked to her left to see that Darren was watching television. Kristen started rhythmically rotating her perfect butt against my dick. I applied more pressure to Kristen's tits and moved my mouth down to her right ear. Kristen's head cocked up, and her eyes fluttered.

"Acapulco!" I whispered.

Kristen's eyes snapped open, and I increased my hand pressure to the nearly painful level on her boobs.

"John, John, please, I was going to tell you! It's for my job," Kristen stammered.

"So tell me, the only work you're suppose to be doing south-of-the-border is on me," I said. I could feel my emotions in flux, anger, pain, sadness, jealousy.

"Is this some rich guy taking you on a fun-filled beach vacation, where he provides the top-of-the-line amenities, and you provide the top-of-the-line blowjobs?" I snarled.

I spun her around and looked deep into her eyes.

"John, it's for work. I got a great commercial, good money, lots of exposure. It plays just in front of the local news, my agency worked hard to get it for me," Kristen said.

Looking away from me Kristen was talking fast.

"It's a great opportunity for me. Really, any good looking girl could do it, I just got lucky. It's for the Miller car dealerships. All I have to do is breeze through their dealerships saying, 'Make it a Miller Mercury, Service, Selection, Satisfaction, at Miller Mercury.' Then I give a light hug and peck a kiss on the dealership owner, Conrad Miller, it's already been shot."

Everybody in the Midwest knew of the Miller car family, they must have had 20 dealerships around the five state area.

Holding her hard by her arms I asked her, "So Kristen, since when does your old pal Conrad sell cars in Acapulco?"

"John, there's a little more to this. You see, ahh, he's giving me a trip to Acapulco because the commercial went so well. Look John, there's a little more I should tell you. Conrad wants me to have a new car, because we worked so well on the ad spot he thinks I should have it. It's a fully loaded Grand Marquis, mint green, with soft white cream leather interior, 460 cubic inch engine. You can drive it anytime you want. Conrad is going through a hard time now. He's getting divorced, he won't even touch me," Kristen huffed.

"Since when did you become so knowledgeable about cars?" I snapped. "Sounds to me that good old 'money bags Conrad' is turning my Kristen into a real gear head. Sounds like Kristen and 'big money Miller' have been doing more than 'light hugging and pecking'."

It was here that Kristen looked away and let out a tired sigh. The kind of surrendering sigh that said, 'Busted' as her hands moved to my belt buckle. Kneeling down she went for my zipper fly.

I seized her by her armpits and raised her up off her feet to my eye level.

"People will see you with him, at the airport. You know what that means. It means that I will be laughed at. I don't like to be laughed at - no man does," I said.

Breathing hard now, Kristen whined, "John, I've tried telling you about how it is with me, I'm 30 next month. Do you know how many girls like me come on the market every year and that's what it is, a market. But all these girls are younger, fresher, firmer, 18, 19 years old, clearer skin, brighter smiles, tighter butts. In another few years I won't be able to sell spit. It's a top of the line Mercury, Conrad says it's one of his most popular models."

"You know what I think Kristen? I think you've become one of Conrad Miller's most popular models. Oh, and he won't touch you in Acapulco? You think I'm that dense? Conrad is going to pump you full of margaritas and spend four days pumping away between your legs. You know it and so do I," I angrily snorted.

I released my hold on her and slammed the door as I left. As I got in my car I thought for a minute about going back and saying goodbye to Darren, but then thought better of it.

34.

DARK IRISHMAN, UNTAMED JEWS, AND THE HAPPY WARRIOR:

Mid December 1977, Four Weeks Before The Super Bowl

I liked working Friday Nights. The band was always jumping and the patrons were freer with their money; better tips. Maxwells was always packed (both the restaurant and discotheque) and time flew by fast. I did not like reporting two hours early because one of the day bartenders had a teacher/parent meeting.

So at 2:00 PM the arctic Minnesota wind cut my throat like a blade as I climbed out of the brown bomber and hustled into Maxwells. There is a term for how we in the north walk in the winter. The Minnesota Shuffle is a cross between a fast walk and slow run. Small quick steps, wide legs, planting carefully, one slip on the ice and your ankle, knee, or shoulder are shot.

I knew that I would be bored for the first couple of hours because the lunch crowd was gone and there were still three to four hours before things got crazy. With almost nobody in the place, the two cocktail servers wandered around chatting, smoking and thinking of their future.

Off in the corner I saw Zeller, the bookie with his vicious trained seal Andy The Axe Kople and Boomer. These three seemed to be spending more and more time together. I really didn't know whether this was a good thing or not. Maybe Zeller could help grow North Star Security. I'm sure that Zeller and Andy had contacts all over the midwest, and maybe even further.

I wasn't surprised to see Big Tom Taylor walk in and sit at my station. I was always glad to see Tom, in his own "working man way" he had a lot of class. My guess is Tom was in his mid 50s, a large man with huge shoulders. Tom would come in on Friday afternoons, order a beer and read the sports section. Quiet, thoughtful and always courteous. Pulling up in his pick up truck and wearing his construction clothes you would think he was some guy ducking out of work early. Truth was, Tom was a plumbing contractor, real estate investor and friend and supporter to all. Tom liked to relax on Fridays when it was quiet in here, then go meet with his wife and large gaggle of kids and grandkids. Like so many WW II vets Tom rarely if ever talked about his wartime experiences.

"I guess you heard that this nightclub is closing for a few weeks?" I mentioned to Big Tom.

"Sure, I heard, what are you guys going to do?" Tom asked.

"Tom, my roommate Tim and I haven't had a vacation in years. We're taking off for parts unknown, probably out west. Maybe in the spring we'll come back and reapply at the new place," I replied.

Without looking up from his paper Tom said, "Sounds like a good plan."

Desperate for conversation I handed Tom his beer and said, "Did you hear that Atlantic City is thinking of getting into the casino business?"

Tom slowly opened his sports section, and without looking up said, "Ya, that damn Hubert Humphrey."

One of the cocktail servers waved me over and asked if she could take a twenty minute break. I just nodded my OK and stopped to think of what Tom had mumbled.

Returning to the corner stool that Big Tom was sitting on I asked, "Tom, what did you just say about our Senator Humphrey?"

It was here the I noticed Tom looking at Boomer, Zeller and mostly Andy Kople.

Turning to me Tom said, "It was Hubert Humphrey that cleaned up Minneapolis back in the late 40s and early 50s. Who knows, maybe we could have been what Las Vegas is becoming."

My mind went blank, I had no idea what Big Tom Taylor was talking about.

Tom could see my confusion and set his sports section aside and took a slow careful pull on his beer.

"John, I'm sure you think of Minneapolis as the clean, fair, law abiding, town that it is, a lot of that is due to Hubert Humphrey," Tom explained.

Now I was really lost, if Humphrey helped make Minneapolis a good place why did Tom Taylor say what he said about, "That damn Hubert Humphrey?"

Tom slid his beer to one side and leaned into me, "There are a lot of things about the Twin Cities nobody ever talks about. I know, I grew up in the 30s and 40s. Minneapolis was a wide open town. St. Paul had the idiots like Dillinger, Ma Barker, and Baby Face Nelson, and any other small time hood and robber. But Minneapolis was a real center of organized crime. Unfortunately, it was also one of the centers of the Silver Shirts.

I had heard that back in the old days St. Paul was a great hideout for criminals. The bad guys would take the train to St. Paul, check in with the local cops and slap an envelope full of cash on the police chiefs desk. The deal was simple, bring the money, don't cause us any trouble, and you're safe in St. Paul. St. Paul was their fall-back, safe haven. But what Tom was talking about organized crime in Minneapolis was new to me, and what was a Silver Shirt?

"Minneapolis had three major gangs, one Irish, two Jewish. Maybe you're heard of Kid Cann Blumenfelt? Davie Berman? Tommy Banks?" Tom questioned.

I shrugged.

Tom continued, "Most of the organized crime back then was gambling, loan sharking, bookmaking, and prostitution. This was before girls grew up to be lawyers, accountants and champions of industry. Hey, a girl's got to eat. Minneapolis had great gambling halls, well run, clean and fair. The polished, spotless brothels were the best in the country. If one of the gangs had a problem with one of the other gangs they worked it out. The only guys that got hurt were the crusading newspaper writers who would be machine gunned in the back. I don't know, maybe it was because there weren't any Italian gangs blasting away at each other like in Chicago, or New York that made everything run so well, I'm just guessing."

"Ya, but what does that have to do with our Senator Humphrey?" I asked.

Tom softly put up his hand, "I'll get to that, you see most of these guys were former bootleggers. The gunflint trail from Canada to Minnesota was the main route for the bootleggers. But, after the repeal of prohibition these guys graduated to bigger and definitely better things."

It was now that I lightly raised my hand and asked, "Tom, how does a guy like you know about this criminal gang stuff?"

Tom grinned and gave a slight shrug and said, "Because, I worked for the boys."

My mouth dropped open, *"Tom Taylor, self made business man, friend to all, supporter of every good cause in the community, WW II veteran, was in the gangs?"*

"Depression John, you did what you did to get by, there was no other way for street kids like me," Tom shrugged.

"How did Humphrey get rid of all these gangs?" I asked.

'It was after Davie Berman returned from the war that everything changed. The Berman brothers were the biggest and most successful gang of them all. They were into everything, and had every politician and cop in their pockets. When Humphrey was elected Mayor of Minneapolis he made it clear that the lawless days of gambling dens, brothels, bookmaking operations were over," Tom quietly explained.

"Berman was one sharp, maybe a little maniacal Russian Jew gang leader. Smart, tough, determined, he couldn't be beat at anything. When Davie Berman got wind of what was going on with the Nazi holocaust he went absolutely crazy. I mean he went insanely mad. Came up with his own plan to get the Nazis. For every Jew that died ten Germans had to die. Ten to one. Whether it was ten German grannies, or ten little German frauleins, or Frederics was of no concern. It was ten Germans for every one Jew. Period," Tom lectured.

"Really, what did he do?" I asked.

"Well you see Berman wasn't like so many of those gangsters who may have talked about killing Hitlers boys. Berman had every intention of doing it. Soon as he heard about the way they were killing Jews in Germany he beat a path to the nearest army recruitment center and tried to sign up. He wanted German blood, lots of it, all of it, and he wanted it right now."

"I'm sorry Tom, you're going too fast for me. What was a Silver Shirt? Sounds like a fashion statement," I questioned.

Big Tom took a deep breath and for a second a faraway look came into his eyes, "John, this is going to be hard for you to understand but for many years Minneapolis, this clean, liberal, unprejudiced city was one of the major centers of the American Nazi movement. The Silver Shirt people with their blazing red "L" on their shirts thought Adolph and his group were the greatest. They hated everybody that wasn't just like them, Blacks, Catholics, Asians and especially Jews. The Silver Shirts would hold rallies and marches around town. Some people liked them, most just dismissed them as a group of nut-jobs. Davie and his brother along with a bunch of their gang members would wait for the rally or march to be over then attack them, beat the hell out them. Bats, clubs, chains, all these righteous, big shot Nazis would be lying around the street beaten and bloody. The cops didn't care, most of them were on one gang or another's payroll anyway. The only rule was, don't kill anyone. Killing makes things messy for the cops."

It was here that Big Tom paused, searching his memory for the Minneapolis of his youth.

"Finally, Davie Berman had had enough of these Silver Shirt assholes and wanted to send a real message to them. He heard they were rallying one winter night at a church up in North Minneapolis. Naturally he slipped some cash to the local cops so they didn't see anything. After all the Silver Shirts were in the church, bam, bam, we, I mean they, crashed into the church and tore into the swastika guys. It was something. Most of them ran out of the church into the woods, a few got away in their now smashed up cars.

The rest were held captive in the church. This was funny. Davie now got on the stage and laughing and grinning took the microphone and announced, 'that the Silver Shirts were finished. If he ever hears of them in his town again they'll get it twice as bad next time.' Then we, I mean, they, finished them off. The doctors and dentists around town were busy for weeks."

"Did you say this Davie Berman tried to sign up for the Army? What do you mean tried?" I asked.

Tom gave me a sly smile, "Berman had done seven years at Sing Sing prison for robbery, just a few banks and post offices, that's all. So he goes into the Minneapolis Army Recruitment Center and tries to enlist. He tells them that he's ready to go now, today."

Tom had a slight chuckle, "I think he wanted to skip boot camp. Berman didn't want to waste any time. Just give him the guns and ammo and he'll take care of the rest. He would have done it too."

Tom took a small sip of his beer and gave another thoughtful stare at Boomer, Zeller and Andy The Axe off at the end of the room.

Big Tom continued, "Berman passed all the tests, had his paper work done, and stood up with a bunch of other guys to be sworn in to the army. Just then the Officer-In-Charge stopped them and had Berman come into his office. Because Davie had a criminal record the army wouldn't take him. They had some silly rule that real tough guys, who wanted to kill the enemy couldn't serve. Boy, was I glad I wasn't around Berman that day. They said he flew into some kind of homicidal rage. The Officer and Desk Sergeant went white as a ghost. They thought that Berman might shoot them both dead on the spot. Davie called them every dirty name he could think of and roared out of the recruitment center."

"So he wasn't able to fight the Nazis, that's too bad," I said, and made a move to leave.

"Oh, he fought the Nazis alright, nothing was going to stop Davie Berman from kicking German ass," countered Big Tom.

"Huh?"

"If Davie Berman wanted to kill Germans nothing was going to stop him including the United States Government. Davie had dual American and Canadian citizenship. So when our Army wouldn't accept him he just took a train to Winnipeg, Canada and enlisted in the Canadian Army. He didn't care who he fought for, he just wanted to kill Germans. After two years of wiping out the Nazis he comes back to Minneapolis and was told by Mayor Hubert Humphrey that everything is different. No more gambling halls, brothels, bookmaking operations, nothing. Humphrey wanted a clean town and an honest police force, and he got it."

"They call Humphrey the 'Happy Warrior', and he is. He's a 'warrior' for decency, fairness, and honesty. Hubert really is a 'warrior' for the little guy, a great leader with integrity. But who knows, maybe Minneapolis could have been what Las Vegas is becoming, a gambling and entertainment center."

"That Kople guy kind of reminds me of icepick," Big Tom absently said.

"What, Andy Kople reminds you of an icepick?" I asked.

Tom kept looking at Kople, "Not an icepick, Willie 'Icepick' Alderman a member of the Berman gang. He carried around a small three pronged icepick. If a person was to have an unfortunate disagreement with that Jolly Jew, with the pinball eyes, he might be treated like a block of ice."

It was here that Big Tom took three fingers of his left hand and made a motion of them sinking into the side of his head. The thought of it made me temporarily shutter.

Tom continued, "Ever hear of guy named Bugsy Siegel?"

I quickly answered, feeling proud that I actually knew something, "Yes, he started the Flamingo Hotel in Vegas" I gushed.

"Good John," Big Tom patiently said.

"Well, Siegel spent sometime in Minneapolis before heading to Nevada. After Bugsy was killed there was a management vacancy in the Flamingo Hotel for about eight hours. The powers in New York and Chicago knew they had to get somebody to run the Flamingo and a few of their other operations in Las Vegas. Had to be somebody smart, tough and honest. Davie Berman, and a guy named Moe Sedway were sent onto the Flamingo Resort casino floor and in a loud voice announced that they were now in charge. They made it clear that if anyone had a problem with them running things they could take it up with the guy standing next to them, Willie 'Icepick' Alderman. Nobody challenged them."

I could see Big Tom was tired from his week and was ready to go when he said.

"But it was the same thing down in Cuba, where I was stationed during the war." Tom made a move to leave but I stopped him with a question.

"You were in Cuba during the Second World War?" I asked.

Tom gave out a tired sigh and began, "There had been reports of German U Boat Subs down near Cuba. The guys in Washington were sure that the sneaky Huns were planning a southern invasion of the U.S. We would have been easy picks too, our southern border was unprotected. So the Navy had us down in Cuba patrolling in PT Boats. It was scary but fun. We'd take leave in Havana and go to the resort casinos. Havana was an elegant, glamorous city. The east coast mafia was running everything. Beautiful hotel casinos, and stunning Spanish Cuban girls with lush shimmering dark hair, sparkling diamond black eyes, guiltless smiles and hard strong slender bodies."

"Castro threw the gangs out of Cuba just like Humphrey threw the gangs out of Minneapolis. That's what made Las Vegas. Now you have to fly all the way out to that miserable, baking desert just to flip a card, roll a dice, or pull a slot machine."

"Just think John, somewhere down in Havana there are guys just like me walking around the waterfront going 'that damn Castro he ruined everything.'"

Big Tom paused and then almost absently said, "But you know what scared us the most down in Cuba? Not the crooked Havana Police that would shake you down or throw you in jail for anything; not the pistol packing Mafia enforcers, not even the German U Boats. It was the snakes, they were all over the place. We were always afraid that the poisonous snakes would slither into our tents and nail us. Snakes, scary snakes! John I have to go, hope to see you in the spring, who knows, maybe our Twins won't stink so bad next season."

With that Big Tom Taylor slowly got out his wallet and with as little attention as possible did what he always did, tucked a ten dollar bill under his beer coaster. Big Tom never tossed the money on the bar, that would be disrespectful. I guess growing up in the Great Depression respect was something important. Tom took one last look at Zeller, Kople and Boomer.

As Tom started past me I reached out to shake his hand, he paused, and then grabbed me hard, almost pulling me over the bar. I could feel pain shoot up to my arm socket. This was the handshake of a man who'd spent thirty years cranking on a pipe wrench.

"John, just one thing, wherever you go, watch out for the snakes, the snakes are everywhere."

35.

THE AXE MAKES A VISIT:

Little Carl Mattson thanked John for calling and letting him know that he could expect a visit soon from Zeller's highly trained muscle Andy The Axe. Carl slowly put the receiver back on the phone cradle and reviewed his options. He looked at the three assistants that he'd hired in less than four months, and turned and viewed the group picture of the 41 Security Officers that now worked for him. Last week Carl had met with Government representatives to patrol the Federal Reserve building in downtown Minneapolis. He had already secured a contract with the State of Minnesota to work at the Capital Building. State and Federal checks don't bounce. City and County projects would be next, but there were other concerns.

"Should I ask Einer to come and protect me from 'The Axe'? he asked himself. *"Damn that Boomer, getting mixed up with Zeller. Well, unlike Boomer, and me, Einer has never ever been in the Minnesota Correction System, and if I involve him in this*

problem, that might change, No, that is too big a risk to Einer, plus, he's big, but no match for 'The Axe'.

"*Every small man in the world suffers certain indignities that big men never think of. Would it have been nice to be part of a sports team? Would it have been nice to get one of the leading roles in the school play? Would it have been nice to just once be listened to at a meeting? Ever notice that in the movies when the Officer reviews the troops he's always looking down at them. Why is it that when a large man makes a joke he's considered outgoing, ingratiating, gregarious and spontaneous. When a small man makes a joke he's considered a little smart ass!*" These were the thoughts of Little Carl Mattson as he sat in his office chair. "*Maybe it is time for payback!*"

Carl had heard that 'The Axe' was fast and quick for a man his size. He'd also heard that Kople's favorite move was to smash his victim with his mighty fist, then pick him up, slam him down on the floor and stomp on a hand, and wrist. The healing process for crushed scaphoid break could be long and painful. Carl knew that his small bones would break easily, and had no intention of letting that happen.

Carl told his staff that he would be back in a few hours, and if Einer came in the office to send him away for the rest of the day. Carl then drove over to a gun shop in St. Paul. Not only had Carl never shot a gun, he'd never even held one. The shop clerk took him through many hand gun options none of which worked for Carls small hands and slim arms.

Finally, Carl looked at a display that advertised, "Woman's guns." "The Taurus PT 25 caliber, very small, light, easy to conceal with almost no recoil," explained the knowledgeable sales clerk, "Is this for your wife or girlfriend?"

Carl grinned, "Yes, that's it exactly, you know your job well." The sales clerk blushed and asked if Carl would like a demonstration in the firing range.

"*A ladies gun, or a man's gun, who cares, this isn't the Gunfight At The OK Corral.*"

"That would be most appreciated," Carl responded. The clerk took him to the back and showed the functions and cleaning procedure for the weapon. Then after discharging the nine bullet clip and checking to make sure the chamber was empty he handed it to Carl. It fit like a glove. Popping the chamber and loading the clip was a snap, the slide pulled hard but would not be an issue. On the range Carl went through two clips but wasn't concerned about any distance shooting. The target that Carl was going to hit would be big, close, and mean.

Carl than drove across the Minnesota River about twenty miles out of town. On an abandoned winter road with cornstalks poking out of the snow Carl Mattson stopped to think. Carl had done this before when he had to make an important decision. Killing Andy Kople qualified as an important decision. He decided that he was left with only one option. Einer must not go to prison, where he would easily me manipulated by hardened cons, and North Star Security was not up for grabs. Paul Zeller was a bookie and a crook. Andy The Axe Kople was an enforcer and a thug. Nothing good would ever come of doing business with these two criminals. If he let the barbarians in the gate once, there would be no stopping them. They'd kill him and very possibly Einer too. The cops or anyone else for that matter would never miss Andy Kople. This would prove to everyone that North Star Security was not to be messed with. That Carl Mattson was not to be messed with. He would make sure that Kople made the first move. Carl knew that Andy The Axe Kople was never sent out to negotiate. A simple case of self defense. A known shake-down artist against a successful business manager. Carl would make sure that there was one and only one witness. Little Carl was now at peace. The decision was made. This afternoon Andy Kople would get three in the chest. Carl drove back to town and entered his offices.

"Mr. Mattson, a Mr. Kople has been waiting to see you, he said he would be back around two," said the assistant.

"Thank you Ruth, I would like it if you would join us in the conference room when Mr. Kople and I meet," said Carl.

"Really," responded the assistant, now feeling very important.

"Ruth, as you know this is a growing business, my brother Einer and I are counting on you to grow with it," offered Carl.

At exactly 2:00 PM the massive frame of Andy The Axe Kople slowly entered the offices of North Star Security. Ruth jumped to her feet and escorted him into the conference room.

Carl was impressed with Andy's punctuality. *"Nice of Kople to die on time,"* thought Carl.

The two men sat across the conference table from each other with Ruth three feet to their side. Carl opened his brief case with the back of it shielding Kople's view. Taking out a paper and pen Carl brought down the lid of the attache case leaving it open with his right hand lightly gripping the Taurus PT 25.

Kople began, "Do you know why I'm here Mr. Mattson?"

"I think I do," responded Carl.

"Should I have brought references or recommendations?" Kople asked.

Carl's index finger snared the trigger, his small paw tightened on the gun handle. *"This Kople was good, trying to confuse me before he pounded the first punch."*

"I think your vast reputation has been seen by everyone," Carl countered.

Ruth started to squirm, this was not exactly the meeting she was expecting.

"Well then, would you at least give me a chance? I'll be the best employee on your staff. Honest, Mr. Mattson, I can work anyplace in the five state area. Any shift. I don't have a family so you can count on me for overtime, weekends or holidays," Kople said.

Carl kept his hand on the PT25.

Andy continued, "I've talked to a lot of your Security Officers, Mr. Mattson, really I have. They all say the same thing. This is a great company to work for, great training, plenty of work and the checks always clear. Could you at least think it over?"

Carl paused, thinking, *"Either Andy Kople is a great actor or he really does want to work for us. Call it 50-50."*

Ruth spoke up, "Mr. Kople, this is a question we always ask our applicants. Why would you want a career with North Star Security?"

Carl was glad Ruth joined in. It gave him a few more moments to measure Kople.

Andy Kople took a deep, long, sigh, "As I said, this is a fine Security company that is growing, but, ahh....can I be completely honest with you two?"

"Absolutely, Mr. Kople, honesty, integrity, and trust are the foundations of our business," Ruth explained.

"That's what I want too! The people I work for now make me do bad things, and now they want me to really cross the line," Andy said.

"Go on," Ruth asked.

"Ahh, it's like this, you know the girls that you escort, and protect. You know the ones in the hotels. The guys I work for want me to hurt them. They want to break North Star by hurting the girls. They said I have to mess 'em up a little."

Kople was getting more and more agitated. He started to gasp, and it looked like he was going to start crying.

"They say I should break a few of the girls noses, chip a few teeth, bust a few lips. I could never hurt a girl. That's not me! I've never done anything to any woman. Never! Honest! Who do they think I am? If I did anything like that my parents would come down from heaven and strike me dead. Not that I ever would, I just couldn't. If my two sisters found out I hurt some lady they would never have me over for Sunday dinner again. I wouldn't be able to play with my nieces and nephews."

Ruth moved to him and put a consoling hand on his bulky shoulder. Then ran for a tissue box for both Andy and her.

"You see Mr. Mattson, I just want to do the right thing, and that's what you guys are all about. See, I know these escort girls are in a tough spot. But the guys I work for think I should hurt some little 120 maybe 130 pound girl that's just trying to make her rent and car payment. I just want to get away from those guys."

Andy The Axe looked like Andy The Basket Case. Ruth moved to him and smoothed his back and neck with her hands, looking down as Andy blew his nose.

"Oh Mr. Kople, I'm sure we can use you here at North Star. I'm sure Mr. Mattson will hire you, won't you Mr. Mattson," Ruth implored.

Carl thought, *"Yes I will hire Andy, and he will be perfect for a very specific job indeed."*

Carl Mattson paused and stared at the now nearly crying Andy Kople, then said, "Mr. Kople your application comes at a time when we are expanding, Ruth will set you up with orientation."

With that Carl slid his hand out from his brief case and snapped it shut, setting it on the floor. Standing up he offered his hand to Kople.

"Let's give it a try, just one thing, from now on you can call me Carl, you can even call me Little Carl, just don't ever call me Runt," said Carl Mattson.

As Kople was being escorted out of the conference room he turned back to Carl Mattson and said, "Ah Mr. Carl, I mean Mr. Mattson, er, Carl could you do me one small favor. Could you not refer to me as The Axe, it seems to scare people, and when that happens it makes me sad."

36.

THE BIG GAME, THE BIG BET, THE BIG PAYOUT: VIKES/STEELERS EVEN, OVER/UNDER 42,:

Thursday, Three days before the Super Bowl: Vikings vs Steelers

What a great season our Vikings have had. Rolled to an NFL Central Division title beating our hated rival Green Bay Packers in both match-ups.

Then in the playoffs, quarterback Fran Tarkenton, running back Chuck Foreman and tight end Stu Voight had played fantastic football making for easy victories. On the defensive side the famous Purple Gang had not only stopped everything the other teams had thrown at them. But the crashing, slamming defense also had been able to harass quarterbacks, intercept passes, and cause fumbles with their smash-mouth, in-your-face, take-no-prisoners defense.

My roommate Tim spent hours pouring over the Vikings and Steelers rosters. He thoroughly studied both teams' entire season, game by game looking for similarities and trends. Tim meticulously examined what the two teams rushing, passing, and scoring was for the year. What teams they had success with but more importantly where they had stumbled and why?

Finally, it was Thursday afternoon as I was getting ready for one my last shifts as a bartender at Maxwells when Tim had me sit down and listen.

"So Tim, you think you have this game analyzed, categorized, sanitized, and homogenized?" I teased.

Tim gave me a disapproving smirk and shook his head.

"Well, John, here's how I'm planning to play it. Naturally, I would never expect you to contribute your hard earned tip jar money without reviewing the game-plan with you. I will say this, if I have the Super Bowl game handicapped correctly we should be relaxing on Hawaiian beaches for some time. If I'm right we can land in Maui and pick our spot. By that I mean we won't be desperate for moola. For the first time in our lives we can wait and search out the best employment opportunities that fit us."

The thought of smoothing it out on a palm treed island with warm Pacific breezes bathing my body rather than another winter of a driving arctic wind in my face made me listen even more intently.

Tim continued, "First the teams similarities: Both teams have a stop-you-in-your-tracks defense. I'm sure you knew that. Maybe the Vikes have a better pass defense with the run stoppage needle pointing to the Steelers. But really, both teams defense are top-notch so I call it even. What that tells me is it's going to be a low scoring game. Nobody has run-it-up on either of these defenses all year.

Special teams are much the same. Good field goal, kick off, and punt teams. Here again, I rate both teams even.

Coaching goes to the Vikings simply because they have been to a Super Bowl and this is the first time the Pittsburgh staff has been in the big one.

That takes us to the offense. Neither team turns it over much. Both have great players at every position. Some day the Vikes Fran Tarkenton and the Steelers Terry Bradshaw will be enshrined in Canton, call that equal. But here is where I see an edge for Pittsburgh. Franco Harris, is a banging, blasting, bulldozing, fullback that makes defensive backs wake up at night in cold sweats."

"In conclusion, I like the Steelers and under, way under. I don't think 30 points will be scored by both teams. I want a bet a thousand apiece, what to you say?" Tim finished.

I stared back at Tim and gulped, "You mean you want to bet a thousand total, like five hundred on the Steelers and five hundred on the under, right?" I said hopefully, knowing I was pretty sure wrong.

"No John," Tim replied, "I think we should bet a thousand on the Steelers, a thousand on the under and a thousand to parlay it. If we lose, we lose three grand, if we win we win...."

My mouth went dry.

"Five thousand dollars," Tim concluded.

A two play parlay paid three to one. A thousand win on the Steelers, another on the under and then a three thousand dollar pay out for the parlay.

I think my eyes glazed over thinking about all that money.

With the seven thousand we had and the five thousand we could win, Tim and I would be set for months in Maui.

"John, John, did you hear me? are you OK?" Tim questioned.

"Huh," I came back to reality. "Ya, sure, if that's what you think we should do. You've been winning all season long. What, something like 70 per cent right?" I responded.

"73 per cent," Tim corrected.

I nodded, and got up from my chair. Tim called in the bet, placing it in the cover company name with several different bookies. "Now remember John, be sure to stay very quiet about this strategy;

we don't want other betters diluting it, and also even though we are with several bookie outlets, I suspect that Zeller will end up taking the hit on this action. So MUM is the word, right?"

"Right - o Tim."

37.

BIG SHOOTERS NEVER DIE,
THEY JUST PASS OUT:

Friday, Two Days Before The Super Bowl, 1977

The Twin Cities is buzzing. All the bars, restaurants, and hotels are packed. If you weren't a big enough hitter to get a ticket and take a flight to the Super Bowl, you partied in the Twin Cities. Everybody wants to be out and about for the big Super Bowl Game on Sunday. Parties, parties, and more parties, everywhere.

Naturally, everyone at Maxwells has been busy searching every watering hole in town looking for a job, since the place closes for the big redo after Sundays Game. Everyone except Tim and me that is. I'm sure there are a few people wondering why we're not out banging on doors and calling on bar managers around town. Tough shit!

I can almost hear the imploring sounds of my Maxwell coworkers begging for a job, "Is there anyone quitting your bar? I'm ready and raring to go. You know I can work any shift. I'm available for part-time. Weekends, holidays, swing shifts, doesn't matter, I can do it. You know I'm very flexible and can be trained for any job, or even various jobs. Just say the word and I'll be over." Man, this recession really bites.

Because I worked early on Thursday I was able to score a few hours off on Friday night for some serious Super Bowl fun. I hit a few bars on the strip and was surprised to run into Boomer. "I heard there is huge bash out at a swanky house on Lake Minnetonka, you want to go for it, John?"

The Lake Minnetonka and Wayzata area of western Minneapolis was where the senior corporate executives of Fortune 500 companies and silver-plated trust babies with inherited wealth lived. Lavish homes, expensive yachts, and turned up noses. If Edina was where the "cake eaters" lived: medical, legal and business professionals. Lake Minnetonka was where the the Chocolate Truffle crowd hung out, and let it all hang out. Partying was a competitive sport for the ultra rich.

Big parties near Lake Minnetonka meant three things, free top shelf booze, plenty of great free chow and lots of desirable, desperate woman looking to score in the big leagues. I had already poured plenty of low rail bourbon down my throat and was ready for action. How Boomer scored an invite to that party was not my concern.

"Sounds great Boom, I'll follow you there," I said.

Thirty minutes later I passed my keys to a parking valet and was greeted by three members of Carl Mattson's North Star Security staff. Wow, Mattson's crew were all over the Twin Cities. Fantastic!

The home was amazing, big, refined, stylish, fill in the blank. Overlooking one of the many Lake Minnetonka bays you could see the large boat house rising after the endless snow covered yard. Shoulder to shoulder, elbow to elbow, butt to butt most of the areas elite were present, everybody sporting their best purple Viking garb. Dazzling girls in Viking mini skirts passed trays of bubbly. There were walls of hot and cold eats and two bars where purple clad bartenders hustled drinks. Even a few guys dressed up like Viking Warriors including swords, shields and battle axes would clown around with the crowd. Every few minutes some drunk would climb up on a chair and sing the Vikings chant, "From Out Of The North Comes The Vikings." Great party.

Finally I spied Boomer talking to a bunch of guys that included Zeller the bookie. Boomer waved me over and gave me a big hug.

"Just to let all you guys know, John here was one of the guys who started North Star Security. John and his friend Tim were the guys behind the original business, can you believe it?" Boomer boomed.

Looking down I tried to change the subject but Zeller gave me a cool, detached look and commented.

"Ya, I hear you and that roommate of yours are quite the brainiac team. Must be nice to always be the smartest guys in every room."

"Well I'm just glad we could help some people get a start in business, you know, that's all," I stammered.

Zeller's eyes never left mine, "My aren't you and your friend the magnanimous team. Smart, caring, giving, you must be great guys. Speaking of giving, perhaps you could give that Carl Mattson a little advice. I'm having a problem making Boomer's brother understand how important growing a business can be. Five years ago I was taking bets on Cedar Ave. and Lake Street. Long hours, cold sidewalk, small time players. Now I'm the biggest bookie in the Twin Cities. Caring and giving were not part of that equation."

Just then I looked to my right and saw her. Hair was a thick swirl of cashmere and caramel, vigilant alert eyes, face of an amused empress, dressed in a long shimmering purple clinging dress. As always, there was a solar system of admirers, and adulators, grooving on her presence. Then, as always, there were the lustful, wanton stares of the men. Some obvious, some evasive, a few totally failing at concealing their craving. Kristen was doing what she did better than anyone: bring a crackling sexual charge to the room.

Kristen eyes met mine just as Conrad Millers' hand caressed her neck. It was then that I figured it out. This was Conrad Millers' home. Wow, must be nice. Very nice!

Miller bent down to sniff Kristen's hair and then moved up to take another slurp from a bottle of Old Grand Dad that he had in his other hand. Nothing like having one hand on the most beautiful woman in the state and another holding a bottle of top shelf booze. *"Life is just a bitch isn't it, Conrad."* I said to myself. Yes, John's jealousy meter was rising. Like everyone, Miller had been drinking for hours and was starting to wobble.

Turning to Boomer, me, Zeller, and a few of their thuggish pals, Miller waved us forward and called in a commanding, sinister voice, "You bums come with me, I have something to show you clowns."

As Conrad waltzed Kristen ahead, we followed him down a long hall and entered a dark room. Closing the door, Conrad Miller switched on the dimmer lights of his study. What we saw was a surreal monument to Miller's days at Yale. Blue Yale college jerseys draped the walls, blue embroidered furniture, inscribed cocktail glasses, in a Yale logo adorned cabinet behind a small walnut bar. Even blue Bulldog curtains draped the windows. On the bar was a large bottle of Jack Daniels with a Yale University baseball cap on it. Pictures of Yale football teams, and sports action photos hung on the walls.

Miller went behind his desk and pointed to a large picture of a Yale Football Team. "That's me, number 17, Yale '58." With a drunken, wavering finger he pointed across the room to a large framed picture of number 17, holding his helmet in one hand and a football in the other. Handsome, confident, with a patrician, aristocratic smirk on his face.

Miller decided to lecture us, "You know what we did after the football season was over? We studied, we learned, we got a real education. Some of you out here in this Big Ten waste land might think this was unfair. The field is definitely not flat. We Ivy League athletes were expected to perform on the sports teams and in the classroom. Outrageous! I Know! True scholar athletes, I bet that's a term you prairie plucks never heard of. Finance, business, economics, investment, not how Holsteins screw or whatever they teach at that hack U across town. My Dad sent me out here to this terrible tundra to grow the business and grow it I have. Thirty seven dealerships in fifteen states."

I could feel my inebriated back go up. As a bartender you learn early to let people talk. Keep slinging the booze and let the drunks brag. At the end of the night the register should be full and the bottles empty. Bartenders have thick, teflon skins. But Conrad Miller had zinged a sensitive nerve that midwesterners in general and Minnesotan's in particular have. We're taught to keep our mouths shut, carry jumper cables, and extra bottles of anti freeze. Pompous, arrogant, conceited behavior never got your car or your neighbor's out of a snow bank. He caught my attitude and upped his game.

"Williams? Right? You're a funny guy Williams. Did you really think you had a chance at an unreal beauty like Kristen against me? Delusional! You remind me of that bitch ex-wife of mine. She thinks she's going to take me down. I got news for that greedy slut. My lawyers will burn her at the stake before she gets one thin dime of our family money."

Miller took a long, slow pull from his Old Grand Dad bourbon bottle. Then turned to me, "I know your type Williams. Nothing matters to losers like you. How 'bout we play for her? One game, for one night with Kristen, your call! Poker, or billiards?"

I turned to Kristen, the only girl in the room, "Look Kris, he's drunk, you don't want us to....."

"Zip it Williams, I didn't ask her permission. What! Are you scared?" The condemning pitch of his voice made my irritation rise again. "Billiards," I uttered without fully realizing it. Miller led us to his game room. Disgusting! Why bother describing it. More Yale bullshit, another small bar, TV, family photos, replicas of old cars, vintage airplanes. I'm sure his rich family owned all this stuff.

"One game, straight eight ball, with one small caveat," announced Miller.

With that Miller went behind the small bar and got a fresh bottle of bourbon, and four shot glasses.

"Every time your opponent, and that would be me, knocks in a ball, the loser, that would be you, has to take two shots of bourbon. First one to win the billiards game, and stay on his feet is the champ," Miller slurred.

Miller pointed a demanding finger at Zeller, "Rack'em up, bookie boy."

Now gesturing in my direction while bracing himself on the billiards table Conrad sneered, "Williams, considering the only thing you're good for is tending bar you can do the pouring. Filling a couple of shot glasses with bourbon will undoubtedly maximize your minor league intellectual capabilities."

I momentarily wondered if this is the way he treated his hoards of employees. But if you're as rich and entitled as Conrad Miller I guess you think you can do and say anything you want to anyone.

I took the bourbon bottle and carefully poured two shots for me and two for Miller.

"Wait a minute," I said. "Who gets to break?"

Miller set his stick down. Heavily sighing he said, "Who's house is this? Who's table is this? Who's bourbon is this? But you think you deserve honors?" Now turning to Kristen, "You actually spent time with this idiot?"

Miller now ceremoniously took one of the shot glasses and motioned me to do the same.

"Courtesy!" We both drank down the shot. I immediately refilled our glasses.

Miller broke and then ran two in. I took four shots of Old Grand Dad Bourbon and steadied myself. Got lucky and rammed in three in a row.

Conrad got to his fifth glass of bourbon and slumped, then staggered to a reclining chair. Game over, I had outlasted a guy who'd been drinking since noon.

I vaguely remember somebody helping me to my brown bomber. Kristen digging out the keys from my pants pocket.

The hard cold air momentarily reviving me as I lurched into my townhouse. Then Kristine helping me into bed and feeling her take off my shoes. Out!

38.

HANGOVER, CONCERTOS, AND A BACK STABBING, TURNCOAT, RAT BASTARD, SON-OF-A-BITCH:

Saturday Morning, 1977, One Day Before The Super Bowl

Kristen Bennett had a rare talent that in forty-two years of having sex I have never seen emulated. Kristen liked to wake me up by slowly, carefully, meticulously giving me head. It was as if an orchestra was warming up for a symphony performance. First Piccolos, then clarinets, followed by swooning violins, bring on the bassoons, now the trumpets are waking up, the conductor addresses the podium, trombones are sliding in-and-out, the orchestra is falling into an even pace, cue to cellos, double bass, and harp. The orchestra is wailing now, everyone wants out, the crescendo is near, I feel the percussion man grip the cymbals. Finally, the conductor points a long demanding finger at the kettle drummer who lets loose with a vicious, thumping roll, and the cymbals crash, crash, crash, again and again, and Kristen is there swallowing every note.

As the audience stands and applauds our Kristen is not finished. The orchestra evenly takes it to a slower, smoother beat. Serenading the blowjob as my Kristen tempos to a kinder, gentler finish. Finally, the curtain comes down and then back up to the roaring approval of the audience. The conductor asks Kristen to step forward. The first violinist hands her a rose, the conductor ceremoniously hands her an ivory white handkerchief. She graciously smiles, spits and releases into the hankerchief accepting the thundering applause from the crowd. There isn't a man in the symphony hall that doesn't want her or a woman who doesn't want to be like her. Shimmering in her purple gown she slightly blushes, smiles, and nods her acceptance to the roaring audience. The men start to loudly whistle, the woman are all digging in purses for tissues to dry their eyes. Before them is a triumphant warrior queen for love, passion, romance and sex.

Pain, pleasure, pain, pleasure, galloping headache, fantastic oral sex. My mind and body are somewhere in between. Fully erect now, if I could only grasp an aspirin bottle. Kristen is about to challenge the trombones, when she stops and asks, "John, John, I don't have much time. I have to be home when that evil ex-husband of mine brings Darren back."

If purgatory is between heaven and hell then I'm temporarily a resident.

"John, my son Darren wants to put a little action on the Super Bowl. Could you help? You know, just his allowance money. Which way are you betting the big game?" Kristen asked while still hovering over my cock as her right hand griped and slowly pulsated my balls.

"Huh, oh, okay, ahhh, ahhh, please don't stop. Oh Kristen, that is so good. You have such great skills. Ahhh, Tim has us going Steelers and under," I moaned in ecstasy and anguish.

Kristen's head snapped up, "What? What did you just say?"

"Ahhh, Tim has us at Steelers and under, say, could you keep going," I begged.

Kristen's eyes glared at me, her hand now gripping my shaft. "Steelers! Did you say Steelers? You're going against our Vikings?"

"Ahh, ya, Steelers and under, could you start again, I really like it when…." I pleaded.

"Now wait a minute John, you're not serious? A lot of those Viking players are our friends. Great guys. We've partied with them, hung with them, cheered for them. You're not really betting against the Vikes in the biggest game of the year?" Kristen questioned.

"Well, ahh, that's the way Tim has it figured. So, ahh, ya, Steelers and under," I struggled out.

Kristen looked seriously mad. Flinging my cock away like it was disgusting trash she said, "What kind of traitor are you and Tim? You're betting against our Vikings? Our team? Our state? I don't believe this! What kind of rat bastards are you two?"

With that Kristen jumped out of bed and threw on her cloths. Marching out into our living room she grabbed her winter coat and snarled at me, "John, I think you and your friend Tim have some serious loyalty issues. What kind of turncoat goes against our team now?"

Kristen looked around and noticed two suitcases standing by our front door.

"Are you and Tim going somewhere?" Kristen asked.

"Ahh, ya, after the bar closes tomorrow, Tim and I are going on vacation, to like, ah, Maui," I groaned.

I was now standing naked in our living room while Kristen continued to rip into me. My headache was fast reaching full throttle.

Kristen seemed more puzzled now, "But what about last night? What about me? Maui?"

I quickly responded, "Great, did you want to come along?"

Kristen's temper gauge was rising, "Go on vacation now? You know I can't do that, Darren is in school. If I leave the state I forfeit my alimony and child support. You know I can't leave now."

Kristen grabbed her purse and moved to our front door, "John Williams I hope you and that nasty friend of yours drop every dollar you bet. Fran Tarkenton is going to throw for three hundred yards and four touchdowns, easy! Chuck Foreman will make that Pittsburgh steel-curtain defense look like it was made out of sawdust. Do me a favor, 'traitor John' don't bother calling me for at least three months. That's how long it's going to take me to get over your back-stabbing, turncoat, cut-and-run behavior."

"Wait a minute, did you say you wanted Darren to get down on the Super Bowl?" I asked.

With that Kristen violently reached into her purse and threw two twenty dollar bills on our living room floor. She always had plenty of twenties.

All I heard was our front door slamming, as the gust of glacial air smashed against my naked body. I shivered and wearily went back to bed, knowing now that I may never understand women.

39.

PACK THE BAGS, SELL THE CAR, PAY THE RENT, SURFS-UP, HAWAII CALLS:

Later That Afternoon, The Day Before The Super Bowl

I flopped my long body out of bed and headed to the medicine cabinet. Is this a three aspirin day or four? Shaking the pills down I carefully walked into the kitchen worrying that any sudden movement might result in permanent life long cardiac or skeletal issues.

Tim was siting at the dinette table reviewing Maui Hawaii brochures and maps. By the time we get to Maui in a few days Tim will have all the roads and streets ingrained in his head. We never get lost. I was always so grateful that Tim was such a thoroughly organized person. Of course I was the complete opposite. But tough shit! I had Tim.

Slumping down at the table my eyes felt like a Roman Legion was attacking the Gauls, both armies were losing.

Tim looked at me and smiled, "My aren't we leaving Minnesota with a bang Mr. Williams!"

"Let's not talk about it," was my only reply.

"When you were dragged in here last night I think you dropped some money on the living room floor? I picked up a couple of twenties," Tim said.

"No, that's from Kristen's kid. He wants to get on the Steelers and under with us, that's all," I slurred.

Tim paused and looked at me.

"Ahh John, you didn't tell Kristen which way we're going on the Super Bowl did you? I asked you not to tell anyone."

'Tim please, it's just little Darren's allowance money. So he gets to buy a few extra comic books and candy bars. What's the big deal?" was my exhausted response.

I think Tim could see I was too tired to listen to any of his 'little man's paranoia'.

Tim thought a second and then said, "OK, when you get cleaned up I want you to sell the brown bomber today. Try to get a good price on it, but more importantly get it in cash."

I nodded.

Tim continued, "I'll drop off the rent check for next month and wrap up our travel plans. Remember to pack light. Just leave everything here.

We won't be back for a long time if ever. One bag. Hawaii is warm, and we'll be in a hurry to blow out of here, so let's keep it thin. If we have this game right we'll have plenty of money and we both will be in need of a Hawaiian wardrobe."

I always liked the way Tim said, *"If we have this game right, as if I did any of the handicapping work, but it was nice he included me.*

Ninety minutes later I was standing in front of an ice and snowed caked used car lot off the 494 freeway. The glaring cold wind made me want to stay in the car, *"Has anyone ever sold a car while sitting in it with the windows up?"* I wondered. A ruffled man approached me in an old heavy green parka, and completely ignored me while looking over the bomber.

"Give me the keys," he demanded. (Not, *"Could I have the keys please? Or, 'Would you like to come into my office for coffee and we can discuss how I could help you today?' Just, 'Give me the keys'."*)

He started the car up, read the odometer, looked over the interior, shut down the bomber and got out. Opening and closing all four doors he looked at me past the hood and said, "Seventeen hundred."

I looked back at him and replied, "I was hoping for $2,500.00."

"I was hoping to get laid last night, didn't happen, didn't happen the night before and I don't think it's going to happen tonight, seventeen hundred," the dealer said.

"How about if we meet in the middle, call it $2,100.00 even?" I said encouragingly.

"I think my office phone is wringing, I got to go," he said.

"Okay look, I need the car until Tuesday, and can I have the seventeen hundred in cash?" I dejectedly replied.

"Cash is all I deal in, bring it in Tuesday morning, I like to turn these cars over fast," he said.

40.

THE BIG GAME, THE BIG STORM, THE BIG BET

Super Bowl Sunday Afternoon, 1977

Tim and I rolled into Maxwell's parking lot knowing that after tonight the big lighted purple football would be turned off forever.

All the news on the car radio was about today's Super Bowl game and the monster storm that was brewing out west.

"Minnesota and the entire Midwest is in for another Siberian Express with record levels of snowfall by Monday. This will be the largest storm of the year, and folks, as most of you know, a big storm like this is usually followed by a paralyzing arctic air mass with temperatures well under 20 below. Now here's Catherine with your up-to-the minute road conditions report." I snapped off the radio and just hoped the Minneapolis/St. Paul Airport wouldn't close before we escaped.

As we got out of the car and sustained the blustering frigid Canadian wind Tim raised his hand to me.

"John, I almost forgot to tell you, I've changed our travel plans. Win or lose we leave tomorrow. We collect our pay tonight, square up with the bookies, and drop off the car at the dealership tomorrow morning and then taxi to the airport. You're packed? Right?"

"Ya, I'm ready, but why the change? What's the hurry?" I asked.

Tim chose his words carefully, "Ahh, look, I think it best for us to get out of here as soon as possible, I'll explain more after the game."

I looked at Tim and smiled, "Tim, do you still think there are monsters in your closet when you go to bed at night?"

"Absolutely, big ones," said Tim.

Together we did the Minnesota shuffle into Maxwells and got ready for a busy afternoon.

There are few things that bore me more than pre-game analysis by former players and finely groomed announcers. Tim knew more than most of these guys anyway so I rarely paid any attention to their oh-so-insightful, nonstop, time filling, bullshit. They literally make my eyes glaze over. By the time the Vikings and Steelers were ready to kick it off every angle, or thread of the game had been dissected ten times by these dudes.

With three and four deep drinkers at every inch of the bar I knew I wouldn't be able to keep up with the game anyway. The best I could do is after a big play catch the instant replay and then keep pouring. I also knew that by the time the bar closes at midnight I would be flush with tips.

The first quarter went just as Tim had figured. Two experienced, bruising defenses stopping everything the other teams offense could try. Halfway through the second quarter it was still scoreless and Tim's call on the under looked locked. I started to think of what kind of car we should buy in Maui. I'd never driven a Corvette, but I assumed they were a total beach bunny magnet. Two single guys pull up to the surf in a red 'vette convertible and the string bikini's will be flying to us.

My hands never stopped, pour, pour, pour, mix, mix, mix, "Here's your change."

"Thanks for the tip."

"What is that Ma'am? That Golden Cadillac had too much cream in it, oh dear me, I feel so bad."

"How kind of you Sir, I can always use another quarter."

"Hope the Vikes figure it out at halftime."

"Blah, blah, blah."

The bar manager already figured that halftime would be a good slot to give the bar staff a quick smoke break. We each took a turn and when my time came I bolted to the storage locker to clear my head, Tim quickly approached me.

"John, we need to talk, I know you don't have much time."

"Tim, the game is going just like you said. Low scoring with the Steelers looking a little better than the Vikes. What do you think of a Corvette, maybe red is a little too much, how about burnt orange or maybe dark blue?" I asked.

"John, ahh, look, ahh, there is still a half to play, we're not there yet, and what's more…." Tim seemed to be having trouble getting his thoughts out.

With that I could see the bar manager wave to me to get back to my station.

"John, ahh, meet me here after the third quarter, we have to talk," Tim yelled as I bolted back to the chaos.

Bedlam continued, drink, drink, drink.

"Did you see that call?"

"What kind of glasses are the refs wearing?"

"The Vikes are getting jobbed."

"Worse call I ever saw!"

"Tarkenton isn't getting time to throw."

"We've got to stop Franco."

"The Vikes have been coming back all season."

"This game is not over yet!"

The third quarter ended but I couldn't get away from my station. I peaked over my head with four minutes to go in the game and saw the score, Steelers 16 Vikings 6. Tim tapped me on the shoulder and said, "We need to talk, NOW."

I motioned to the bar manager and signaled a break with my hands. He nodded knowing that if the score held up this was going to be a very quiet empty bar as soon as the game ended. I followed a very nervous, agitated Tim to the storage locker and he began.

"John, John, you know we've always been good friends, right?"

My only thought was, "Huh?"

Tim continued, "Good friends, right? For a long time, right? Real pals, buds, right?"

"Tim, of course we're good friends, we're like brothers, where are you going with this?" I questioned.

Tim continued, "We've always been straight with each other, right? Above board? Honest?"

"Tim, are you telling me you didn't take the Steelers and under?" I asked.

Tim kept looking around, then said, "No, no, ahhh, John, you know how I said we were going to put a one thousand on the Steelers, and one thousand on the under and one thousand to parlay the two?"

"Yaaa."

Tim, with his head on a swivel, "Well, ahhh, I didn't exactly do that, I put, ... two thousand on the Steelers, two thousand on the under and two thousand to parlay."

For a minute I blanked. Simple math has always been very simple for me. We had seven thousand saved, we sold the car for seventeen hundred, and now Tim had just won us.....ten thousand dollars. Eighteen thousand seven hundred dollars! With our last checks and the tips from today we were headed to "Surf-City-U.S.A." with about twenty thousand dollars. The thought temporarily captured me.

"Look John, the score is going to hold up, just don't tell anyone," Tim pleaded.

I peaked around the corner and could see patrons disgustedly shuffling out. A few folks looked ready to cry. I could hear, "It was the refs."

"Our offensive line sucked today."

"Where was our running game?" and a whole lot more.

I looked back at Tim, he mouthed, "Ten thousand dollars."

41.

BAM, BAM, BAM:

This was hard, very hard. As I was cleaning up my station and getting ready to walk out of Maxwell's for the last time, my feet were dancing and my mood was high. Everybody else I worked with was feeling the serious blues. Last night on the job, last check, unknown future during a hellish economy, hugs and shakes goodbye, and what's worse, the Vikes lost the Super Bowl. Tim came into my station and put his index finger over his lips signaling for me to keep quiet.

As always the head bartender had combined the eight tip jars and went to work breaking down the booty. Finally he motioned us forward, handed us our last check, slid our tips forward, shook our hands and wished us well.

Boomer approached me, reaching behind the bar he grabbed a bottle of top shelf bourbon and said, "C'mon John, let's have one last drink together in the office, what are they going to do, fire us?"

Skipping down the hallway I couldn't believe my luck. $10,000.00 wager victory, $20,000.00

in our bank account, A future of palm trees, beach bunnies, warm breezes, and a hot sports car. As I entered the office I was wondering if Tim could get us upgraded to first class on tomorrow's flight to Hawaii.

The blast hit my left kidney like a wall of boulders roaring down a mountain. The forearm smash to the back of my neck put me out. Evidently I hit my forehead on a table corner as I went down.

I came to in a filthy panel truck. Looking up I could see a smudged sticker that read, "Mattson Hauling, You Won't Lose It, If Mattson Moves It."

It was a total toss-up as to what hurt most, my kidney, the back of my neck or the front of my skull. I rolled over and hacked out a little blood. Trying to sit up I felt another person next to me. Tim was either dead or real close. It was here I noticed our hands were taped behind us.

The wall of cold air brought me to the second they opened the truck doors. Grabbing our feet they jerked us out of the truck and pounded a fist in each of our guts, just to make sure we had nothing left. Throwing us on the concrete floor of Conrad Miller's boat house I started to realize what was going on.

Zeller looked down at us and for a second I thought he would kill us right there, "What the fuck were you two thinking? William's I could understand, you're an idiot anyway, but Langford, really, there is no excuse."

Tim rolled over, at least he was alive, I started to come around. Why was I here? Why was Zeller, and Boomer, mad at us?

I could hear the now howling wind picking up, the Siberian Express was roaring down on Minnesota.

"73 per cent! 73 fucking per cent! Langford nobody wins 73 per cent and lives. $10,000.00 dollars! Are you crazy? What gives you the right to put me out of business?"

"OK, fine, just don't pay us, we won't tell anyone," I said as well as I could considering my condition.

"Bullshit, everyone will know I didn't pay, besides, I need all the money we're getting to kill you two," Zeller laughed.

"What?"

"Oh you two college boys are so smart. Win all the money, drive every bookie in town crazy. Put every pimp in town out of business. Steal all the good looking hookers."

I had no idea what Zeller was talking about.

"Every bookie in the Twin Cities wants you two dead. Every pimp in the Twin Cities wants you two dead. Conrad Miller wants you dead, I want you dead. You're not skipping to Maui with ten grand," Zeller said.

"Is that it, you're being paid to kill us, by all these guys?" I asked.

Boomer picked up an ice auger, Zeller grabbed a sledge hammer, talking was over.

It felt like a blast of ice coming through the boat-house door when Little Carl, Andy The Axe and Nazi Steve Lynch smashed their way in.

"So you two thought you were going to have all the fun, not very nice not including us," Little Carl said.

With that Little Carl bent down in front of me, slowly opening that vicious Philippine knife he grinned at me.

"NOW," snarled Carl.

The next few minutes seemed to last for hours. I saw Andy Kople and Steve Lynch attack Boomer. I saw Boomer doing his best to fend them off with the ice auger. I felt Carl heave me over and slice the tape unstrapping my arms. I saw Zeller bolt for the door but Kople caught him slamming him to the floor. I saw Boomer pick Lynch up and throw him against a wall. I saw Lynch thrust a knee to Boomer's crotch. I heard Carl yell at me to, 'help out'. Zeller was off the floor, desperate, grabbing an ice chisel he went for the throat of Kople but Carl was able to trip him up. I was fast coming around and needed to do my part. Boomer was in full fury, throwing the auger at Lynch and Kople knocking them both down. Boomer and Zeller were both fighting like men with nothing to lose. At best they would go to prison, at worst they would die. Boomer picked up the sledge hammer and like a Nordic Warrior came right at us. With bodies flying around the boathouse I looked down to see Zeller beneath me holding Little Carls blade. I fired a straight right fist to his head that temporarily stopped him. A hard left, right, left combination with a kick to his face put him out. I stepped forward, grabbing the knife and pounded my heal into Zeller's bleeding face. I was going for another killer foot stomp when I was knocked down by a slumping defeated Boomer Mattson. Steve had nailed the hammer swinging Boomer by stepping to the side and ejecting a karate thrust to Boomer's left knee. I could hear the bones, muscles, and cartilage all snap. Boomers knee jutted out at a 45 degree angle. The pain must have been well north of excruciating. Lynch paid for the kick by taking a glancing blow from the sledge. With Boomer on one leg Kople finished him off with a roundhouse to the head.

Together Carl, Steve and I looked over the now out cold Zeller and Boomer. I handed Carl his Phillippine knife and he uncut the still sagging Tim. It was then that I noticed the pain in my right hand. I must have broken a bone or badly sprained something when I was fighting Zeller.

"We have to finish and fast," said Carl. Little Carl then went over and unhooked a large fire extinguisher canister and smashed it first on the head of Zeller then going over to Boomer he looked down and muttered, "Who's the runt now?" BAM, that was hard to watch. So much for brotherly love!

Kople picked up Tim in a fireman's carry and said, "We better get out of here, I think they both might be dead. Carl, you better wipe everything down and slop some motor oil to cover our tracks." The snow and wind pushed against us as we fought our way up the hill to Steve's car. One problem, the car was stuck in the snow.

"John, get back there and push," commanded Lynch.

The snow was already over my knees. I positioned myself next to Kople and Carl and we all leaned in. A bolt of pain shot up my arm, I'd hurt my hand worse than I thought.

"Steve, I can't push, my hand is hurt," I yelled through the raging storm.

"Well then get in here and drive," Steve roared.

Minnesotans learn at an early age that brute force is not always the answer for a rear wheel drive car submerged in snow. A rocking motion with a big final shove usually does the job. On the fourth rock I could hear Carl yell, "This will do it."

I spun the car out and wobbled down the hill. Coming to a skidding stop a small voice in my head tweaked, *John, keep going, just keep driving, there's two dead guys back there. Why are you stopping? In the end all that matters is 'YOU'. You could freeze to death tonight, you could go to prison, a long stretch. The money is gone, you can't collect the ten grand from a dead bookie'.*

It was then that Steve jerked the car door open and ordered me in the backseat. The right back door flew open and a merciless blast of Alberta Clipper whirled into the car. Kople gently laid Tim in the middle and Carl got in next to him.

Andy hefted his huge body into the front seat and the five of us drove off in the worst winter storm of the decade. The great Super Bowl storm of 1977.

After I caught my breath I leaned past Tim and asked Carl, "How did you know we were in trouble?"

Carl calmly replied, "We've been keeping an eye on you two."

I looked at the front seat. Can you drive a car with more than 100 per cent intensity? If you can, Steve Lynch was doing it. Luckily for us Steve had been a stock car driver at an earlier time. Kople had his face plastered into the front windshield signaling Steve right or left as best he could. In this blasting storm we were lucky to average thirty miles an hour.

"Why were you watching us?" I asked.

"We were pretty sure you two characters would get yourselves into trouble. But more importantly we wanted to get even, nobody likes to owe any-body for anything," Carl said.

Bumping and swirling in the storm I tried to figure out what Carl was talking about. Finally I said, "Why would you think you owed Tim and me anything?"

"John, we owed you everything," Carl said.

"But we're even now, Williams, I don't have to put up with you anymore, I don't owe you spit," barked Steve from his driver position.

Hopelessly confused.

Carl looked over at me, "During the Packer/Viking brawl at Maxwell's it was you that jumped over the bar and freed Steve. It was you and your dangerous scotch bottle that kept him from getting hurt. It was you that jumped on my brother Einer and took the kicks and blows that probably saved his life. There were at least 40 Maxwell employee's that night but you were the only one willing to help. It was you and Tim that started the Security business, and you were the guys who brought me into it. Now it's a success and we need to move on and expand, but now we're even."

"What do you mean, move on?" I asked.

"We're separating the Security Business and moving into other cities, Milwaukee, Madison, Fargo, Sioux Falls," said Carl." "We're not going to be North Star Security anymore, now we're Midwest Security. That's how we turned Kople, right Andy?"

"That's right Carl, and I'm mighty grateful," said Andy The Axe.

More hopelessly confused.

Carl could see my confusion and continued, "The Escort business is too good to let go, but it conflicts with some of the clients we have secured. Government Offices, College Campuses, Banks, and Hospitals. Somehow protecting Grannies' checking account and making sure some guy got laid didn't mesh. Blowjobs and biopsies, not a good fit. My sister Gretchen has studied this stuff, says that the business climate is at it's low ebb, 'the bottom of the economic wave' she calls it. It's going to be up from here and we should be able to catch the ride."

Tim's battered head rose and he was able to gargle out, "Your sister is right, and you're smart to listen to her."

Carl continued, "Kople is taking over the Escort service, we're focusing on everything else. Andy will be good at it too."

Still lost I said, "OK, but that was your brother, what is your sister Gretchen going to say if she finds out you, ahh OK, we killed him?"

Carl eyes rolled over to me and he gave me a slightly amused smile, "It was her idea."

Huh!

Carl went on, "Since day one Boomer's been nothing but trouble to everyone. Then when he couldn't get us into enough hot water to have us sent to Granite he tried to kill us. The Packer/Viking brawl was not what you think it was. We did some checking. Boomer said that he'd herded the other bouncers out into the parking lot because he needed some help with a fight. We checked, there was no fight. Boomer wanted Steve and Einer to get hurt bad so that he could move in on the rest of North Star. Fact is, we found out that Boomer had slipped some bucks to some Wisconsin guys and fingered Steve and Einer. Then when he came back into the bar that night he puts on this big act with the barstool, bullshit. Naturally, Boomer's been trying to get to you and Tim forever. Now he wants to get Mary Tyler Moore, the Minneapolis cops and City leaders aren't going to like us messing with that statue. It was just a matter of time before he would try and get me, but I got him first."

"Well how did Zeller and Boomer know that the ten grand was won by Tim and me?" I asked.

Tim's head rose and he fought for words, "Because, my fuckup roommate told them."

It was then I started to put the building blocks together. The only person I told about the Steelers and under bet was my now ex-girlfriend Kristen. Come to think of it, it was Zeller who introduced me to Kristen in the first place. There was no way that Zeller was going to let us skip all the way to Maui with ten grand. I started to get queasy and nervous.

Steve piped up from the front seat, "All week you've been telling people that you and Tim were going on vacation. You didn't actually tell anyone that you and Tim were heading to Maui? Did you?"

Tim gulped, "Sure he did, he told his traitorous girlfriend Kristin, that's why they had to get us tonight."

Tim rolled his battered head toward me and slurred, "Well we can kiss Maui goodbye Williams, once the cops find those two dead guys they're going to beat a path to everyone they knew, that would include your back stabbing girlfriend Kristen. Guess what genius? She's going to tell them exactly where to find us."

Steve had us on East 494 and finally we saw another car going west. This was good, the cops weren't pulling over anyone for being crazy enough to drive in this storm. Finally, Steve skidded in front of our townhouse. Stopping the car he turned to me, "Listen up, Williams! Here's how this is going down! Give me the keys to your Toronado, and help me get Tim in the back seat. We're going to the Holiday Station on Lyndale to gas up and grab some sandwiches. You're going to get the travel gear and meet us here in twenty minutes. Carl and Andy are taking off in this car. The storm has covered our tracks out at Lake Minnetonka. We were never there. If you're not outside waiting, Tim and I are leaving without you. You can be hauled in by the cops and questioned for hours about two dead guys, and it won't be Granite, it will be thirty to life in Stillwater. Enjoy all the boys!"

"We're leaving in this storm? Are you nuts? We might not make it, and why in my car?" I responded.

"Because dumbass, your car has front wheel drive. Now get out," Steve ordered.

The storm nearly blew me over but I struggled to the townhouse door and fumbled out my keys.

Tim said to keep it light, I looked around. Opened my bag, I guess I was ready. Opened Tim's suitcase, feeling around I felt the money envelopes. Opening them I could see the seven grand in cash. *Great! Enough for a new start somewhere. Just because we can't go to Maui, doesn't mean we can't go somewhere else nice.* I didn't know where, geography never interested me.

I zipped through the kitchen, bedrooms and bathrooms, saw nothing that I couldn't live without. It would not look good to the cops when they see that we banged out of here without taking most of our stuff. *"What was the hurry guys, running from something?' I didn't like the sound of that. Stillwater Prison! Man, I'd heard stories. Steve is right, we got to go!"*

I could barely make out the headlights of my Toronado when Lynch pulled in.

I motioned Steve to pop the trunk but it wouldn't open, frozen shut. *No problem, I'll just put the two bags on the backseat floor by Tim.* Steve got us onto Highway 494 and then skittering down the loop ramp we slid our way down 35W heading south. South to where I had no idea. Definitely time to go.

42.

NO HAT, NO GLOVES, BROKEN SHOE:

Monday Morning, The Day After The Super Bowl. 1977

"Get Out."

"Get Out," Steve commanded a second time.

I had fallen asleep, man was I tired. I looked out the car window, I couldn't see anything but endless mounds of snow. Looking up I just saw more falling waves of the white stuff.

"Huh! What? Why do you want me to get out?" I asked.

With that Steve Lynch All-American Asshole got out of the driver side, walked around the coupe, threw open my door, grabbed my suitcase and flipped it against a gas pump.

"Get out Williams, now, or I'll throw you out," yelled Lynch.

I tepidly got out and asked, "What's going on?"

"We're breaking up, the cops just might be looking for us. Better we split up," said Steve.

"Wait a minute, why here? This is my car, you can't just leave me here," I said.

I looked around again, my eyes were waking up now. I looked out onto the freeway, torrents of snow was flying past the road. I looked around behind me. Lynch had pulled into a large truck stop. There must have been twenty big rigs parked alongside and behind the cafe and small shop. Obviously everyone had taken refuge inside. We were the only ones crazy enough to drive in this weather.

Steve looked back at me, "Oh, I guess you missed it, ten miles back we flipped for the car, you lost."

"Well, why do we have to split up here?" I asked.

Lynch was getting cold standing by the car and was impatient to cut me loose. "I'm taking Tim with me, if he gets better he can hang with me as long as he wants. If he gets worse I'll drop him off in front of a small town hospital and keep driving. Tim's going to be a successful businessman, I'm going to pharmacy school. You are a life time loser, a druggy, a drunk, a slut loving idiot. Your complete lack of discipline, and dedication speak for themselves. You're going to either overdose on something or be shot by a jealous, pissed off husband, just wish I could be there to see it."

With that Steve ran into the truck stop office to pay for the gas, and then sprinted back to the Toronado.

Steve made a move to get in the driver side of the Toronado when the door creaked open and Tim crawled out. I was sure that Tim was abandoning Steve to be with his life long pal. Steading himself on the car door, Tim said, "Ten thousand dollars the biggest score of my life, you can't imagine the hours I spent studying that game. Ten thousand dollars, gone because you ran your mouth to that back stabbing bitch."

My only response was, "Tim, it's me, John, you won't leave me?"

Tim was mad, really mad, he was hurting from the beating and he looked like hell.

"John, we must never see each other again. In sixty years you must still never contact me. For the rest of our lives we will never know if some smart-ass detective isn't going to crack this double murder cold case. I'm not going to prison because of your big mouth, and the seven thousand is all mine," declared Tim.

Tim started to gingerly crawl back in the car but stopped, poked his head out again and said, "Oh, and John, just one more thing, that championship fight back in High School with Robinette! You took a dive, and I should have known then that you would always cost me!"

With that the rear window of the Toronado snapped up, and Tim laid down in the backseat, mumbling, "Ten thousand dollars." Steve took off his coat and covered Tim and started to sit in the driver seat.

"Look, ahh, Steve, can you at least tell me where I am?" I pleaded.

With a now amused smile on his face Steve Lynch looked back at me and said, "John, can't you see? You're in the snow."

There they left me, freezing, and alone. It was here that I realized that when Tim told me to travel light he meant to Hawaii, not wherever I was. No hat, no gloves, thin coat, hmmmm! I stood there at the pump watching my Toronado and best friend disappear forever in a blur of snow, ice and wind. It was here that I noticed I had cut my right shoe open, probably in the fight. I took out my cigarettes and stuffed one in my mouth. Pawing around I came up empty for my lighter. Great! Lost my lighter, the one that Tim gave me for my twenty first birthday, engraved JW. If it was at Miller's boat house I could be cooked, Paul Zeller and Boomer Mattson did not match JW.

I picked up my grip and was blown into the truck stop cafe by the unrelenting January prairie blast.

43.

TRUCKER'S HUMOR, IN PRAISE OF DUCT TAPE:

Monday, One Day After The Super Bowl, 1977
Somewhere....

Since few were braving the highway conditions the cafe was packed. I waited about ten minutes for my chance at the mens room. 'OH BOY' did I look bad. I was a perfect candidate for a post office most wanted board. My bruised forehead bump had colored into a gray and purple welt. A few minor facial infractions outlined the picture. I could just see the write-up:

Wanted: John Williams

Involvement In A Gruesome Double Murder. If You See Him Do Not Attempt To Approach. Remain Vigilant And Contact Your Local Law Enforcement Agency Immediately.

"How could this have possibly happened to me?"

A counter stool at the cafe opened up as I finished in the well appointed truck stop mens room, and I slid onto it shielding my face.

A tired waitress landed a glass of water and cup of black coffee in front of me and told me to hurry up and order because they were almost out of everything.

I looked at the stained menu:

First Item was, The Hungry Highwayman's Hash.

Wow, and I thought Tim had an alliteration problem:

I pointed to the first item and said, "I'll try the Hash, thanks."

"We're out of that," the waitress snapped.

I went down to item two:

The Big Rig Scramble.

The waitress just shook her head.

"OK, how about some pancakes?" She wrote it down and left without even nodding to me. Trapped for hours with a bunch of tired, frustrated, horny truckers had worn her out.

I took a sip of coffee and reached for my wallet. Big surprise, things were not looking good. Folded inside was my final check and my share of tips from my last shift at Maxwells. One hundred and twenty three dollars. A broken shoe, a thin coat, a packed truck-stop somewhere in the midwest with the windows shaking from the pounding Siberian Express.

I looked at my watch, 9:45 AM, my flight to Hawaii should be boarding now. I leaned over to the guy sitting next to me and asked, "This may sound strange, but could you tell me where we are?" Without looking at me he said, "We're at a truck stop."

My head was hurting, kind of a sting. My pancakes arrived. Sausage links too, wasn't expecting that.

Halfway through my refined breakfast I tried the guy next to me again, "Excuse me, do you know what state we are in?"

Again without looking at me he said, "Yes I do."

This was getting harder by the moment, "Could you tell me what state we are in now?"

"Yes I could."

I gave up. I took the tiny napkin and dipped it in my water to massage my pinging forehead.

It was here that I felt a small tap on my shoulder and the guy next to me was looking at me with a grin on his face, "Just having a little fun," with that he stuck out his hand, "Ed Gagnon, nice to meet you."

"Look Ed, I hurt my hand yesterday I really can't shake yours, but it's nice to meet you, and yes I can take a joke," I said.

Ed told me that we were about twenty miles west of North Platt Nebraska.

Of course that meant nothing to me, but Ed was nice enough to give me a quick update on our location.

Hmmm! Steve had done better than I thought.

Then Ed asked, "How did you hurt your hand?"

"Fight after Super Bowl with a friend," no point in lying.

"Where are you going?"

"I don't know, lost my job," no point in lying.

"What are your plans?"

"Just to go out west and look for work," somewhat true.

Finally after scooping up my bills for the pancakes I leaned forward and in a confidential quiet voice asked the waitress if I could borrow a little masking tape.

Career waitresses at truck-stops have heard everything, nothing surprises them. In a loud voice she yelled back to the cooks, "We got any masking tape back there?"

"We're out," said the waitress.

Ed could see my frustration and asked, "What do you need the tape for?"

"Cut my shoe, in the fight," I replied.

Ed paused a minute and then grinned, "Let me guess, you should see the other guy's shoe!" For some reason this brought on great guffaws from most of the truckers.

"Here, let me see what I can do about that shoe," Ed said.

Without thinking I took off my black shoe and handed it to him. Ed left the cafe and disappeared into the storm.

For a minute I thought, *"How really stupid that was. Ed was obviously a joker, he might just think it was funny to take my shoe and drive away. There's John, somewhere in Nebraska, during a storm, with one shoe on and one shoe off."*

A few minutes later Ed came back with my duct taped shoe. I must say he did a real good job of it. Even took some black electrical tape and put if over the gray duct tape so I didn't look two toned. It fit great, and I told him, "I am very grateful, thank you."

The storm was finally lessening and guys were stomping out to their massive trucks to prepare to leave.

"I can take you for a ways, cause me any trouble and I'll drop you in the middle-of-nowhere. But because of the storm I'm running late and I could use someone to keep me awake," Ed Gagnon said.

44.

GOBBLE, GOBBLE, GOBBLE: - 315

Wednesday, Three Days After The Super Bowl, Three Days After John Williams, Spoiled Suburban White Boy Participated In A Double Murder.

I had never seen real prairie until Ed Gagnon soared us through the rest of Nebraska and into Wyoming.

Stops were infrequent at best. When we did stop it was gas up, hit the biff, grab some snacks and kick it down the road. Ed had to be in Sacramento and fast. The way Ed explained it, if the term, "Time Is Money" was not invented for the over-the-road trucking industry, it certainly applied.

The prairie turned into mountains and then to north Nevada desert. We stopped in Ely, Nevada at a place where we could take an hour break and they mercifully had showers and facilities. First time in three days I was able to scrub down, floss and brush. Did that feel good! Back on the road we were about 40 minutes from Reno Nevada when Ed asked me a question.

"Listen Williams, I don't know your situation and it's none of my business but you look like you're running from something. My guess is you either tried to rip-off your last employer or you got your best friend's girl knocked-up. Whatever! It's no concern or business of mine. I have this run at least once a month. There's a large turkey processing operation about ten minutes up the road. I've heard the work is hard, but the pay is good and they provide housing and meals. If you need to lay low and make some dough this might be the place for you. I can slow her down, and you can give it a try if that's your call."

I gave it a few minutes thought, and realized that Ed might be trying to either help me, or get rid of me.

"Come to think of it nobody would ever think that a guy like me would be doing hard labor. I'd never done hard labor in my life, always avoided it, and definitely no one would think I was alone. Tim and I had always been locked together. Steve was right, best that we broke up."

"Ed, I want to thank you, and I'll try the turkeys," I said.

Just like Ed said about ten minutes later we saw an unbelievably large turkey operation up the freeway.

Ed slowed down and pulled off to the side, I thanked him, and grabbed my bag and jumped down.

The turkey ranch, what else would I call it, was maybe 12 minutes hike from the road. As I walked into the first set of buildings a guy looked at me and nodded me over. Arvid Schwall was about five feet high and about as wide. Evidently part of his job was to wait for guys like me to wander into the Schwall's Turkey Plant and get them started. Without shaking hands or even introducing ourselves he just had me follow him to a backside corner of some building and pounded on a doublewide door.

"Gerdie, you got a live one," he yelled.

A few seconds later an older, bitter looking woman with curlers in her hair and a Chesterfield in her mouth opened the door and glared at us.

"Send him in," she said.

"Sit down," she ordered.

Taking out a white piece of paper and pen she said, "Name?" I said my name, "Social Security Number?" I recited my Social Security Number.

That was the application, done.

Gerdie continued, "We work twelve hours on, twelve off, nine days on, five off. Three meals a day, never complain about the food. Never! I have five rules. No drinking, no gambling, no fighting, no stealing and never come back to my house again."

Just as she finished with her five golden rules to happiness at the Schwall's Turkey Ranch an attractive teenage girl in a nightgown popped into the kitchen and said, "Grannie, can I take the bus into Reno to get some things?" Maybe seventeen years old, pretty.

Just then another girl, maybe fifteen entered the kitchen and opened the fridge for some juice.

"No, and this one's too old for you. Now finish up that homework, and get started in the mess hall," Gerdie commanded.

I didn't think I was too old for her, but I was broke and needed a job so I kept my mouth shut.

"Alright ahh Williams right?" she nodded.

Reaching behind the double wide door Granny Gerdie pulled out a pump action shotgun, probably 20 gauge, it was here that I noticed both teenage girls rolled their eyes.

"Follow me Williams," she ordered.

Stepping out in the mid morning north Nevada air she looked at Arvid who simply nodded to her. Evidently nodding was a major form of communication out here in northern Nevada.

Gerdie led me away from her luxurious double-wide and had me about twenty feet from three fence posts with pumpkin shells on them, "Here, hold my cigarette," she said. "Now, what were the five rules of working here?"

I started to stammer them out, "No gambling, no drinking, no fighting, no stealing and never....."

Boom, Boom, Boom. The three pumpkin shells exploded. From off in the distance I could hear all the workers yell out, "Welcome!"

"Give me back my cigarette, and follow Arvid around, he'll show you everything." With that, she turned and stomped back into her doublewide.

It was pretty obvious why "gun packing Gerdie" thought she needed to demonstrate her weaponry expertise. If some lonely night one of the workers figured they could chat up one of her granddaughters they just might end up like a pumpkin shell.

Arvid showed me where I would eat, sleep, shower, and work. 'Ugh!'

Arvid began his diplomatic tutorial on the career requirements needed for working at the Schwall Turkey Ranch. "Everyone starts as a cleaner. Turkeys aren't potty trained. You'll shovel turkey poop, and spray out the barns, and trucks at least once a day. After two months if there's a new arrival you can bid on something else. Carpentry, auto mechanics, supply, or anything. But you'll pull the first two months cleaning turkey barns, and trucks, any questions?"

I shook my head, I was fast learning how to express myself with my head.

"This is important, you cannot work in the barns without the right coat, pants, gloves and steel toed boots, the State Inspectors would fine us if they caught you without them. The bus to Reno goes every other day. You're in luck because I'll be driving in there in about an hour. We drop off the guys who have finished their nine day shifts, pick up supplies and collect anybody coming back."

Arvid looked at my feet.

"I don't know, we may have to wait an extra day to two to get your size. You might as well stay in Reno until you're outfitted, nothing for you to do back here."

An hour later I was thumping toward Reno, Nevada, Arvid at the wheel of a clanky old school bus. Eight really tired looking guys about my age bumped along, worn out from nine twelve hour shifts. My guess was they would either take a bus or plane somewhere to see family, or hide in one of the cheap hotels, drinking, gambling and trying not to get VD.

Reno, Nevada was coming into view.

45.

1977 RENO NEVADA, NO BOOTS,:

Arvid dropped everybody in front of an old building that was now a strip club. Right away I noticed three things about Reno. The buildings looked old, rusty and dusty. The casino's looked small and there seemed to be more strip clubs per acre than any place on earth.

After everyone left the bus Arvid took me over to the uniform shop and showed me to the guy who outfitted the turkey workers. Without saying anything the shop clerk looked at my feet and slowly shook his head. Arvid gave him knowing nod. I didn't know what to do with my head.

"Monday at the earliest, more likely Tuesday or Wednesday," said the clerk.

Arvid just nodded, the clerk nodded back.

"I'll measure him for his coat and pants today, and have his gloves and hat ready, but the shoes, the shoes will take a few days," said the clerk.

Arvid nodded.

After we were through with the shop clerk Arvid said, "Williams if we're lucky I can take you back Monday afternoon and put you to work on Tuesday. More likely I'll pick you and your gear up Wednesday and you'll start on Thursday, see you then."

I nodded.

46.

BUMP AND GRIND, $96.00,
NO LAP DANCE, BUFFET WARRIOR:

What to do for the next three or five days. Things were looking grim. For now I felt safe from the tentacles of Minnesota law enforcement. Sitting on a bus bench I gave Reno some serious thought. No one I had ever met while in Minnesota vacationed in Reno, everyone went to Las Vegas. In fact, I can't remember Reno ever even coming up in conversation. Finally, I don't think I ever heard of any flights here. Reno was just not on any Midwesterners' radar.

I checked my resources: $96.00. I wasn't stupid enough to think I could improve my finances by gambling at any of the casinos. If Tim was with me we would combine our money and he'd conquer a poker table. I was not Tim!

I was thirsty and the north Nevada wind was wearing me down. Relaxing with a cold beer at a strip club might make things better.

'Girlzxxx Girlzxxx Girlzxxx,' advertised itself as having, "The finest exotic dancers in all of Reno." *Dancers? maybe. Exotic? probably not.*

The beer wasn't that cold, on top of that I ticked off management by not tipping and, I couldn't afford a lap dance because money was tight and what's more the size of the behemoths strutting around could have done permanent damage to any number of my vital organs.

I knew I had to eat, sleeping someplace was going to be tough. I'd never been to a homeless mission. *John how far have you fallen! There is one thing that Tim always made clear to me,* "John, no matter how low you may think you are, the bottom can always fall out and you can zoom down further than you ever imagined." Words of wisdom.

I walked into a hotel casino and was greeted with the usual clatter, buzzing and ringing of slot machines. At least I was out of the wind and didn't have a Guernsey on my lap. I checked my watch, 6:18 PM on Friday evening with $94.50 on me.

My parents never ate at buffets, they said they were for lower class people, I felt I qualified.

All You Can Eat, $2.19

I figured I might be down to one meal a day. I would try to eat enough to get me through to about 3:30 PM tomorrow. I had to plan my buffet strategy. Don't skip the fruits and vegetables, salads, lots of them, plenty of hot veggies, pack away the proteins, skip the potatoes. Go slow, it's warm in here, cold out there. Beverages, have to stay hydrated. As for desserts, no point in missing them. I lucked out and found a used newspaper and pretended that I was entranced with every word.

Here comes the coffee girl, big surprise, she looks bored. A little chubby, hair out of place, her legs are hurting. I've done worse. How bad is it for her? She's not even a real waitress, a coffee girl at a low budget buffet at a cheap hotel. She's like me, she's hit bottom. Well, I've hit a lower bottom than her.

"Is this the best buffet in Reno?" I asked.

She stared at me as though nobody had ever tried to engage her in a conversation before.

"New here?" she asked.

"Just got in, scored a job out of town, hope I can make it," I said.

She sat down and we talked. Her name was Rhonda. Time for me to sell the, 'golly-gosh-midwest-shy-boy' routine.

Her tiny trailer was about three miles out of town. Looked like there was about 100 of them out there. I told her that her swell couch was good enough for me and that I wasn't like any of those other guys.

She told me that her ten year old son would wake up around 7:30 in the morning.

Six foot four, sleeping on a four foot couch. It was free!

Lying on Rhonda's tiny couch I stared at her "single-wide" ceiling. Somewhere in the decrepit trailer court a hungry dog was barking. I kept staring at the ceiling, and thinking.

"I don't know why everyone is mad at me! What did I do that was so terrible? Oh sure, blame John for everything. Was it my fault that Kristen sold Tim and me out? Did I ask for Boomer to try and kill his brothers and me? I don't think so! I never asked Zeller to try and move in on North Star Security. Not my fault that Tim was so good at betting sports! While we're on the topic of Tim, I never told him to win ten thousand dollars, that wasn't John Williams' idea. This is the thanks I get for saving Steve Lynch and Einer Mattson in the big fight. When you get right down to it, I'm just a fun loving guy who likes to have a good time. For this I have to suffer! Real nice everyone! Real nice! I'm the victim here!

*There, now I feel bette*r."

47.

JUMP SHOTS, HOOK SHOTS, AND A BAD DRIVE BELT:

Morning, I noticed four things, two good, two not so good. First, I didn't seem to need a cigarette, (It had been four days since I last light up), and my hand that I thought I had broken had stopped hurting. However, there was no coffee, and there was nothing to eat.

Rhonda's keys were on the counter. Hmmmn! The car was old, in bad shape. For a minute I thought to myself, *"How far would I get? I think I'll go for a ride."* Then I decided, *"Oh, scrambled eggs for breakfast would be nice."*

As I drove back into Rhonda's lovely trailer court I thought I was going to have a heart attack. A cop car was parked across from the driveway with its bubble gum lights flashing. Just as I braked in the parking drive I could hear Rhonda shout at the cops standing in front of the trailer, "There he is officers, that's the guy who stole my car!"

Two cops, one about 55, fleshy, jowly, mean, and the other young, a rookie, maybe 25 ordered me out of the car. I could see the older one reach for his cuffs.

"Is there anything I can do to help officers?" I asked.

"Did you steal this ladies car?" snarled the older cop, Officer Powell.

"Ahh, no, I just thought I should get some groceries for her and her son. She let me sleep on her couch last night and I wanted to thank her," I said.

I motioned to the back seat at the grocery bag of food, as I did I could see both of them put their hands on their holsters.

"What do you got in there?" the head bull asked as the younger one grabbed the bag.

"Just some eggs, coffee, donuts, a little juice, a few oranges," I said.

The young cop inspected the bag contents and handed it to Rhonda, and closed the car backdoor.

"Where you from son?" the jowly cop asked.

No point in lying, "Back in the midwest, Minnesota," I responded. *"Hell, I guess they will figure out I must be wanted there. Should I run now? They might just shoot me. No point in getting hurt."* I took out my driver's license and showed it to them.

"What are you doing here?" Officer Powell asked.

"Ahhh, just looking for work, got lucky and scored a job out at a turkey processing ranch this week, just waiting for my uniform to be ready," I said.

Hearing that the older cop immediately put away his attitude and sighed, "Oh you're one of them!"

After a little more talking the older cop turned to Rhonda and asked, "Is everything OK here Ma'am?"

Rhonda smiled and said, "Yes, sorry to bother you officers."

"OH, sounds like I will make it through this encounter okay. I must convince them I am just a decent hardworking Midwesterner as cover so there will be no doubts." It was here that I noticed Rhonda's maybe ten year old son dribbling a basketball. Almost instinctively I signaled him to pass it to me. With the basketball in my hand I started twirling and spinning it, took a few quick dribbles and slipped a behind-the-back pass to him, all the time grinning.

I could see that the younger cop still had some questions about me. I popped open the hood of Rhonda's old Chevy and started examining the engine, "Rhonda, I think you have a slipping drive belt, and what's worse I'm pretty sure your oil pan gasket needs to be replaced. I get five days off in a few weeks and I'll bring in my tools and get this done for you."

That seemed to convince the younger cop that I was an OK guy.

Slamming the hood of Rhonda's car down I noticed that her son was now shooting hoops at the trailer community playground. I walked over and joined Rhonda's son and started shooting with him.

For some reason I just could not shake these two cops. They followed me over and watched me shoot with Rhonda's son. After a minutes the older cop motions me over and asks, "Can you shoot from the outside?"

"Sure, I played basketball in High School and a little in college before I flunked out," I truthfully said.

"What college was that?" asked the young cop.

"Dang, I over sold it. What did actor Terry say at the bar? 'Don't push it, John.'"

"St. Olaf College, back in Minnesota. But I haven't played in two or three years," I said.

The old cop put his hand out like he wanted the ball and I flipped it to him, "Williams, right?" he asked.

I nodded, "Yes sir."

"Let's see you shoot," he said.

"Sir, like I said, I haven't played …."

"Shoot now!" demanded the senior officer, and fired a hard pass into my gut.

Turning to Rhonda's son the old cop said, "Boy, you feed him."

These guys will just not go away. I clanked the first two off the back rim and then found my range. 'Swish' went the sixteen footer from the corner; 'Swish' went the twenty-two footer from the top of the key. After a few more I was really in a zone. Couldn't miss! I even did a few of my favorite running base line hook shots. Loving it! Filling it up! Pouring them in! For a second I was wondering if I would be the only white player on the Stillwater Prison Basketball team.

Showing off now I took the ball out near the forty foot mark and swished in a long set shot like it was the easiest thing in the world. With the ball in my hands I faked like I was going to throw a pass to the young cop, moved left, slanted right, ran the ball around my back, flew past the basket and spun home a reverse layup.

Rhonda's little boy crowed, "Wow, mister! Can you ever shoot."

"OK Williams, we get the point. Give the kid his ball back. I guess you are who you say you are," said the older cop.

"Anything else, Officer Powell?" I asked huffing a little.

"No, but next time you take someone's car, leave a note." With that the two moved to their cruiser.

Rhonda yelled that breakfast was ready and her son and I walked to the trailer. But then I noticed that the cops hadn't left. They kept staring at me. A few minutes later I peaked out the trailer window and they were still there. *"This is nerve wracking, but I should just stay cool here,"* I thought.

It was about three in the afternoon, Rhonda's son and I were watching an NBA game when there was a loud knock on the trailer door. Ronda looked back at me and said the young Reno Police officer wanted to speak with me and to bring my bag.

"Holy shit, I suppose they nailed me."

I motioned a goodbye to the kid, grabbed my stuff and met with the young cop.

"Williams get in my cruiser," said Officer Stevens. *I thought it a little strange that only one cop came to arrest me but maybe that's how they do it out here.*

I had totally resigned myself to the fact that I was going to prison. "Look, I feel terrible about what happened, things just kept getting away from me," I said.

"It happens Williams," replied Stevens.

"I would do things so differently if I only could have seen how things were going to work out," I said.

"Work out they did," said the officer.

"I somehow got on the wrong path," I said.

"Don't you think you're being awfully hard on yourself Williams? You just went for groceries. You chose to help this lady, and you're to be commended for it," said Stevens.

It was here that I decided to shut up.

48.

GREASY RIBEYE'S, A LOSING TEAM AND COMMUNITY SERVICE:

Stevens began, "So Williams here's the deal. The coach wants you on our team. Coach says you could really help turn us around. I know I sure would like you to play for us. Already you would be the best player on our squad. Positive of it!"

"Play what?" "On what team?" I asked Officer Stevens.

"Our city basketball team, the coach was really impressed with your shooting," said Stevens.

"Who's the coach?" I asked.

"You met him this morning, don't you remember?" replied Stevens.

"Officer Powell is your basketball coach?" I questioned.

"Ya, but it's not his fault we're so bad. We just don't have anybody who can shoot," said Stevens.

"You guys have a basketball team?" I asked.

"Sure, a bad one. No point sugar-coating it. Haven't won a game yet this season. The police superintendent is getting really mad at us. Says we're a disgrace to his department. The Reno Gazette calls us the 'Cops that can't shoot straight' Officer Powell is taking a lot of heat," said Stevens.

"I might as well tell you now the Coach is going to offer you two different jobs," said Stevens.

"What?"

Call me confused.

Officer Stevens continued, "You can work in administration or college security. I'm sure you'll go with administration. It's easy, filing, answering the phone, setting up meetings, hey can you type?"

"Tell me about college security," I asked.

Stevens began, "It's like this, The University Of Nevada here in Reno was having some problems. You know, theft, breaking-and-entering, wild parties, abused coeds, fights at the games, I could go on. So the City Of Reno Police Department was asked to provide more help. Well, we're already stretched thin. So the police and college got together and created a campus security program. You would not be a Reno Police Officer, however, you would be working as a Police employee under the guidance of the Reno Police. That's close enough to be on the team. There's about twenty Campus Security Officers that report to the police. Always on patrol around the University, checking doors, greeting visitors, working sporting events, escorting coeds, a million other things. But you don't want that job."

"Why not?" was my reply.

"Because, you'll be at the bottom of the seniority list. You'll work nights, weekends, holidays, all the bad shifts," said Officer Stevens.

My mind went into overdrive. Reno Nevada, nights, weekends, hmmm! Maybe this would even be a better way to hide. Besides, if anyone is hunting me, they wouldn't think of me as working for a police force.

"There is one advantage to being a University Campus Security Officer. If you ever wanted to join the Reno police force it's a good entry path. You've already got a lot of the training. Some of the guys have done that already," said Stevens.

Stevens started his cruiser up and pulled out of the lot. A few minutes later we stopped in front of an older looking cafe. This was where the cops, fireman, and city employees hung out.

"Now Williams, say what is your first name anyway?" Stevens asked.

"John," I said.

"Great, John, try to hear the coach out, he's in a tough spot. Nobody likes to get laughed at, and no coach likes to have his team made fun of," said Stevens.

With that we got out of the car and entered an old, weathered, looking cafe.

Officer, I mean, Coach Powell got up to greet me and shook my hand.

"Thanks for coming Williams, can I get you anything to eat?" Coach Powell said.

Without waiting for me to reply he told the waitress who looked as weathered as the building, "Jen, get Williams here your ribeye dinner special."

Jen looked me over and asked, "Are you the new ringer? These guys sure need you. What do you want on your salad?"

Without thinking I said, "Ranch, and thank you."

"Stevens filled you in on what this is about?" Powell asked me.

"Yes sir," I said.

"OK then, I have to tell you, we can't pay you the kind of money you'd make out at the turkey ranch. But we sure could use you on our team. Also this could be a step toward joining the City Service in the department of your choice. Finally, you would be doing the City Of Reno a real community service," said Powell.

"What community service?" I asked.

"This is how it's done, this recession has bitten hard out here. There's not even a minor league baseball team here anymore. The whole city is at a real emotional low. Unemployment and inflation are way up there. So the Mayor and Council organized a basketball league for people to cheer for. Police, fire, emergency medical, administration, water, school, sanitation, maintenance and repair, and janitorial service have teams. Everybody plays everyone else twice and then has the playoffs, winner is City Champs. This is to build moral and collect money for the kids," said Powell.

"Collect money for the kids?" I asked.

Officer Powell went on, "Times are tough Williams, a lot of these kids parents can't afford school supplies. Everyone throws a dollar into a basket to watch the games. All the dollars are put into an account for poor kids to buy pencils, pens, notebooks, schools supplies. Before you ask, this area must lead the nation in dead-beat-dads."

Powell then leaned in and said, "I have to ask you one question Williams, you don't do drugs do you?"

How would Terry the actor handle this question.

"Sir?" I questioned.

"Drugs!" said Powell, "you don't use drugs do you?"

I gave Officer Powell a blank look, "Sir, drugs are illegal and bad for your health, I don't even smoke."

It was here that I noticed my right leg was shaking. The idea of playing basketball and escorting college coeds versus shoveling out turkey manure had started to take hold.

Jen served a fatty, greasy ribeye (I was never a fan of this cut) with a huge pile of steak fries. The salad consisted of a small plate of old lettuce. Reno Nevada was a long way from haute cuisine.

I slowly started eating. *"Keep it slow. Deliberate."*

Powell was wrapping up his pitch, "Now if you say 'No' I'll understand and we'll get you a ride out to the turkey ranch, it's your call, but we sure need you."

My mind rolled back to what Terry the full-time actor, part-time bartender at Maxwells taught me. *"Must be calm, must not over sell it, must be the most heartfelt guy in the room."*

I slowly set my knife and fork down and said, "All the money goes to help the kids, right?"

Coach Powell nodded his head up and down.

I nodded slowly and said, "Count me in."

49.

BRUISERS, LOSERS, AND THE ZONE DEFENSE:

I liked being a University of Nevada Security Officer from the first moment I put on the uniform. Black shoes and socks, deep brown pants and shirt, brown cap, big star badge on my belt. The job was easy and from the beginning I noticed a lot of the coeds liked looking at the tall Security Officer. I liked looking back.

Because I worked at the college I got to stay in a dorm room with another officer and got to eat at the University cafeteria at a deep discount, anything was better than Jen's beat up cafe.

The Police basketball team was another matter. After the first couple of practices we played the all black janitorial team. It did not go well. I could see the frustration with the players, coaches and fans. Surprisingly, I didn't think that we were that bad offensively. The next day I called coach Powell on the phone and asked him to meet me for a (greasy) ribeye.

Taking out a notebook and pen I explained what I thought needed to be done. There has never been a coach at any level of athletics that likes to hear a new player tell him how he's messing up, so I was prepared to be tactful and patient. As we ate, I thought, *"OK, in a situation like this you have to lay it on thick. You're about to tell the boss he sucks as a coach."*

"Coach Powell, I first want to thank you for letting me be part of your team, your police department and this fine University. Your dedication to the community is highly commendable. Also your determination to make our team better is admirable. After being on the team for a few weeks now I was wondering if I could run a few ideas by you," I said.

I quickly opened a notebook and grabbed my pen. Coach Powell leaned in, I could see he was desperate for any help.

"Our guys are big, powerful, some might say they're a bunch of "knuckle draggers." Whatever! We have more size than any other team. That's good! But our players are a little on the slow side. Quickness is not our strength. Strength is our strength. So I was wondering if I could run some ideas about our defense by you," I asked.

Officer Powell nodded. Big surprise!

I continued, "Because of our size, rebounding is not a problem, but getting back in transition is.

Also our guys are getting beat on give-and-goes and are late on switches. Our man-to-man defense is not very good, would you like to hear how I think we can fix that?"

Powell enthusiastically nodded.

"We need to teach the guys to hustle back on defense and set up a sagging zone. With our power, height and length we can force the other teams outside, and not get beat on switches. To be clear Officer Powell, I want our team to seal-the-door shut," I said.

The rest of the dinner consisted of me outlining the basics of the same sagging, match-up, lockdown zone defense we used in high school and college. Coach Powell wanted to try it, that day.

The police force started winning. My status kept rising. Sixteen months later I was sworn into the Reno Police Department.

I started to change my appearance. I went gray and then light blond. I always tried to wear sun glasses during the day. But while hiding in plain sight one must make even bigger changes. I would have to get married and have a family. No one would believe that a guy like me would ever consider such a cause.

50.

ARIZONA SKY, BALLROOM DANCING AND PAR THREE GOLF:

September 2018

I like sitting by the community pool watching the girls run through their water aerobics routine. I bring my wife down here to the community pool in our golf cart and stretch out and let the Arizona sun bathe me. I often review the things that I'm grateful for.

Three healthy daughters and five healthy grandkids.

A wife that still laughs, and hasn't bitched at me once in thirty two years.

A defined benefit retirement plan with an annual cost of living adjustment.

My father-in-law's money.

The thin western air that still allows my golf ball to zip.

Then there's the thing I have never told my wife Lois that I'm grateful for. When we first first retired to southern Arizona I took us to a small Mexican resort town on the Pacific. One day I told Lois that I needed to find a drug store and I'd meet her at the resort pool for a late lunch. It was then that I slipped into a bank and reserved a lock box. Twenty two thousand in cash would last me awhile, and give me some breathing room if I ever saw a curious Minnesota detective down here. Call it my "Stay out of jail card." There are lots of stories about long closed cold cases that some detective finds a new slant on and cracks open. It's fifty minutes to the border and another ninety to the bank.

With the career and kids I soon left my adventures in Minnesota behind. The drugs, the woman, the partying, the gambling, all had to stop. However, leaving a double murder is very hard. One morning Lois looked at me over coffee and asked, "Who was Boomer, and why do you keep talking about him in your sleep?"

Lois could see my face freeze, "Honey, when I was young I watched a lot of cop shows, fact is I still like CSI. That's all this is." I could not tell whether she bought it or not.

As the girls finished with their water aerobics, I bent down to help Lois out of the pool. Draping a large towel around her I rub her shoulders and pat her butt. Some of the others don't like it, but Lois does. Maybe it's the attention that she gets and the jealousy she see's in the other gals that lights her up. It's our way of saying, 'we're still into each other'.

After dropping Lois at the house, I head to the grocery store for party supplies for our evening cocktail party. Every three months there's a big formal ballroom dance down at the community center and Lois likes to have our friends over for cocktails and snacks after the dance. As we bid everyone a goodbye at our front door Lois will sling her arm around me and lay her head on my shoulder. Here again, she likes to advertise that we're still connected: that John and Lois Williams are not just going through the motions.

As I am standing in the checkout line with my shopping cart someone taps me on the back. At first I ignored it, then another tap, harder. I took my hands off my cart and turned around to see the big, dumb, smiling face of Boomer Mattson.

Slouching forward with his four pronged cane he reaches out with a handshake, and tries to give me a hug without falling forward. "I thought that was you, John Williams!" *"My God, BOOMER Mattson- How . . .?"* I tried not to allow my panic and astonishment to show.

"Goodness, Boomer, let's talk in the parking lot," I say. *"My God, I can't believe BOOMER Mattson is alive!"*

Immediately I started to search for any kind of weapon. The best I could do was a small can of pineapple tidbits. I made sure they were on top of my bag. I waited for him at the door and noticed he can't carry his groceries. A kid is helping him and he gives me that same big sloppy midwestern grin and asks, "Where are you parked?"

"Let's go to your car," I say. As I slumped behind the carry-out kid its obvious that Boomer is hurting. One look and you can tell the hips are gone, knees are shot. Typical of a powerfully built guy like him, age takes its toll. Boomer punches open his car and the kid puts the groceries away and leaves us. My panic is now just surprise.

"Great to see you John, what have you been up to all these years?" asks Boomer.

I tell him as little about myself as possible. Boomer tells me he's living in a great little trailer court on the edge of town.

I'm starting to let my guard down.

"Let's play golf sometime and then have the wives meet," says Boomer.

"That would be nice," I reply.

"Of course I can only play nine holes, and only the par three courses. Oh, and I need a cart. But hey, it still would be fun. Let's get together soon, we've got a lot of catching up to do, don't you think?" says Boomer.

"Yes, yes, lot's of catching up," I replied.

I turned toward my car when Boomer called to me and waved me back. I was no longer afraid of him. If you can't handle your groceries you're probably not much of a threat.

Boomer seemed very serious now, "Just one thing John, that big brawl out at Lake Minnetonka all those years ago?"

I nodded.

Boomer continued, "That was the best thing that ever happened to me. Maybe a few knocks on the head was what I needed to pound some sense into me. Changed everything. I took over Dad's trucking business and did real well. Never got into trouble again. I always said to myself if I ever saw you again that I would thank you for helping me straighten out."

"Thanks, but it was you that changed your life, nice to see you," I said.

"Unbelievable!" With the pounding southwestern sun broiling the roof of my car I can't seem to find the hand coordination to press the electronic ignition switch. Stunned and shocked I thought of all these years looking behind my shoulder. *"I could have stayed in Minnesota!"*

Driving back to our gated over-fifty-five community with everything anyone could want including hardworking Mexican housekeepers and landscapers I get lost in thought.

"Those years and that girl, Kristen Anne Bennett. The very thought of the girl still made me hard. Some would want Kristen to have a difficult life, fall on

hard times and pay for her treacherous behavior. I knew better.

A girl like Kristen knew the angles and knew most men's weak spots. It could be any late spring afternoon, Kristen would get invited to some Country Club bash, or maybe just show up looking great and explain that there 'must be some mistake'. After a Minnesota winter of heavy coats, and hair hiding scarfs, she would swirl and twirl in a printed dress during cocktails. Not enough to be slutty, just enough to show everyone she was fun. Men's eyes would get lost in her rich, flowing caramel hair. Because Kristen was the best looking woman in the room, there would be jockeying for position to sit next to her for dinner. Kristen would do just enough talking to seem interesting without revealing how limited she was. As before, she would placate and then ingratiate all the woman starting from the bottom up. Dancing would bring forth a lonely retired executive or a recently divorced super success. Kristen would be on her game, a game that girls like Kristen always win."

THE END